When we got LOST in DREAMLAND

D0100974

When we got LOST →in←

DREAMLAND

Ross Welford

HarperCollins *Children's Books*

First published in Great Britain by
HarperCollins *Children's Books* in 2021
HarperCollins *Children's Books* is a division of HarperCollins*Publishers* Ltd,
1 London Bridge Street
London SE1 9GF

www.harpercollins.co.uk

HarperCollins*Publishers*
1st Floor, Watermarque Building, Ringsend Road
Dublin 4, Ireland

1

HB ISBN: 978-0-00-844718-2
SIGNED EDITION ISBN: 978-0-00-847024-1
TPB ISBN: 978-0-00-845190-5
BOOKCLUB EDITION ISBN: 978-0-00-846958-0
PB ISBN: 978-0-00-833381-2

Ross Welford asserts the moral right to be
identified as the author of the work.

A CIP catalogue record for this title is
available from the British Library.

Typeset in Adobe Garamond by Palimpsest Book Production Ltd,
Falkirk, Stirlingshire

Printed and bound in England by CPI Group (UK) Ltd,
Croydon CR0 4YY

MIX
Paper from
responsible sources
FSC™ C007454

This book is produced from independently certified FSC™ paper
to ensure responsible forest management.

www.harpercollins.co.uk/green

If a man could pass through Paradise in a dream, and have a flower presented to him as a pledge that his soul had really been there, and if he found that flower in his hand when he awoke — Aye, what then?
— Samuel Taylor Coleridge (1772–1834)

I've still got teeth-marks in my arm from a massive crocodile called Cuthbert that only ever existed in my head. Aye — what's all that about, then?
— Malcolm Gordon Bell (aged 11)

BEFORE IT ALL STARTED

I've got to tell you about a bad dream. Only . . . it's real as well.

That's okay – it didn't make sense to me either, at first.

When I was very little, I had this dream about a crocodile coming down the railway track where we lived, and chasing me round the back garden. (This was where we lived before Dad left. Seb was still a baby.)

I'd wake up and shout for Mam and she'd come into my room and say, 'Shush, Malky, shush. You'll wake Sebbie. It's just a bad dream,' and she'd sit on the side of the bed and stroke my hair and sing the song that went, '*Let it be, let it be, let it be, let it be . . .*'

But the crocodile kept coming back.

Then Mam had the idea of buying me a stuffed toy crocodile and giving it a funny name and we chose Cuthbert. Nothing called Cuthbert could be scary, she said.

So one night (I must have been about six) I dreamed that the crocodile was there, back in our old garden, chasing me like before. I stopped and pointed to it and said its name: 'Cuthbert!'

In seconds, the beast in front of me turned into my toy. I watched – there in the garden in my *Star Wars* pyjamas – mesmerised, as the horny, scaly, knobbled skin became the soft green fur of a cuddly toy; the yellow razor teeth transformed to little white triangles of felt. Everything about him shrank till he was a furry toy.

All in my dream.

When I woke up the next morning, Mam says, my arm was slung round toy Cuthbert. The nightmares went away shortly after that.

This was my first experience of controlling a dream, and I kind of forgot all about it. Then the Dreaminator came along, and Cuthbert came back and, well . . .

The next time I saw Cuthbert – the real Cuthbert, not the toy one – was a few years later when I was with Seb, and the crocodile flopped out of the boot of a car belonging to one of the most evil men ever to have lived.

I should have quit then. But I didn't.

I was somewhere bigger, more mysterious, and scarier than anywhere on earth you could possibly dream of. I guess you'd call it Dreamland – and that's where I lost Seb.

CHAPTER 1

This is my dream, I've been here before, and I'm furious and scared.

Furious because this is not meant to be happening, and scared because it *is*. It's Sebastian's fault, of course. *Why does he keep doing this?*

Even I could tell that things were getting better. Seb and I hadn't fought in weeks. Mam was happy. I had made friends at school. (Well, *a* friend, sort of, but still . . . You'll meet her.) Dad had called for the first time in ages.

I stand in the mouth of the cave, wondering what to do. A massive seagull circles high above me in the cold blue sky. In the distance, down by the shore, the same pair of woolly mammoths as before munch lazily on the same oversized birthday cake.

I tut and think: *Why does Seb have to ruin everything?*

I could just wake up. In fact, that's exactly what I'm going—

'Oi, Dog-breath!'

I turn round to see my brother standing behind me,

in the cool shade of the cave, wearing his green goalkeeper's top.

'What's going on?' I snap at him. 'I turned the Dreaminators off.'

'I know. Why did you *do* that?' he whines. 'I turned them on again cos I couldn't fall asleep. My sleep rhythms are out of sync with yours.'

My thleep rhythmth are out of thync with yourth. I know it's tricky to speak properly when you're missing three front baby teeth, but he doesn't even try. Anyway, I'm not going to write it out like that every time he says something, so you'll just have to imagine that he speaks like a dog's squeaky toy.

'Seb, man,' I say, trying not to shout straight away, 'it isn't safe. There's something not right and I think we should . . .'

'Not right with what?'

'Not right with the Dreaminators. With . . . with everything . . .'

'Come on, Malky. You *said* we could. You *promised*!'

I didn't, actually, but he's getting more whiny. I hate it when he gets whiny.

'Seb . . . I'm telling you, something is wrong.'

He's not listening. 'Where are the others?' he asks. I shake my head. I am still thinking about stopping the whole thing right there. Seb starts sniffing. 'They've been here. Not long gone, in fact.' He points to a fire smoking in a pit. The sharp wind outside the cave rattles the bunches of seaweed, hanging in long strings like little grey-green flags, that are drying by the cave mouth.

'They have gone to steal food,' I say, a bit grumpily. 'You know how it goes.'

One last dream together? A short one. No more after that.

'What, without us?' says Seb. 'That's not fair. Come on, Malk. We'll just wake up if we need to.'

From somewhere – my conscious mind, wherever that is right now? – drifts a warning. How did it go? *Inside your mind is bigger than the outside, Malky . . .*

'Malky!' shouts Seb. 'Come *ooooon!*'

I give in. He's right on one thing: we can wake up and come out of the dream whenever we want. That bit I can still control, at least. And the minute the crocodile appears we're out of here.

I have never made a bigger mistake.

'All right,' I say, quickly, before I can change my mind. 'We can catch them up. They won't have got further than the lake. And promise me: when I say we quit, we quit, okay?'

'Promise,' says Seb. But I'm not sure he's really listening.

CHAPTER 2

We set off at a trot, each of us clutching a spear with a tip of sharp flint, and a thick wooden club with a fist-sized rock securely tied on one end with strips of leather.

We get to the end of the beach – exactly like the real beach where we live in Tynemouth (apart from the mammoths, obviously) – and run up the hill until we're staring out over the huge plain where, in maybe ten thousand years' time, there will be a wide road, and a pub playing live music, and a housing estate of low-rise flats. Now there isn't any of that. There isn't *anything* made by humans – apart from an old-fashioned airship that's floating past in the sky above, shaped like a giant goldfish. Don't ask me what it's doing there. Dreams are weird like that and, by now, I'm kind of used to it.

There is no sign of our friends, though.

I say, 'Super-sprint. Dream-style. You up for it?'

Seb grins gappily, and in an instant we are sprinting across the windy plain like a pair of Olympic runners battling for the finish line. Side by side, weapons in hand, I'm edging ahead of Seb, and then he pulls level as the

Gravy Lake comes into view in the far distance. Then he's ahead of me. He remains ahead as we descend the side of the shallow canyon where there is a green river of minty custard (this is a dream, remember?) and we hop across the exposed rocks and up the other side.

I let him get a good lead so that he will think he is winning. Then it'll be an easy matter to lengthen my stride, judging it finely so that I can overtake him and win at the last minute, but not humiliate him so that he won't want to race again.

And so, as the Gravy Lake gets closer, and I can see the shapes of our companions gathering on its shore, I begin to exert myself a little more. I deliberately make my strides stronger and longer . . . but still Seb is ahead of me. I drop my weapons and pump my arms more, thrusting my chin out, and run harder. And harder.

It's happening again. My dream is not doing what I tell it to do.

What's wrong? I'm not gaining on Seb at all.

I have no idea exactly how fast we are running, but the ground is whooshing past under my feet at a terrifying rate and, however fast I go, Seb is managing to keep ahead of me.

It is not meant to happen like this. I don't understand it.

Kobi and the others are in full view now, and I can't stop in time. I'm going so fast that I run right past them and into the shallows of the freezing-cold lake where the watery school gravy finally stops me and I fall forward, sinking under the surface before rising, gasping for air. The others point at me and laugh, while Seb bounces on his feet, arms raised in victory.

The cold of the gravy has shocked me.

Being beaten by Seb has shocked me more.

I'm still standing in the shallows of the brown lake, and I look round at the group: there's little Erin, old Farook and, of course, Kobi the Cave Boy who looks like he does in Seb's book, which is cartoonish. He's basically a walking, talking drawing. He is wearing a fur thing that only covers one shoulder and he has a club-and-rock weapon like the one I just ditched. Looking at his fur makes me feel even colder because I'm just wearing my soaking pyjamas. I close my eyes and say, 'Change pyjamas to fur,' and wait.

Nothing happens. I try again, but I'm already losing confidence.

Seb hasn't seen any of this: he's a few metres away, talking to the others. I call over to him and he saunters back, all cocky after beating me in a running race.

'What's up, loser?' he says. 'You not cold?'

'Seb,' I say, 'it's going wrong again.'

'What do you mean, "again"?' says Seb.

'I've told you: the dream doesn't always do as it's told, and it's happening much quicker now. Look!' I point upwards. 'Turn green!' The sky does not turn green. I don't want to scare him, though. Instead, I say, 'Shall we wake up now?' It's really the only safe option.

He wrinkles his nose and pouts. 'I don't want to. What's wrong with you? You said it yourself, Malky. We haven't got much time. I want to get to the bit when I ride the mammuf, at least!'

He's in such a good mood, and he's probably right. Even if I can't direct things perfectly, we'll both come out of the dream cycle, anyway, waking up normally in our beds at home, in about twenty minutes. I'll soon dry out.

Relax, Malky! It'll be perfectly safe. Just like a normal dream where weird stuff happens.

I try to convince myself, I really do. I tell myself, *Let it be . . .*

'Come on, Malky,' he says. 'We're on a food raid, remember? Just like in the book!'

'Yeah, yeah,' I sigh. 'You win.'

I move forward on to the lip of the low cliff, where the lake tumbles over the rock in a massive waterfall, like the drawing in the book. I release the big breath that I took and sniff the air, turning my head completely in line with the horizon.

The smell is coming from where the sun is just beginning to set, painting the Gravy Lake brownish-pink. Someone is roasting meat. Mammoth? I turn back to the others and nod. 'Meat,' I say. Kobi's cartoon lips part in a wide grin and he sticks out his tongue with pleasure. He has no fear about what might come next. He never does. Beside him, Erin stands up and holds her hand out to old Farook who waves it away and gets to her feet with a small grunt.

(Seb made up most of the names, by the way. Just thought I'd say that. Erin is a kid in his class.)

Through the trees, there's a huge rock and, a little further on, the faint glow of a fire.

Stealing meat from another tribe is a huge risk. In the book, it's all fine and happy-endy: the tribe gives us meat because we're hungry, then Kobi gets to ride on a mammoth. We've never actually got that far in the dream, we've always been side-tracked. It's probably why Seb doesn't want to leave. He really wants to ride that mammoth, and I can't say I blame him.

I crouch behind the rock and pick up a lump of dirt and sniff it, recoiling at the foul smell of dog poo. 'Dogs,' I whisper, wiping it off my fingers. Even in the dark, I see a flash of fear pass over Erin's face. We all know about the dogs. The other tribe travels with them. They can talk to them, give them names and commands, just like we do in real life. The dogs attack when told to. They are terrifying, even in a dream.

Then from behind me I hear a sound: *r-r-r-r-r-r-r-r-r-r-r-r-r*. I swallow and spin round: there it is. An old black-and-ginger hound with a grey muzzle. Its head is held low, ready to pounce; its eyes flash amber in the low sun. It lifts up one misshapen front paw, twisted from some old injury, and growls again.

R-r-r-r-r-r. There is another one now, and another. We turn . . . but they're behind us too. The five of us – me, Seb, Kobi, Erin and Farook – are blocked from retreating.

Trapped.

CHAPTER 3

We face the dogs, our backs to the tribe's camp.

I hear a branch swish behind us, and a shadow is cast by a flaming stick. We turn to see them standing there: five men, lips parted, thick, stinking furs tied at their waists, all bigger than us. Much bigger. The sort of big that you only get in dreams.

Okay, now is probably a good time to wake up. I try to catch Seb's eye.

The nearest man whistles, and the dogs respond by taking two paces towards us, growling louder. Beside me, little Erin whimpers. Another whistle, and the dogs creep forward, forcing us to retreat towards the biggest man. Then he gives a command and the dogs stop. We are the length of two people from them and the big man grins and nods. Without turning his head, he says something in his own language to the others and they laugh and point their spears at us. One of them has a short bow and arrow, and the leather string creaks as he pulls it back.

The tall one takes three strides until he's in front of

me. His flaming stick smells of burning fat: a strip of something is wrapped round the end and it spits as it burns. He moves the flame close to me and I arch backwards.

'Seb,' I murmur. 'Get ready to wake up. I don't like this.'

I stare back at the man. His big eyes, like the others', are almost black, topped with a single, dense bush of eyebrow, and below his hooked nose is a tangled, square moustache. He steps closer and moves the flame from my feet to my head, then he reaches out his hand and I try not to flinch as he runs it over my chest, then across my chin. I hear myself squeaking with fear.

'Seb. He's just touched me. Let's get out of here!'

The man growls slowly and then says two words, in English this time, that send a chill through me.

'Take them.'

CHAPTER 4

The tall man's companions murmur and nod. He straightens up, lowering his flaming torch. Then his arm darts out and grabs Seb roughly by the hair, making him squeal, and in one quick movement he throws Seb, staggering, towards his companions who grab him roughly.

'Hey, stop it!' cries Seb. His eyes meet mine and we know what to do. 'Wake up!' we both shout.

Only nothing happens.

'No!' shouts Erin and takes a step towards the men, but their spear points stop her in her tracks. The leader says something to the dogs and they gather round him without taking their amber eyes off us. Meanwhile, he grabs Seb's wrists and starts tying them together with a rough rope made of vines. His big arm muscles flex beneath his skin and I see a rough, smudged tattoo of a swastika through the hair.

I'm properly scared now. 'Wake up!' we both shout again.

The tall man bares his teeth and steps towards me,

leaning close enough so that, when he laughs, I can smell his stinking breath.

'Too late,' he says. 'You didn't listen to the warnings, did you? Try it again, strange, modern pyjama-boy, ha ha!'

'Wake up!' I shout for the third time, then I do the hold-my-breath thing, releasing the air after a few seconds with a *paaaah!* right in his face.

He sniffs my breath then sneers, 'Toothpaste, hm? Yet you're still here. That's reassuring. To me at any rate. Welcome to my world – a vast dimension filled with anything you can imagine. But unfortunately for you – *I can imagine too.*' He draws himself up to his full height – enormous now – and addresses his companions. 'Take the little one away!'

'No! Malky! Stop them! Wake me up!'

'I can't, Seb, I can't! Do the breath thing! Wake up!'

Seb's cheeks are bulging, but then I have to look away as the dog with the damaged leg lurches unsteadily towards me and I have no choice but to run.

This is just a dream, I keep telling myself. *What's the worst that can happen? Seb will wake up naturally soon.*

I run through the line of trees, pursued by the dog, my chest aching with fear and breathlessness, until I reach the clifftop and I turn round to see the huge grey-muzzled beast hurtling towards me. Below me is . . .

Nothing at all.

Not sea, not rocks, not a canyon, not even something silly and dreamlike, like a trampoline or a big pile of autumn leaves: just an endless, grey, fuzzy emptiness like a television that is not tuned in to a channel. It is as though Dreamland has just given up trying. As I look back, the dog is in the air, its front paws stretched out, and they hit me – *oof!* – straight in the chest, sending us both tumbling into the greyness.

I start to shiver: a small trembling that becomes a shake. My teeth are chattering and my whole body begins to twitch in huge convulsions; my stomach starts to spasm and I feel as though I'm going to throw up, and I grip the sides of the white toilet bowl and up it comes.

And again.

And again.

And I don't know how long I'm there, on the bathroom floor, resting my head against the cool porcelain, in my still-damp pyjamas.

My breathing returns to normal. I spit the last of the puke into the bowl and flush, then spin round in fright in case a crocodile comes through the door like it once did.

But no. I'm not dreaming. I punch the wall.

Ow.

I'm in my bathroom at home. I jump and try to float downwards to the floor, but land with the usual force. I am awake.

I am not . . .

. . . *definitely not* . . .

dreaming!

I'm still shaking with fear, but everything is as it should be. I manage a wobbly grin in the mirror, rinse my mouth from the tap and head back to bed. I peel off my pyjamas and throw them in the corner.

That's it! No more. Never, ever, *ever* again! That was just horrible, and I'm furious with Seb for persuading me, and with myself for giving in to him. It's nearly time to get up, anyway.

'Seb!' I hiss, angrily, when I get back to our room. 'Seb. Hey, Seb! Wake up!'

He lies there in the same green goalie top, twitching his head from side to side occasionally, his face grey-blue in the glow from the Dreaminators hanging above our beds: the devices that I had switched off, but that Seb switched back on again, once I was asleep.

Annoying little brothers do stuff like that.

'Seb, man, stop messing about. Seb? Sebastian. *Sebastian!* Wake up!' I shake him roughly. 'Seb! *Seb!*'

He doesn't wake. It's like he's dead but still breathing. I shake him some more – I even slap him.

'Wake (*slap*) up (*slap*)!'

My stomach flips over, and, if I hadn't already thrown up, I feel like I might do again. I grab him by both shoulders, shaking him against his pillow. Nothing. I shout louder, I slap him harder – too hard, in fact. There's now the red mark of my fingers on his cheek.

'I'm sorry, I'm sorry,' I sob. 'But just wake up!'

From across the landing I hear Mam's sleepy voice. 'Boys? Malky? What's going on?'

In those few seconds before Mam comes in, I begin to regret all the bad things I had thought about Seb.

I sink to my bed and hold my head in my hands. I can hear Mam coming.

What have I done?

CHAPTER 5

Can you divorce your little brother?

Daft question, I know, but until fairly recently I really wanted to. I didn't exactly think through the practical side. I mean, it's not like we could live in separate houses, is it? I guess Seb could go and live with Dad and his girlfriend and choke on her fruity perfume, but he'd only wail, 'That's not *fair*!' and cry, like he always does, and somehow it would end up being me living in Middlesbrough with Dad and Melanie.

There's a photo of us in a frame on the kitchen windowsill, and I've got my arm round Seb's shoulders. We're in the old back garden. Once or twice Mam has looked at it and said, 'You used to be *such* good little mates,' with a sad expression, and I usually try to be nice to him after that, but he always – I mean always – spoils it.

And then there was the time I hit him. Okay, okay . . . bear with me. It wasn't my fault. Have you ever hit someone? I mean properly, when you're angry? Say when someone tries to grab the game controller from your hands when you're just about to reach the next level of *Street Warrior*?

Take it from me: it's very easy to hit someone with a game controller a bit harder than you mean to.

That was not long after Mam and Dad split up, and we had moved to the tiny house in Tynemouth. Mam tried to make a thing of it, like adults do. 'We're going up in the world, boys!' she said, because Tynemouth's a bit posh compared with Byker, but I knew she was putting it on. Moving from a house with my own bedroom to having to share with a whingeing snot-ball isn't my idea of 'going up in the world' and, when I complained that all my friends were staying in Byker, Mam said, 'If they're real friends, they'll come and see you, Malky.'

They never did. We don't have a car and Mam wouldn't let me ride on the Metro on my own till I was ten, and by that time I hadn't seen Zack and Jordy and Ryan for ages.

A new school then, nearly two kilometres from my house, where the kids all talk differently, and they play rugby instead of football in the autumn term. (I hate rugby.) But I could have dealt with all of that.

Everyone – Mam, Valerie the school counsellor, Mrs Farroukh – thinks that what they call my 'behaviour issues' are all because of Mam and Dad, and the move, but they're not.

They're all down to Sebastian. If it hadn't been for

him, none of the bad things – the crocodile, the Stone Age, Adolf Hitler – would have happened.

He would have woken up as normal.

And the Dreaminator? Okay, I'll grant you that. The Dreaminator *was* my fault, but I'd have probably got away with it if it hadn't been for him.

You'll understand when I explain – but to do that I'm going to have to go back to when I found the Dreaminators, and Seb and I first discovered Dreamland.

Just don't start being all judgy with me when I tell you what I did, okay? Because I'll bet you've done stuff that's bad yourself. And everything is more complicated when you have an annoying younger brother.

Just clearing that up before we start.

FOUR WEEKS AGO

CHAPTER 6

It's early September and school starts tomorrow. Kez Becker and I are in the empty back lane behind the row of big terraced houses that overlook the river. It's about seven p.m. and still fairly light. Between you and me, I don't think I really *like* Kez Becker, but she's an alternative to whiny Seb.

In order to 'celebrate the end of the summer', she has just dared me to commit a robbery.

I'm pretty sure she doesn't mean 'robbery' or 'celebrate' exactly, and I am about to point that out, only now she's got my phone, the one Dad sent me for my birthday last month, and she's refusing to return it. She's my friend (sort of) so I'm pretty sure I'll get it back at some point, only she's *also* the weirdest kid in the school and you can never be quite sure.

('Weird?' you say. 'How?' Well, Kez's dad is a funeral director, and Kez has offered ten pounds to anyone who'll spend half an hour alone in his workshop after dark. I think there are dead bodies there. It's another of her dares. She calls it 'the Halloween Challenge'. That's weird if you ask me.)

Kez is in the year above me and she has taken my phone because . . .

Banter.

That's what she says, anyway. 'Only bantz, innit, Bell! Lighten up!'

Kez was sitting at the top of the stone steps that lead up from the bay, examining the purple-dyed ends of her blonde hair, when I ran into her earlier.

'A'reet, Bell?' she grunted, barely looking up. She calls me by my last name. I don't like it, but I haven't said anything. Then she said something about a 'nice evening' and the sunset behind her turning the river-mouth a sort of brownish-pink. It was so unlike her that it should have made me wonder, right there and then, but my guard was down. So when she said, 'Ha'way, I'll take your picture! Your mam'll love it,' I handed her my phone . . .

. . . and ten minutes later she still has it. Like a hostage.

'Please, Kez. Give it back. Me mam'll kill me . . .'

I stop myself. *Please?* To Kez Becker? She's got me now, and I know it, and she knows I know it.

'Go on then, Bell. You've gorra do it. It's the rules. Or you're not gerrin' this phone back. Or don't you trust me?' She leans against the high brick wall, arms folded across her beefy chest, my new phone clutched tightly in her fist. Kez talks with a strong accent, more like my old friends in Byker than most kids at school, although I think she puts it on a bit.

Next to us the wooden door to someone's backyard is open a little, and my heart is thumping.

'It's easy, man,' she says. 'Just gan in, take somethin' and come oot again.'

'But take *what*?' I'm trying not to sound scared, but I am: my voice has gone all high like it does sometimes. Kez wants me – requires me – to go into someone's backyard and steal something. And I've never stolen anything in my life – well, nothing big.

'*Anything*, y' great chicken. Anything that's there. I bet there's a bike. We can take that. Oh, don't look at me like that: we'll put it back. Honestly, we're not thieves, man. It's just borrowin'. This is a test of your courage: a "rite of passage" they call it. Years ago, they'd make you swim across a river with crocodiles in it, so count yourself lucky. I'll wait here and keep watch. Off you go.'

'But . . .'

Kez bends her head close to mine and I can smell her chewing-gum breath. 'But what, soft lad? You scared? Good. You should face your fears! Stand up to them! Welcome to the grown-ups' club.'

She prods me in the chest with a thick, nail-bitten forefinger.

'Now *go*.'

CHAPTER 7

I've opened the squeaky door as much as I need to squeeze through when Kez says, 'I'm not lettin' you back out unless you've got something.' She pushes me hard, then pulls the door shut behind me with a loud bang, disturbing a seagull from a shed roof.

I look round the space: there's nothing to steal. I'm quite relieved.

I'll just go back to the door and say, 'Kez: there's nothing to take.'

Doesn't sound good. I glance around again. There's a big green wheelie bin, and next to it a smaller black one with a recycling symbol on it, some bin bags, and some flattened cardboard boxes. That's it: a few square metres of cracked, swept concrete.

There's a small kitchen window and a back door into the house and to my right is a narrow shed. I try the door and it opens. It's dark inside, but I can tell it's just shed junk. Kez said 'anything', though, so . . .

I put my hand out. A thick cobweb flaps into my face. On the floor there's a paper carrier bag with handles.

It's going to have to do. There's a box in it or something, but I don't wait to look – I just want to get out of here. I squash the whole thing down inside my hoodie and zip it up to my throat.

I shut the shed door behind me and I'm ready to run for it when the light in the kitchen window comes on. I press myself against the side of the shed, squeezing myself into a shadowy corner of the wall as I hear the back door open.

From inside comes a woman's voice.

'Go on out, you smelly old thing.'

The biggest dog I've ever seen shuffles out and starts sniffing around. The kitchen light goes off and I hear an internal door in the house shut as whoever let the dog out goes back inside.

The massive beast has got coarse black-and-ginger hair in tight curls. It doesn't notice me. It sniffs around on the ground and then squats to do a poo. It's in the middle of its business when it turns its head towards me.

If fear has a smell, then I must stink.

Slowly, the old dog finishes, rises off its haunches and ambles towards me, leaving a small mountain of steaming poo behind. I'm wondering if it is one of those 'friendly to everyone' dogs like Tony and Lynn's collie over the road, and I'm getting ready to pet it when it pulls back its top lip and emits a growl that makes me go cold.

R-r-r-r-r-r-r-r-r!

Its head dips, as if it's going to leap at me. It's between me and the door leading to the back lane.

'Kez! Kez!' I'm sort of shout-whispering, but she doesn't hear me.

When I hear the kitchen door open again, and the light comes on, I have no choice but to run, in a kind of backwards arc round the dog. In my panic, my foot squishes right into the mound of poo. I slide but remain upright and make it to the back door past the dog who has started a loud barking, but is probably too old and slow to chase me. Turns out I'm wrong about that.

'What is it, Dennis?' says a woman from the house. 'What's up?'

The dog has made a late start, and has followed me, growling, as I wrench open the door to the alleyway. Dennis is coming for me and I only mean to shut the door to keep him in, but I pull it really hard and something is stopping it, so I pull still harder, and that's when I hear a crack and a howl of pain. I look down and, horrified, I see that I have trapped the dog's front paw, and one of his claws is bent at a horrible angle.

Immediately, I let go of the door, which springs open again, but I can't stop. Dennis doesn't stop, either, and limps after me, barking and snarling and trailing drops of blood. I run down the back lane, clutching the paper bag under my hoodie. I've run about twenty metres when I realise that the dog is gaining on me in spite of its injury.

Kez is nowhere to be seen. (I find out later that she legged it the minute she heard the back door to the house open. 'Test of courage.' Yeah, right.) She's still got my phone.

I look behind me. A woman has followed the dog out of the backyard and is coming after me. 'Hey! Stop! You little—' she swears at me.

There's a bend in the lane that takes me out of sight of my pursuers for a moment, and, while I'm running, I unzip my hoodie and chuck the bag I'm holding as hard as I can over the wall. It is evidence of my crime, and I want rid of it. It sails through the air and I hear it land. Still, Dennis is getting closer, probably seeking revenge for his injury, and I know I won't be able to outrun him. I get to a pair of big wheelie bins and clamber on top of them. On the other side of the wall is a garden belonging to a house that's been empty for ages, so I grip the top of the wall and haul myself over.

It's a long drop on the other side. My T-shirt and hoodie ride up and I scrape my belly and chest hard as I lower myself down behind a big bush. On the other side of the wall, the dog is barking and its owner has caught up with it. 'Where's he gone, the little toerag? Oh my God, Dennis, you poor thing, you poor thing!' Then she says something that makes my stomach turn over with fear. 'We'll find him, won't we?'

They'll find me?

I try to push my fear down.

There are loads of blond kids.

The evening's getting darker.

She can't have seen that I've stolen anything because there was nothing in my hands – it was inside my hoodie.

She'll not do anything . . .

It's working. My breathing settles. Everything's quiet, apart from some traffic a couple of streets away.

Wait.

I touch my head. There *are* blond kids at my school . . . but almost everyone has their hair short. Mine is a bit of a haystack, and it makes me stand out.

Still, I can't worry about that now.

My chest is stinging like mad where I scraped it. I realise not *everything* is quiet: there is a gentle, rapid flapping noise coming from the other side of the bush. Nervously, I peep out and see a big overgrown garden with a flagpole in the middle of it. And now I can see what is causing the flapping sound: countless strings of little flags all tied near the top of the flagpole are rattling in the strong evening breeze. They stretch out from the pole to ground level, forming a large colourful cone like a circus tent. Next to them is what appears to be a bundle of rags.

As I watch, the bundle sprouts a pair of short, skinny legs, and in seconds it's on its feet and a head pops out of the top and glares at me. I shrink back, but it's too late: I've been spotted. It's a tiny old lady with deep lines in her dark-skinned face. Her hair is straight, shiny and black with streaks of white. She releases the fabric over her thin legs and I see she has been gathering up a long sarong in her hands.

She waddles towards me, saying something fast and quite angry in a language I don't recognise. Then there's another voice, also coming from beneath the canopy of little flags. A girl emerges, holding my tattered paper bag by the handles.

'Is this yours?' she asks.

CHAPTER 8

Obviously, it *isn't* mine, because I've just stolen it, but I can't say that, can I? The girl squints, first at me, with small almost-black eyes, then at the bag. It's bashed up now, and its bottom is ripped.

Did this girl hear the commotion: the dog barking, the lady shouting at me? If she did, then she's not showing it.

'Erm . . . no. That is, y-yes. I-it's mine,' I stammer. She smiles and holds it out to me. The old lady in the sarong exchanges a few words with her in a language that sounds sort of Chinese, but how would I know?

Then the old lady points at me. I look down at my chest, which is stinging from the bad scraping it received. You know when you graze your knee? It's like that but about a hundred times bigger and more painful. My hoodie's flapping open in the breeze, and blood is starting to ooze through my T-shirt.

'Are you all right?' says the girl. Her voice is concerned and kind of posh: she's definitely not from around here. She steps forward, then from a pocket in her skirt she takes out a glasses case and carefully puts the specs on to look at my bloody T-shirt. 'My grandmother says you should come inside. We can put something on that. We were meditating, but we can carry on later.'

Meditating?

I just want to get out of there as quickly as I can, so I say, 'No thanks. I'm fine. Really I am.' I even manage a brave grin. 'Just a little scratch.'

She nods, then looks at me very directly. 'What were you doing?'

'Erm . . . nothing, really. You see, I . . . erm . . . I was heading home when this dog started chasing me and, you know, I had to get away from it, so I got rid of the bag so I could run faster and then I jumped over your wall, and sorry to intrude, and . . .'

Stop babbling, Malky!

'. . . And, anyway, I'd better be off. Thanks. Ha ha!' I start walking down the path that runs round the garden.

All the way through this, the girl has let me talk, a peaceful half-smile on her face as if nothing surprises her and nothing bothers her. Her blacker-than-black hair is similar to the old lady's but longer, and her skin shines as though she has just stepped out of the bath. In fact, everything about her looks new: her freshly pressed tartan skirt, white knee-socks, plain blue sweater. It's like she has dressed in her best clothes just to sit in the garden under some flags.

The old lady's angry face has gone, and she now has the same expression as the girl. 'Serene' I suppose you'd call it. (Also 'unnerving' and 'maybe slightly unhinged'.)

'You are going the wrong way,' the girl says, and points to an iron gate in the wall, twisted with weeds. 'Follow me, I will let you out. You need to make sure the dog has gone.'

I walk after her. She punches a code into a pad at the side of the metal gate and it pops open as much as the weeds will allow. I slip through into the back lane and glance up and down: there is no sign of Dennis, or his owner. In the half-light of the evening, I can see drops of blood leading back along the lane.

The girl holds out the bag. 'Don't forget this.'

'Oh, er . . . thanks,' I say.

'What is so valuable?' she says.

I look down. 'Ah . . . it's just, you know . . . stuff. Some stuff. I erm . . . found it.'

She knows you're lying, Malky.

She nods as if I'm making perfect sense. 'Stuff? Well, goodbye then. I expect I will see you at school, assuming you are at Marden Middle School?'

I nod. 'How did you know?'

She points at my hoodie. It's a faded school one, with the school's crest printed on it. Mam bought it at a second-hand sale last year.

'That's a clue.'

She holds out her hand to shake, like she is a grown-up. 'Susan,' she says. 'Susan Tenzin. I am in Mrs Farroukh's class.' *Clahss*. Her hand is still held out, so I shake it.

'Hi. I mean, how do you do? Very pleased to meet you. Malcolm Bell.'

Perhaps the 'how do you do' is going a bit far, but she just says, 'I hope the bleeding stops soon.' She is about to shut the gate when from the other direction the old lady reappears, holding something in her hand and scuttling along on her little legs at a speed that would be impressive for someone half her age. Susan's shoulders drop and she mutters, 'Oh no,' almost under her breath.

The old lady draws level with me and holds out a small package of brown paper.

I take it warily. She scrunches up her round face in a smile, showing yellow teeth, and then mimes rubbing something into her chest. I look at Susan, puzzled.

'It is . . . a remedy. You should rub it on your chest,' she says, 'for the wound.' Susan sounds doubtful.

'Oh, erm . . . thanks. What is it?' I lift the packet to my nose and sniff, and immediately wish I hadn't. I get a whiff of cheese and old trainers.

'It is what we call *dri*. It is yak's butter. Erm . . . rancid yak's butter.' Susan sounds a bit embarrassed.

Well, this is awkward. I look between the two of them. Remember, I've just dropped into their meditation session, I'm now hurrying away and I've been given a stinking packet of rotten butter, like the world's worst party bag. The old lady is clearly thrilled and says the first words in English I've heard her speak.

'You will be better soon. *Dri* is best!'

I nod, more enthusiastically than I feel, but it seems polite. As she goes to shut the gate, Susan leans in and says in a quiet voice, 'To tell the truth, you may be better off with something else. Savlon, antiseptic spray, anything, really.' Then she gives a little half-smile. 'See you tomorrow, smart and shiny!'

She closes the gate and I'm back in the lane, as though I've just woken from a strange dream.

There's something still bothering me, though, as I wipe the last of Dennis's poo from my shoe on a patch of grass. 'Smart and shiny!' the girl had said. She means the school uniform, I guess, and it makes me swallow nervously. I'm wearing a maroon hoodie with MMS – the school's initials – in big white letters on the back.

Which means the woman with the dog will have seen it.

What with my hair, and the school hoodie . . . she's bound to find me.

And did I mention that I'm on my last chance at school? Probably not, actually. It's a bit of a problem. Well. More than a bit.

Not as much of a problem, though, as what is inside the bag I stole. But I only find that out later.

CHAPTER 9

Tynemouth is a jumble of houses, big and small, old and new, its streets connected by a warren of back lanes crammed with bins and parked cars.

I've emerged at the end of the street that leads to our tiny terraced house, clutching the paper bag, and I'm thinking, *I'll just dump the bag in the recycling bin on our street.*

It's stolen goods, right? Only I'm not a thief. I haven't even had a proper look at what's inside, and Kez Becker ran away at the first sign of trouble, so if I just casually drop the bag here, in the bin, *without even knowing what it is*, then no one will know and everything will be fine, won't it?

'What you got there, Malky?'

Dammit: Sebastian. Just my luck. Half a minute either way and I'd have missed him. Less, in fact. Mam has just started to let him walk back on his own from his friend Hassan's house a few doors down, and he's swaggering along the pavement, hands in his pockets, like he flippin' owns it.

He's seven.

Well, what would you do?

'Oh, *this*?' I say, looking a bit like I didn't know I was carrying a bashed-up paper bag. 'It's, erm . . . not mine. I, erm . . . found it. I was just about to throw it away.'

Seb just stands there, blinking rapidly at me, trying to work out whether I am lying. Most of his experience will tell him that I probably am. I am his big brother, after all, and telling lies to younger siblings is one of the few privileges we have.

'You *found* it? Where? What is it? And why were you going to chuck it if you've just found it?' Sebastian has a nose for a dodgy story, despite his age. He tries to look inside the bag, but I hold it closer to my chest, and silently wince as it rubs against my scraped and bleeding skin. At least the bag conceals the bloodstains on my T-shirt.

Seb reaches into the bag and starts to pick at the box inside, which is sealed with tape. Suddenly I feel very jealous: I want to be the one to discover what I've been stealing-not-stealing. I snatch it away from him.

'Leave it alone, you little pest!'

'Did you nick it? You did, didn't you? What is it? Who'd you nick it from? Tell me or I'm telling Mam.'

Aaaagh! It's like he's got some sixth sense.

Fit Billy next door is standing on his front path, holding a massive dumbbell in each hand and performing arm curls, shirtless even though the sun has gone down. He grunts as he lifts the weights and says, 'Hi, lads! How's yer mam?' He always wants to chat.

Mam reckons he's lonely since his mam died and his girlfriend moved out, so I feel bad hurrying past and saying a quick, 'Hi, Billy.'

'I've got something for you,' he says to me. He puts his weights down and takes my phone out of his trackie bottoms pocket. 'Friend of yours came past a few minutes ago. Said she found it at the top of the beach steps, and knew it was yours because of the case. You wanna be careful with it, son. Canny phone, that is!'

'Oh aye . . . thanks, Billy,' I stammer.

At least that is one less thing I have to worry about.

Some hope. I look at the screen and there's a long, fine crack across the glass. My phone! (It was a present from Dad, so we could FaceTime, he said, although we hardly have.)

I don't hear the rest of what Billy says. Something about a new World War Two film he's got off Amazon. He's obsessed with the war, is Billy.

I get the package in the house and upstairs without Mam seeing. It isn't hard – she's asleep on the settee because she had an early shift this morning. I've zipped up my hoodie to hide my bloody T-shirt from Seb and now the carrier bag sits on the floor between our beds.

'Open it then,' says Seb.

'Okay, okay.'

I told him that the bag was by some bins – and that was sort of a bit true-ish. Even as I pick up the bag, I work on my conscience.

If it was by, well, okay near *the bins in that yard, then it must be rubbish. Nobody wanted it. It belonged to nobody. Probably.*

Therefore it is definitely not stealing. You cannot steal something that has no owner.

Seb and I sit opposite each other while I run my thumbnail through the tape on the top of the cardboard box and tip the contents on to my duvet: two slim packages about the size of a small pizza box, each bearing an identical coloured label.

CHAPTER 10

KENNETH 'the Mystic o' the Highlands'
McKINLEY

presents

THE DREAMINATOR

Live Your Perfect Dreams!
Dream Your Perfect Life!
MAKE YOUR DREAMS COME TRUE!

100% Safe — 100% Restful
— 100% Money Back Guarantee

There's a picture of a grinning middle-aged man with a luxuriant swept-up hairstyle, the goldish colour of a pound coin; he has dazzling teeth of a whiteness I've never seen for real. His eyes peer out from the picture over the top of round, coloured glasses. The design of the label looks pretty old-fashioned. Definitely from way before I was born.

I ease up the lid of one of the packages and there is another label resting on top of the contents.

USE ONLY AS DIRECTED IN THESE INSTRUCTIONS

Underneath this is a clear plastic bag containing lots of bits and pieces: strings, sticks, a plastic hoop made to look like bamboo, feathers, a circular disc the size of a saucer with threads woven in a pattern, like the head of a tiny, intricate tennis racquet.

There is yet another sheet labelled:

ASSEMBLY INSTRUCTIONS

On the other side is a drawing of the finished object, which at least gives me something to go on. Bit by plastic bit, taking about twenty minutes and watched by an awestruck Seb, I shove 'Stick A' into 'Slot B', and thread 'String C' through 'Hole D' and so on until I have something that looks exactly – okay, *almost* exactly – like the illustration. I hold it up for Seb's approval, dangling it from my finger, and he sighs in admiration.

'Awethome!'

Round my finger is a hook leading to a short plastic chain attached to the top of a pyramid about twenty centimetres square, but without a base. The sides of the pyramid glitter a dull gold ('suffused with crystals of pure pyrite' according to the sheet). From each base corner comes a wire: from these hangs the plastic-bamboo hoop. The woven disc with the coloured glass sits in the centre of the hoop, and from the hoop hang feathers and beaded wires with tiny, jewel-like stones at the end. Just visible inside the rim of the hoop is another wire that leads to a small, empty battery pack sitting inside the pyramid. Dangling from the centre of the whole thing is a wire with an on-off switch.

It is a strange cross between one of those mobiles that you hang above a baby's cot and a wind chime. It's quite pretty, I suppose, if you like that sort of thing.

Seb reaches over and plucks the thing from my hands.

'Hey! Careful!' I say.

Seb stares at the Dreaminator, allowing it to hang from his finger, and then at me. There's something in his eyes that I don't like: an accusing look.

'You nicked it, didn't you? I know you did.'

That's the problem with Seb. He's far, far too smart. I can beat him in a fight, but he's clever with stuff like this.

'There's two of them,' he says. 'Put the other one together and let me have it, or I'll tell Mam you've been stealing stuff.'

I don't really have a choice, do I?

I sigh. Then, sullenly, I get to work on the second package. And it's maybe exactly *then* that everything starts to go wrong.

Like I said – sort of Seb's fault, really.

CHAPTER 11

When both Dreaminators are assembled, I pick up the instructions again – they're pretty short. On the first side of the single sheet is a repeat of the photo from the box cover, and 'a letter to the buyer' that gives me a pang of guilt, because I didn't buy it at all. Still, I'm too excited to find out about it to worry that much, and I read the whole thing aloud to Seb.

THE DREAMINATOR (™)

A Letter to the Buyer

Hello!

Thank you for buying the Dreaminator! You are now the proud owner of a revolutionary concept in sleep and dream management. I am delighted that you have made this purchase and I am confident that a world of amazing adventures awaits you – and all while you are fast asleep!

My name is Kenneth McKinley. You may know me from my appearances on stage, radio and television . . .

I glance up at Seb. He shakes his head.

He's never heard of this fella, either, but then it must have been ages ago, judging by the yellowed paper and the design and everything. He's probably dead by now.

Based on teachings and traditions from all around the globe, the Dreaminator (™) harnesses the deepest powers of your sleeping brain to allow the user to become conscious in his or her dreams – yet remain asleep!

THESE ARE WAKING DREAMS!

That's right! With practice, you will be able to recognise when you are dreaming while you are dreaming, and make choices about what happens.

Say goodbye to frustrating dreams that you do not understand!

No more nightmares! When you literally control your demons, you can send them packing!

Happy dreaming!

Kenneth 'the Mystic o' the Highlands' McKinley

Seb is doing his rapid-blinking thing as he tries to take in what I have just read out.

'So . . .' he begins and then trails off. He tries again. 'So . . . you can be awake even though you are asleep?'

'Sounds like it.'

'But that doesn't make sense.'

I shrug. I have to say it doesn't make a lot of sense to me, either. I turn the sheet over and start reading again.

What are 'waking dreams'?

Waking dreams are sometimes called 'lucid dreaming'. This is a term devised in 1867 by the Frenchman the Marquis de Saint-Denys who first described the extraordinary ability to be fully conscious and direct your dreams while you are asleep.

The Dreaminator™ combines the teachings of Saint-Denys with philosophies and traditions from other cultures – such as Native Americans, West African animist religions, Buddhist meditation and Western 'New Age' thought – to create a powerful tool.

The Dreaminator™ uses the unique and mysterious properties of crystals to create a charge of ultra-low-level energy around the sleeping person. Coupled with the ancient power of the pyramids – known since the time of the Egyptian pharaohs – this creates an astonishing combination of forces.

Now you can have 'waking dreams' whenever you sleep!

Fulfil your wildest desires, enact your craziest fantasy! All from the safety of your own bed.

When you wake, you will be just as refreshed as after a good night's sleep.

'Awethome!' breathes Seb again. 'I wanna try it!'

The instructions say to position the Dreaminator above your head while you sleep, and, minutes later, we have found four triple-A batteries in the kitchen drawer and put two in each unit. Then, by balancing the little bedside cabinet on each of our beds in turn, I have fixed the screws into the ceiling, and hung the contraptions over our beds with the little on-off switch hanging down within reach of my hand.

I read out the last bit.

How to dream the Dreaminator way!

1. Go to sleep as normal, at your normal time, with the Dreaminator™ turned on.
2. During a dream, you may become aware that you are dreaming. To test this, simply ask someone else in the dream, 'Am I dreaming?' They will almost always answer with the truth.
3. Another dream test is to look at a clock or to read. Numbers on clocks and printed words are usually jumbled or indistinct during dreams.
4. Finally, try to float! Even the laws of gravity are under your control!
5. To wake up (for example, if you do not like the dream and no longer wish to control it) simply say to yourself, 'Wake up!' If this does not work, try holding your breath for a few seconds and then expelling it forcefully.
6. If you do not wake yourself up deliberately, your dream will end naturally as your sleep cycle finishes and you will wake up as normal.

Remember – perfect results may not be achieved straight away.

Happy dreaming!

I put down the sheet of instructions and puff out my cheeks. 'Well,' I say to Seb, who is gazing up at the Dreaminators hanging from the ceiling. 'What do you make of that?'

'What does he make of what?' says Mam, standing in the doorway.

CHAPTER 12

We were so absorbed that we didn't hear her come upstairs. She sees the new additions to the room, hanging from the ceiling, straight away. 'What the heck are they?'

If I was going to come up with some explanation that wasn't the whole truth, then I'm too late, because Seb answers immediately.

'They're called Dreaminators. They . . . give you better dreams.'

Mam rolls her eyes and goes, '*Pfft!*', the way she does when one of us says something so unbelievable that she can't even be bothered to argue. 'Where on earth did you get them?'

'Malky found them!'

Mam narrows her eyes. She's suspicious. Seb continues. 'At the Lifeboat Nearly New Sale. This afternoon. Hassan's mam was running a stall. A pound for them both. Weren't they, Malky? What do you reckon?'

He's such a convincing liar, I'm almost envious. But here's the thing: I owe him now, and he knows it.

Mam shakes her head and smiles. She picks up the

sheet of instructions from the bed and glances over it, far too quickly to read it properly, and I know I've got her. 'They look ridiculous. Do they play nursery rhymes?'

Seb is defensive. 'No! They allow you to control your dreams.'

'Oh aye? You did that with Cuthbert the crocodile when you were little, Malky. Do you remember?' I bristle. I haven't been troubled by crocodile dreams for ages. Mam is properly chuckling now. 'Good luck with that, boys. If it works, let me know – I've got a couple of dreams myself that I wouldn't mind coming true!'

I smile back at her little joke. I like making Mam laugh. She doesn't do it often and when I asked her why, about a year ago, she got really sad so I never mentioned it again.

She's being normal Mam again soon enough. 'Now, Sebastian, have you finished your holiday project? Well, *why not*, Seb? It's only stickers. And, Malky, when did you last wash your hair? It's like a ferret's nest. Don't forget – tonight, please. First day of term tomorrow.'

Later that evening, I'm in the bathroom, looking at my chest. It's scabbed and raw and still oozing blood in one or two places. I've tried to dab at it with a clean sponge. There's no antiseptic spray in the bathroom cabinet so I've smeared a bit of the yak's butter on the deepest scratch.

'Outta the way, Malk. I'm dying for a wee! Oh! What you done to . . . ugh! That looks *gross*. And what's that smell?'

Told you. Totally annoying.

'Get lost. I'm . . . I'm not well.'

One of the many problems with Seb is that he's not easily put off when I snarl at him. 'What did you do?' he says. 'That's blood, that is.'

'I *know*. I fell over, okay? Just . . . don't say anything. Mam's got enough to worry about.' That's good, I think. I sound responsible, big-brotherly. From the look on his face, though, Seb has joined the dots: he knows my injuries and the Dreaminators are connected.

I pull on my pyjama top carefully to avoid the huge graze. I roll up my T-shirt so as to disguise the bloodstains, and put it at the bottom of the laundry basket.

When Mam comes into our room to kiss us goodnight, she leans over me and tightens the duvet across my chest and I have to remember not to wince in pain and to smile as she says, 'New school year, boys. Shall we have a story?'

I reply, 'No,' so quickly that Mam blinks in surprise. 'I . . . I mean, not tonight, Mam.' I force a little yawn, but I can tell Mam's a bit hurt. She likes reading us stories, even if it's *Kobi the Cave Boy* for the billionth time.

'I'm working lates a lot this month,' she says. 'There may not be as many chances.'

I certainly know the thing by heart, and at least it's not long. Seb reaches under his bed and pulls out the very well-used picture book. I always thought he'd grow out of it, but he never did. I can't even remember a time when he *wasn't* obsessed with it.

Mam settles down on Seb's bed and begins reading, and Seb mouths along with the words, while I stare at the Dreaminators, silently urging her to speed up.

'In the shadows of the cave, the fire flickers red,
And Kobi lies down with a rock beneath his
head . . .'

It's the story of a boy in the Stone Age who lives with his family in a cave, long before houses and cars and aeroplanes and machines and clothes were invented. There's a lake, and another tribe of Stone Age people, and he rides on a mammoth . . .

I yawn again, a big one this time, and Mam pauses.

'Aww, I want the end,' says Seb, but I manage to catch his eye and I flick a glance upwards. He gets it. 'But if Malky's tired that's okay.'

Mam closes the book and looks between us, with mock surprise. 'Hang on – have you two just agreed on something without arguing?' She runs her fingers through her short curls and shakes her head. 'I hope it lasts! Sweet dreams,' she says. She always says that: it's like an unreliable magic spell that only sometimes works. Then she switches the light off and the twin circles of dull blue light hanging over our beds stand out in the dark.

'Do they stay on all night?' she says. Then, before I can answer, she starts to sniff the air. 'What's that smell?'

'Yeah – I noticed that as well,' says Seb. 'I thought it was Malky's socks!'

It's rancid yak's butter, but obviously I'm not going to say that. Instead, I say, 'Dunno. I can't smell anything.' Mam shrugs and goes out.

We lie awake in silence for a while, Seb and I. I'm staring up at the circles of blue crystals.

Eventually, I hear, 'Psst. Malk. You awake?'

'Mmm?'

'Are you scared?'

'Scared of what?'

'You know. The Dreamylater.'

'Dreaminator. No. Why? You?'

Pause. 'No.'

He means yes.

'Psst. Malk.'

Sigh. 'What now?'

'Good luck.'

I remember the sheet of instructions:

Remember – perfect results may not be achieved straight away.

In order to dream, of course, you have to be asleep. Instead of falling asleep, though, I find my head churning around with the events of the last few hours.

The Dreaminator glows faintly above me.

Kez Becker . . . the empty backyard . . . that poor dog and his broken claw . . . the old lady . . . the flags . . . the girl, what was her name again?

It's gone.

And then I'm gone.

CHAPTER 13

It's the next day. First day of term. I'm in school, in my form room, and Seb is there as well for some reason that I can't work out.

Next-door's Fit Billy is standing in front of the class because he's our teacher, although he keeps talking in a foreign language that sounds like Chinese and everyone is laughing at him as he takes off his shirt and flexes his muscles.

I look round at my classmates: there's Mason, and Callum, and the two Darcys, and Kobi, and . . .

Hang on. *Kobi?* The cave boy from the book. He's not even real: he looks like a three-dimensional drawing, and . . .

We're not in my classroom, we're in the cave, from the first big picture in the book. The cave walls are orangey-red from a fire in the middle of the classroom floor, and . . .

Everyone is gathered at the mouth of the cave and pointing. A huge black-and-ginger dog is walking past on the school rugby pitch outside. When I say huge, it's about the size of an elephant. Is it a dog? Or . . . or . . . a *mammoth*? A prehistoric woolly mammoth, with a long trunk and huge curved tusks, and . . .

And from somewhere a memory kind of swims into my head. A memory of something I need to do. Did I hear it? Did I read it? I turn to Seb – *Why is Seb in my class, again?* – and I find myself saying, 'Hey, Seb. Am . . . am I dreaming?'

And Seb says, 'Yes. Of course you are!' and I grin with slowly dawning relief. I knew it!

That was one of the instructions, wasn't it? Written down on the sheet that came with the Dreaminator: ask someone if you're dreaming and they'll tell you!

Of course, it makes sense now why Fit Billy's our teacher, and why Kobi the Cave Boy is in my class, and why there's a mammoth outside the cave mouth. That is if 'sense' is the right word for nonsense.

Another thought crosses my mind, only it's not the mind that is here: it is like another mind that is observing what is going on. It is this mind that tells me to look at the classroom clock, there on the cave wall, and when I do its hands are moving quickly, but spinning backwards. I know then for sure that I am in a dream. A waking dream!

I turn my attention back to the mammoth, which has cocked its leg on a rugby post and is peeing like a burst water pipe. Everyone is laughing.

There is something I want to try: something else that I recall from the instructions. I stand apart from my classmates, and, while they're looking out of the window, I stand on my tiptoes and tell myself, *Float, Malky, float!* and I do, just a bit, as though a wire between my shoulder blades is lifting me up slowly. I start to laugh, even though, as I get higher, it's a bit scary: if I fall suddenly, I'll crash into my desk and chair and it'll hurt.

Did I just do that? Am I floating?

The feeling makes me breathless with excitement. My mind is overflowing with thoughts. Did I really just control something in my dream? Am I really dreaming?

It doesn't feel like it at all. It feels real – only I can float if I want to.

'Oh, I say! Look at Malcolm Bell!' goes a posh voice. I look down and it's the girl in the blue jumper with the black hair from over the wall. She's pointing and smiling her lips-together smile and everyone else is going, 'Whoa!' and, 'Awesome!' and, 'Check out Malky Bell!'

By the time my head touches the rocky cave roof, I'm getting a bit freaked out, and so I say, 'Down!' but nothing happens. I push with my hand against the ceiling, and descend a bit, but then I bob up again, as though I'm a helium-filled balloon.

Seb grabs my shoe and pulls me down, but, as soon as he releases me, I float up again. This time I bang my head hard on the cave roof.

I don't like this. 'Down!' I say again. 'Let me down!'

This time, though, I really mean it. I am calm. I *expect* it to happen. And so it does. I flap my arms gently by my sides as I float back to stand on top of the school desk, and I do a little tap dance to make my classmates laugh. Mr Springham, the deputy head, has appeared and even *he's* smiling.

Then there's a scream (probably the Darcys), and people scuttle away from the desk, pointing underneath it. I watch from my position on top of the desk as the knobbled grey-green snout of a huge crocodile emerges, followed by the head and finally the whole fat body.

I look around: everyone has disappeared. It's just me and a crocodile I have not seen in years.

'You!' I say, and it curls its scaly lip in response.

I swallow hard, wondering if it will still work. I hold out my hand towards the croc and, trying to stop my voice from quavering, I say, 'Cu-Cuthbert.'

Just then, the school bell rings, making a noise exactly like the alarm on my phone, and keeps ringing and ringing and ringing.

Cuthbert begins to shrink, and still the bell is ringing . . .

It's working!

He's getting smaller and smaller.

I feel a surge of elation, power and confidence . . .

CHAPTER 14

. . . and I wake up, blinking, in my bed, the alarm on my phone ringing and the sunlight streaming through the window.

The top of my head hurts a bit where I hit the ceiling – except that was in my dream, so I must have bumped it on the wall behind my bed.

Turning my head to the side, I see Seb in the morning light, his eyes shut, breathing gently, making occasional little snuffling noises.

Above my head hangs the Dreaminator, the glow of the little stones barely visible in the light. It twists slowly, even though there's no air to move it. Perhaps it's my breath: I am breathing quite heavily, though I don't feel tired.

What the blinking, flipping heck just happened?

It really *did* happen. Didn't it? I 'controlled a dream'. It was like I was awake, but I was definitely asleep.

How long did the dream last? Not all night, surely? Do I remember all of it? Could I do it again?

Gradually, I realise I can recall it all perfectly, which is unusual in itself. Think about it: as soon as you try to remember a dream, it starts slipping away. It's like trying to hold on to smoke. But I just lie there, recalling all the details as if it really happened: the big dog-mammoth peeing like a burst hydrant, Fit Billy talking Chinese, the floating, the crocodile under the desk . . .

My breathing returns to normal and the sunlight gets stronger, and I'm fully awake and smiling. I hear Mam get up and go to the bathroom before putting her head round our door.

'Oh, hi, Malky,' she says. 'You're awake! You look happy. Sleep well?'

It's not really a question. She's gone by the time I answer, 'I think so.'

I look across at my brother who could sleep through an earthquake. 'Seb! Seb! Hey – wake up – did it work for you?'

He rubs his head, making his hair stand on end, and yawns, and runs his tongue round his morning-dry mouth. Then he looks up at his Dreaminator, bites his lip in deep thought and eventually says, 'I'm not sure. I'm trying to remember.'

'You didn't dream anything?'

Then Mam comes back in, saying that Dad's on her phone. (This means *she* has had to call *him* to remind him to wish us good luck on our first day of term because he forgot to call last night, like he did last term. He's very forgetful, is Dad. I'm not sure it's all his fault.)

So it's Dad that I tell first. I tell him I had a really odd dream, and he listens, but he doesn't really get it. I must be gabbling and not making much sense, because at one point he says, 'You okay, Malky?' But then he has to cut the call short or he'll be late and to say hi to Seb from him, that he'll call him later. We both know he'll forget.

The rest is all toothpaste, toast, cereal and Seb's missing gym shoes. I'm up and dressed and downstairs, eating breakfast, before Seb reappears. I haven't said anything to Mam, as I'm still trying to work out what the dream was all about and, for that matter, whether it even happened.

You probably just dreamed it all, Malky.

I mean: that would be possible, wouldn't it? I could dream that I was awake in a dream?

Seb sits at the table and starts to pile butter on to a slice of toast, a smirk playing at the corners of his mouth. Mam notices.

'What's amusing you this morning, Sonny Jim? And easy on the butter. We don't own a cow,' she says, pouring cereal into his bowl.

'I've remembered my strange dream last night,' he lisps, causing toast crumbs to spray on to the table and Mam to tut. I pause, a spoonful of cereal halfway to my mouth.

'Oh aye? Your dream thingummy worked then!' says Mam.

'I was in this classroom with some other kids. And Billy from next door was there. He was the teacher but he couldn't speak English.'

Mam smiles at this. 'His Geordie accent is so strong, I sometimes wonder myself! Sounds like a typical crazy dream!'

'Yeah, and . . . and . . .' Seb was trying to remember. 'There was this massive dog, like . . . like the mamuffs in *Kobi*, weeing all over a football pitch or something . . .'

I have put my spoon down by now. My mouth is hanging open, waiting to hear what he's going to say next, yet at the same time knowing exactly what is coming.

He's going to describe you floating, Malky . . .

'. . . and then Malky was there and he started floating, right there in the middle of the cave-room thing. Oh, and Kobi from the book was there too! And Malky floated higher and higher till his head hit the ceiling . . .'

I instinctively put my hand up to my head where my scalp is still a little bit tender from banging it on the wall.

'And, every time I tried to pull him down, he floated back up again!'

Mam laughs, and I am about to say something when there's the honk of a car horn from outside and everything is in a rush as Seb grabs his stuff and dashes outside to get in the car with the twins whose mum takes them to Seb's school.

'See ya later, alligator!' he shouts, and waits for me to respond.

'In a while . . . crocodile.' I almost whisper it, I'm so deep in thought. 'Mam?' I say after the front door has slammed and Seb and the twins have gone. Mam doesn't look round but gives a distracted, 'Mmm?' as she's clearing up the breakfast things.

What are you going to say, Malky? It sounds ridiculous, doesn't it? Perhaps just say it?

'Me . . . and Seb . . . had the same dream last night.'

'Have you got your clean gym stuff? Oh, did you? That's nice!'

'No, I mean – we had the same dream, and . . .'

'I ironed it for you, by the way. I used to get that with your Uncle Pete sometimes.'

I look at her with surprise. 'You mean you were in the same dream at the same time?'

Her turn to look at me now. She wipes her hands on a towel and her lip curls slightly. 'Erm . . . no, Malky. I've no idea how *that* would work! No, I mean we'd dream about similar things, like . . .'

I interrupt. 'No, Mam, not similar as in nearly the same. I mean *exactly* the same. Seb was *in* my dream, and I was in *his*!'

Mam's eyes crinkle at the edges and a slow smile spreads across her tired-looking face. She shakes her head at me. 'Malky Bell! If you could only turn that imagination of yours in the direction of your schoolwork this year, your teachers will be much happier, and I wouldn't have these worry lines, would I?'

She leans over me and kisses the top of my head. 'And don't forget – you've signed a Conduct Contract. Come on, scoot – or you'll be late on the first day of term.'

Oh yeah. The school 'Conduct Contract'. I hadn't forgotten. I've a horrible feeling that things are going to get difficult.

NOW

CHAPTER 15

Four weeks and many waking dreams later, I'm looking between my little brother – his mouth open, snoring quietly – and the bedroom door. I've been awake a few minutes, but nothing I have tried will wake Seb. The mark on his face where I slapped him to try to rouse him is getting redder. Mam's voice comes again.

'What's the matter, boys?'

'Nothing, Mam. Bad dream!' I call back.

I run through the dream we've just had in my head. The Gravy Lake, the huge man, the dogs . . .

Then I ran away and left Seb unable to wake from his dream.

My dream? My nightmare.

I look up again at the Dreaminators, then reach up and turn them both off in case they're still having some sort of effect. It's already light outside and I pull open the curtains, willing the sunlight to wake Seb, but he lies there in the deepest sleep.

'Come on, come on, Lil-Bro,' I mutter, using the nickname I had for him from ages back, which I'd stopped calling him. Then I start shaking him again and Mam comes in.

'What on earth's going on, Malky?'

I stand there, naked, in our little bedroom. Mam bends to pick my pyjamas up from the floor. She sniffs them and says, 'They're wet, Malky. What's happened? Seb – what's wrong?'

Then she, too, tries to wake him.

How *do* you explain to a near-hysterical parent that you've been sharing dreams with your little brother? That, for several weeks, Seb and I have been having the most incredible, realistic adventures thanks to a strange contraption that I stole/borrowed/found (the distinction is becoming less and less important)?

Answer: you can't, because I've tried. Trouble is, it's all just too . . . incredible. Mam simply can't believe it. Nobody could. Well, apart from Susan Tenzin and her grandmother, whose words now come swirling back into my whirlpool head.

What had she said? Something like: 'You treat this whole thing like a video game. Just press "replay" and everything will be fine, huh? Well, you play with fire, boy! Sooner or later – no more replay. And you will have some explaining to do.'

Right now, though, Mam is shrieking, 'Seb! Sebastian!' and shaking him urgently.

Then she suddenly becomes very calm and quiet. Seb

is on his side. From time to time, he twitches, and his eyeballs are moving behind his eyelids. Honestly, if you didn't know, you'd just think he was asleep – which of course he is, only . . .

'All right, Malky – what happened? Why is Seb's face red? There – look!'

'I don't know, Mam. We . . . we were dreaming . . .'

Mam jabs a finger at the Dreaminator hanging above Seb's pillow. 'If you're talking about these things, then *don't* start that again, Malcolm. It's really not the time.' She turns back to my brother. She lifts up an eyelid with her thumb and his greenish eye stares out blankly. 'Seb! Oh, please wake up! Go and get my phone from beside my bed, Malky. *Go!*'

And so it is that, twenty minutes later, there are two paramedics in our bedroom, doing all of the paramedic stuff like you see on TV – pulse rate, blood pressure, asking Mam if Seb was taking any prescribed medicines, if there were any other medicines in the house that Seb could have swallowed. The redness on his cheek has gone down: they don't ask about that. Fit Billy has come from next door and is making tea.

And the word I keep hearing is 'normal'.

Like, 'Blood pressure, one oh five over seventy, normal. Heart rate, eighty-five, normal. Breathing – normal.'

Mam goes, 'Stop saying it's normal. *He's not waking up!* That's not normal!'

And there's me, just standing there in my dressing gown, feeling helpless, wondering what was happening in Seb's head, in Seb's dream.

Except it was your dream, wasn't it, Malky? How much can he control it?

Is he still being held captive by the main man? He'll be terrified. That is, if he's still dreaming. Poor Seb.

I start crying for him – and for me as well, because it's all my fault.

CHAPTER 16

The next hour is a bit of a blur, to be honest.

There's me getting dressed because I have to go with Mam to the hospital with Seb. There's Fit Billy carrying Seb downstairs and lying him down in the ambulance, Mam crying . . .

There's me and Mam in the paramedics' car following the ambulance to the hospital.

There's Mam on the phone to Dad, shouting, 'I don't know, Tom, *I just don't know*! Nobody knows . . .'

There's the people at the hospital – doctors? Nurses? I can't really tell – who meet the ambulance and rush Seb inside, and then take me and Mam to a little side room . . .

There's Mam asking again and again if Seb is going to be all right, and people being gentle and saying things like, 'We're waiting for results,' and, 'We're doing everything we can,' but even I can tell that they're *not* saying, 'Yes, your son will be all right,' because they can't, can they?

We sit in a beige-coloured room with a faded wall

painting of characters from the Narnia books while Seb is taken for tests, and Mam calls Dad again, and Mormor and Uncle Pete, and her cousin Barbro in Sweden and tells the whole thing again and again.

She's crying a lot, and it all makes me cry once more, and then I start to think again about what might be happening to Seb and I feel sick.

And then, maybe an hour or so later, a lady in a green hospital top with short sleeves comes into the small room, closing the door behind her.

She gives us a nervous smile and introduces herself. 'I'm Nisha. I'm the Emergency Trauma registrar, and I have . . .'

Mam interrupts. 'Is he awake yet? *Can I see him?*' She is on her feet, practically shouting.

'Please sit down, Mrs Bell.' We all sit, and it seems a bit calmer that way. Dr Nisha takes a deep breath and I really think she's going to say he's died or something. 'At the moment, Sebastian is stable, and his condition is not thought to be life-threatening.'

Mam sighs a little and grabs my hand hard in hers. 'So you know what's wrong with him then?'

Dr Nisha pauses, enough for me to know she means *no.* 'We have had the toxicology results back, and there is nothing to suggest that Sebastian has been poisoned. So far as we can tell at this stage, all of his bodily functions are consistent with someone who is fast asleep. He is not fighting any obvious infection that we can see. There is no elevated blood pressure, or heart rate; his blood-oxygen levels are normal . . .'

That word again. She goes on and on. EEG this and ultrasound that . . . I can't remember it all. Then she seems to slow down, like a clockwork toy before it needs rewinding, and then stops. The room is quiet for what seems like ages. Eventually, Mam speaks up.

'Have you seen anything like this before, doctor?'

Dr Nisha glances down, as if embarrassed. She takes a breath and holds it a little before replying.

'No. I have not personally come across a case like this. What we propose doing is keeping Sebastian in for observation, and as soon as possible he will be seen by a neurologist and a sleep specialist to determine the exact cause of his failure to wake up.'

So the minutes tick by in the beige room, and they become another hour while we wait for people to arrive, and I have plenty of time to stare out of the window at an empty paved square and at the Narnia mural and try to work out what I know about the Dreaminators.

It's not much. All I know is that it's not magic. It's *definitely* not magic. How could it be? Magic doesn't exist. What with the crystals and the pyramids and the batteries and everything else, it seems more like science. But it's not like any science I've ever heard of.

Is it possible for something to be . . . both magic *and*

science? Like the two are somehow combined and the result is that Seb now can't wake up?

What's worse is I was warned. I was warned by Susan Tenzin and her grandmother, and all of *that* started the very morning after my very first waking dream when I floated to the cave ceiling.

The problem was – I didn't listen.

FOUR WEEKS AGO

CHAPTER 17

It's the first day of Year Seven. No – this time it *really* is, although part of my head still feels as if I'm in the waking dream.

It's a longish walk to school, but we don't have a car, anyway.

I'm thinking: the big mammoth-dog peeing on the rugby goals . . . Fit Billy talking Chinese . . . Kobi the Cave Boy and his strange cartoon body . . . Me floating up to the ceiling . . . Cuthbert appearing under my desk . . .

But most of all I'm thinking, *Seb had the same dream as me. How can that even happen?*

There is something else as well, though.

I guess now is the time to tell you that my 'behaviour record' at Marden Middle School is, shall we say, 'inconsistent'. I think I told you that everyone's convinced that the reason I've been in so much trouble is because of Dad's breakdown, and Mam and Dad splitting up, but that was all ages ago so I don't see the connection. Besides, half of the things I got into trouble for weren't my fault. Once you get a reputation, though, it's hard to shake off.

'When trouble knows where you live, Malky,' says Valerie the school counsellor, 'it keeps knocking on your door.' She's right about that, at least.

Anyway, I've promised everyone – especially Mam – that things will change this school year.

So I'm scared that the woman who saw me in her backyard last night will report me to the school, or give them my description, anyway. Burglary? Theft? Animal cruelty? That last one's the worst and it wasn't even deliberate.

I'm half-running-half-walking so as not to be late and all these things are going round in my head as I cross the road. I hear a car horn, a screech of brakes and a human scream that turns out to be mine.

A dusty, rusty SUV has stopped about thirty centimetres from me. I look up and gasp. The car appears to have no driver. The electric window hums down and as I look closer I see that there *is* somebody driving, only they're so small that their head barely appears over the steering wheel.

A head pops out of the driver's window: it's the old lady from last night, who gave me the yak's butter. I think she's going to shout at me, but she doesn't. Instead, she just gives me the same intense stare and says, 'Killed!'

I have stopped in the road; there are no other cars around.

'I . . . I'm sorry. I wasn't looking.'

She half closes her eyes and nods as if this explains everything. She wags a finger at me.

'I nearly killed you. Bad boy!'

I nod quickly. It occurs to me to get all smart with her. You know: *'How could you even see me over the top of your steering wheel?'* and stuff like that, but there's something about her that puts me off. I feel I'd come off worse, even though she's tiny and old. So I say, 'Yes, yes. I'm sorry.'

Her gaze seems to bore into me. If this is a telling-off, it is the strangest, gentlest, yet most intense one I have ever had. I feel my knees trembling.

'I'm sorry!' I repeat, and then I hear from inside the car what sounds like *Mo-La!* and some more words I don't understand.

The woman's expression changes, softens a bit. Her eyes, which were screwed up in a glare, relax. She gives a curt nod and a tight little smile, then pulls her head back in as the rear window goes down. The girl from last night with the night-black hair – Susan, was it? – sticks her head out.

'Get in, Malcolm. We'll give you a lift!'

'Ah no . . . no . . . thanks. I'm happy to walk,' I say. I'm embarrassed: I don't know her, I'm scared of the old lady, and I'm still in a world of my own about the dream I had last night which is connected to the Dreaminator, and . . . well, everything.

The old lady says, crossly, 'Don't be stupid! Get in! Hurry, hurry.' She revs the engine, then her angry face changes again to a peaceful smile. It's as though she has flicked some unseen switch and it is very strange to watch. I find myself obeying and I get into the back seat next to the girl.

She looks even cleaner than last night, with her brand-new Marden Middle School uniform: grey skirt, the whitest socks I've ever seen, maroon jumper, all perfect. There's a shiny black instrument case on the floor of the car. (It's not violin-shaped, that's all I know.)

The old lady's head is not much higher than the seat back. I can just see her grey-streaked hair.

'How's that wound you got, huh? Bleeding stopped?' she shouts back at me over the coughing engine. Honestly, it's like I'm being given a lift to school in a tractor.

'Thank you. Yes, much better.' It improved overnight, in fact. I was careful in the shower and I don't think I smell of yak butter.

'Yak butter, yeah? *Dri* is the best, no? You rubbed it in good?'

'Yes,' I say. The packet is still in my bedroom, still smelly. 'I rubbed it in very, erm . . . good.'

Beside me, I hear Susan give a quiet snort, and when

I glance over she has covered her mouth with her hand. Is she laughing at me?

I hope not. I don't even know this girl. Not yet, anyway.

CHAPTER 18

The basic back-to-school stuff is the same every year.

To be honest, I'm still not really paying much attention to any of it because I've already decided I'm definitely in trouble. I'm simply waiting for the call to Mrs Farroukh's office, where there will be (I'm guessing) Valerie the counsellor, plus the policeman who comes to talk to us about drugs and online safety and stuff, and the woman who chased me down the lane last night. They'll bring Mam in, and Mam will tell Dad, and he'll take back my phone because it was sort of given to me on condition I stay out of trouble . . .

And my phone has a cracked screen caused by Kez Becker.

The whole-school assembly's outside in the big playground this year. I'm trying to pay attention, but every time Mrs Farroukh, who is up on the platform, scans the crowd, I imagine she's already received a complaint about last night and is trying to identify a 'medium-height boy, hair like a haystack' and I hunch down, making myself invisible.

Some hope.

'Follow Your Dreams' is the speech Mrs Farroukh's giving.

'Dream big, children of Marden Middle School!' she says into the crackly school PA system. 'And you too can be like these people who had world-changing dreams.'

The big video screen behind her has pictures we can't see very well because of the strong sunlight, but she reads out the names and what they've done.

'Martin Luther King dreamed of an end to racism . . . Albert Einstein was inspired by his dreams to create the Theory of Relativity . . . Paul McCartney of the Beatles wrote "Let It Be" after he dreamed about his mother coming to comfort him in troubled times . . .'

I'm trying to listen, but I have just seen Kez Becker at the end of the row of Year Eights.

Do I mention my cracked phone? Is there any point at all? She'll just deny it.

Then Mrs Farroukh says, 'Let us welcome a new student in Year Seven. Susan Tenzin, please stand up,' and there she is in the middle of the row in front. She stands still, hands clasped in front of her, and turns her head, smiling serenely at the whole school, chin held high.

Mason Todd nudges me. 'Flippin' teacher's pet, I reckon: written all over her,' he snorts. I say nothing. I'm not really concentrating. 'What's up with you?' whispers Mason. 'Are you even here? You look like you're still on holiday.'

Seb had the same dream as me.

'What? No, I'm, erm . . . I'm fine. Yeah – teacher's erm . . .'

Mason gives me a funny look. When I first came to the school, I thought Mason and I would be best friends, but – according to Kez Becker – his mam thinks I'm 'rough'.

By lunchtime, I'm a total nervous wreck waiting to discover if I have been reported.

I'm in the lunch queue and I try telling Mason about my dream. It's not easy. That is, it's hard to make it sound interesting. As far as Mason is concerned, all I am doing is telling him about this strange dream I had and – as everyone knows from about the age of six – no one's that interested in your dreams.

I don't mention the Dreaminators, obviously, because of how I obtained them. That is definitely something I am keeping to myself, at the very least until I know I have got away with it.

Mason's already looking over my shoulder for someone else to talk to when I say, 'Listen, man. I was doing all of this stuff in my dream. I was in control. I knew I was in the dream!' I haven't even got to the bit about Seb yet.

He steps back, kind of dramatically, looking at me through half-closed eyes.

'You *what*? You "controlled" a dream?' he says, making air quotes with his fingers. 'How does that work then?'

'I . . . I don't really know. It's like I was asleep but awake at the *same time*?'

He repeats this back to me, and I feel so relieved that at last *someone* understands that I laugh. 'Yes, man! Yes! That's exactly what happened. I tell you . . .'

'Crazy, you are! That's just not possible. You were *asleep*, Malky, man. You can't be awake and asleep at the same time.'

'But it's true, Mason! I was there. And my brother was too!'

'You had a dream about your brother? Big deal!'

'No! I mean my brother . . .'

I am about to tell him that Seb had the same dream as me at the same time. That Seb was *sharing* my dream. But, as the words form in my mouth, I realise that people have turned to listen, and that it's going to make me sound even crazier.

'. . . Yeah. You're right,' I say after a moment, and I fall silent.

'Honestly, Bell. Summer holiday's sent you soft in the head.' He squeezes his way down the queue past a group of Year Fives. It seems as though he's trying to get away from me, but he's probably just hungry. Still, it looks like I'm going to be sitting on my own for lunch on the first day of term.

Seb had the same dream as me.

'They are called "waking dreams", Malky,' says a voice behind me. 'And I believe you.'

CHAPTER 19

I turn and there is Susan Whatsername who has been standing close by all this time without me realising.

'What?' I say.

'I heard what you said to that boy. I do not think you are lying.'

She has detached herself from her group to stand next to me. The girls she was with – school-orchestra types – eye her carefully and she lowers her voice till it's really hard to hear her over the din of the school dining hall.

'They're called "waking dreams" or "lucid dreams". It is more common than you might think.' There it is again: this girl's precise, adult way of talking. 'My grandmother can do it. Hello again, by the way.'

I half expect her to put her hand out and say, 'How do you do?' but she doesn't. She reaches across me for a slice of quiche and I get a whiff of her personal smell: laundry detergent and apples. Her straight black hair falls in a kind of curtain over the side of her face and she hooks it back over her ear. I can't help noticing that her fingernails are exceptionally neat and clean.

I say nothing, but I follow her to a far table, wondering what people will think. Girls like her and boys like me don't usually mix, not in our school, anyway. Either she hasn't noticed or more likely she doesn't know anyone else. She sits down and arranges her plate and glass and cutlery neatly in front of her and then looks at it all for a couple of seconds as if she's going to say a little prayer, but she doesn't. Instead, she fixes me with her piercing dark eyes and says, 'If you can do that, Malcolm, it is a very special thing. Very special *indeed*.'

She talks as though every word she says is important and she expects you to listen.

'Is it . . . ?' I realise I don't really know the best way to ask this. 'Is it a Chinese thing?'

She screws her eyes up. 'A *Chinese* thing?'

'It . . . it's just, you know, you look . . . I thought . . . maybe your family, you know . . .' Have I offended her? It's difficult to tell. Susan relaxes her eyes and smiles.

'No. Not Chinese, Malcolm. Tibetan. Although my mummy is Chinese, my daddy is from Tibet. And so is Mola, whom you met. That is a Tibetan word for grandmother.'

I nod wisely, as though I had even heard of Tibet, and at the same time I'm thinking *mummy and daddy*? Who says that? She's going to have to lose that if she's to survive in Marden Middle School.

'Do you know Tibet?' asks Susan, as though she's making adult 'small talk'. She takes a tiny bite of quiche.

'What? Oh! Ah, Tibet? Aye, of course. It's over, erm . . . near, you know, that place . . .'

Susan lets me fumble for words, deliberately I think. Then she says, 'It is all right. Lots of people do not know it.'

I nod and frown like I'm taking all this in. 'Pretty small, is it?'

'About five times the size of the UK.' She lets this sink in. 'It lies between Nepal and China. You have probably heard of Mount Everest, the world's highest mountain. Half of it is in Tibet.'

'*Half* of it?'

'Yes. The border between Nepal and Tibet runs across the summit of Everest, although we call it *Chomolungma* – the Mother Goddess of the World. Tibet is part of China now, but it did not use to be. My daddy thinks . . . oh, never mind.'

Yeah, yeah, I'm thinking. *I want to know about the dreams.*

'As for the dreaming?' she says, effortlessly steering the conversation back on topic. 'I cannot say that it is particularly Tibetan or not.' She chews another mouthful and looks upwards thoughtfully. 'I should not think so. But my Mola studies a form of Tibetan Buddhism called "Bon". She grew up years ago in a town called Shangshung. It is a long way away from the capital.'

'And her dreams?'

Susan swallows, smiles, and wipes her mouth with a paper napkin. 'It happens sometimes when she is meditating, or even when she is asleep. She just comes down every now and then and says that she was awake during her dream, and it was fun, or "enlightening". "Dream yoga" she calls it. She says these dreams are better than the old video films she watches! What happened in yours?'

So I tell her, and her dark eyes shine with fascination – which, compared with the reaction I got from Mason Todd, is a big improvement. I'm careful not to mention the Dreaminator because I don't want to answer questions about how I got it. Nor do I mention anything about Seb sharing my dream because that just sounds too mad. (I also miss out the bit about her being in it, because it sounds a bit creepy.)

For a few minutes, in the school dining hall, it's as if all the noise has gone and there's just me and this strange, earnest new girl. At the end, I say, 'So you don't think I'm crazy?'

She winks at me like a much older person would, making me feel suddenly very small. 'You jump into my garden, bleeding; you narrowly escape death at the hands of my Mola's car; and you confess to spontaneous waking dreams? All in less than a day? Perfectly normal, Malcolm Bell!' Then she glides off, smiling her strange, superior smile to herself, and the noise of the dining hall returns.

'Hang on!' I call after her. I want to ask her if she's ever had 'waking dreams' herself, but she can't hear me. Besides, I can see Kez Becker pushing her way towards me, and my retreat is blocked by the waste trolley.

First day of term, and school is taking a turn for the worse.

CHAPTER 20

'When trouble knows where you live . . .' Valerie the school counsellor had said. It has just come knocking in the unmistakable shape of Kez Becker.

'Did you get anythin', Bell?' she says, shoving aside a Year Five and squeezing herself into the space next to me left by Susan. Behind her is Jonah Burdon and they are both smiling smugly. 'Last night? I had to make a tactical retreat, you understand.'

I look at Kez, making my face as blank as possible, and give a half-hearted shrug.

'No. I don't understand.'

She doesn't seem bothered. She turns to Jonah. 'You should've seen his face! Scared as anything he was – of a tiny little dog!' Jonah snorts.

I say, 'How would you know what my face was like? You'd already run away. Oh sorry, I mean made a tactical retreat!'

Jonah Burdon laughs at that. 'He's right, Kez – he's got you there! Nice one, Bell! Top banter. Har har!' He holds up his hand and I high-five him without much enthusiasm.

Kez doesn't like that at all. Her eyes narrow. 'Are you callin' me a liar?'

I just don't understand, I think. How can someone be a friend one minute and so horrible the next? (This is probably why Kez Becker doesn't have many friends. It's got nothing to do with her dad's job with dead bodies, and everything to do with being two-faced.)

'What about this?' I say, taking my phone out and showing her the screen. 'You broke it! Look at this crack!'

Jonah Burdon sucks his teeth and tuts. 'Ooh, brilliant counterattack there by the young Bell!' he says, like he's commentating on the football. It's all just sport to him.

'Don't be daft,' says Kez. 'That was there before!'

'No, it wasn't!' I can hear my voice getting louder and higher, and feel my face turning red. Jonah Burdon keeps up his commentary as people turn their heads. 'It's turning controversial! Becker denies the allegation! What next?'

'Shut up, Jonah,' says Kez without looking away from me. 'It was definitely cracked. I saw it as soon as you lent it to me.'

'I didn't lend it to you and *it wasn't cracked*!' I'm shouting now, and as I wave the phone nearer to her face to prove my point, my arm catches the beaker of water on her tray, knocking it all over her plate and splashing her front. She leaps back out of her seat, bumping into little Poppy Hindmarch and making her drop her tray with a loud crash. This in turn makes everybody look round and cheer and, before I can think about it, Kez and I are tussling, treading in Poppy's gravy. Everyone's jeering and then . . .

The deputy head's standing between us.

Seconds later, he's marching us out of the dining hall to Mrs Farroukh's office, accompanied by the laughter of the whole school. I see Susan out of the corner of my eye. She's just standing at the edge of it all, her serene half-smile in place as if nothing is of any importance at all – or everything is completely important. You can't tell. Her eyes follow us, and I'm a bit freaked out by it all.

Looks like I'm in trouble already.

Mrs Farroukh has a copy of my 'Conduct Contract' on the desk in front of her, signed by me at the end of last term after I had accidentally smashed the glass of the school trophy cabinet on prize day. Long story. Not my fault. (Well, not *all* my fault.) Anyway . . .

'I'm very disappointed, Malcolm,' Mrs Farroukh says. 'I so wanted you to start off this term well. We need to channel your more impulsive energies, but it's far too soon in the school year to start making negative assumptions . . .'

She's been going on like this for a while now and I'm sort of tuning out, but hang on . . .

She doesn't want to make negative assumptions. I think that means I'm going to get let off. I *think* that means she's not going to punish me.

'. . . I have had some rather disconcerting news, however, Malcolm.'

This does not sound good. I straighten up and prepare my innocent face.

She is looking out of her window at the rugby pitch, with her wide back to me. 'I received a telephone call this morning from someone who lives in Tynemouth who believes one of our students here at Marden Middle may have been trespassing in her backyard, and in doing so caused an injury to a dog that has required veterinary treatment. Do you know what trespassing is, Malcolm?'

'No, miss.' I have composed my face to add 'puzzled' to 'innocent', while trying to keep 'relieved' at bay because I know that trespassing – whatever it might be – is probably not as bad as robbery or burglary or animal cruelty . . .

'Trespassing, Malcolm, is being on or in someone's property without their permission.' She turns round and looks at me closely. I don't move. I don't think I even blink.

Blink, Malky, otherwise you look defiant and therefore guilty.

I blink a few times, and add a little smile for good measure.

'Now, she gave me a description of the trespasser.' Mrs Farroukh lets this sink in for a moment. Then for another moment, and I think she adds yet another moment just for extra effect before she says, 'But . . .'

I have started to sweat. I feel a trickle under my arm. I blink again.

'But, as she admitted, it was getting dark. She could not be certain that she would recognise him – or for that matter her – again. From the age of the trespasser, though, and what they were wearing, it would seem very likely that he – or she – was one of our students.'

She hasn't taken her eyes off me. She leans against her desk and her bottom spreads along the edge.

'I like to maintain good relations with the community, Malcolm. I suggested to the caller that perhaps this was quite innocent. Perhaps the intruder was simply collecting a stray football or some such. But injuring an animal, however unintentionally, is quite another matter. I don't like the idea that our neighbours might think of our students as anything other than wonderful. Do you see?'

'Yes, miss.'

'Good.' There's a long pause. Then she lets out a sigh that makes her helmet of silver hair tremble slightly. 'COMMS, Malcolm. Community Outreach Marden Middle School. We'll draw a line under today's incident with Kezia Becker and we'll say no more about it, not even to your mum, all right?'

'Yes, miss.' I can't believe I'm getting away with this.

'But – and it's a very big but . . .'

Now normally, to hear the large-bottomed Mrs Farroukh say the words 'a very big but' would have made me splutter with laughter. Right now, though, I'm too nervous to hear what's coming to find anything funny. '*But* – you have to promise me that you'll become part of COMMS. I have already spoken to Kezia and she will be joining us too. Do you agree, Malcolm? It's a lovely group of hardworking, enthusiastic students and it's a very worthwhile endeavour. I'll email your mum. There'll be a permission form for her to sign, but what you tell her is down to you, all right?'

I'm not sure I have ever heard a teacher describe anything *less* appealing, but what choice do I have? I nod as solemnly as I can.

She smiles warmly at me and claps her hands. 'Excellent! We'll be starting in a few weeks. I'll team you up with Susan Tenzin. She's the new girl: you may remember her from assembly and she has already volunteered. Is that all clear, Malcolm?'

'Yes, miss.'

Susan Tenzin *again*. Susan Tenzin with her super-clean fingernails and apple-smelling hair and make-me-feel-stupid, peaceful smile. I'm beginning to dislike her. Right now, though, I can't worry too much about that because . . .

Seb had the same dream as me.

And I need to talk to him about it.

CHAPTER 21

On the days when Mam's working, I'm supposed to be home when Seb gets in from school. So I'm waiting for him. I wouldn't normally do this, but I've poured him a glass of milk and cut him up an apple when he walks through the front door.

'Oh, hi, Malk . . .'

'Last night,' I say, as he eyes the snack suspiciously.

'I know,' he says and after taking a cautious sip (in case I've put salt in it again – it was *just a joke*) he downs the milk in one gulp. 'It was *awethome*! I've told everyone in my class. They all think I'm lying. But I don't care: it happened, didn't it, Malky? We were in the same dream. Was that *meant* to happen? It wasn't in the instructions. Was it?' He lets go a massive burp, wipes his mouth on his sleeve and starts in on the apple.

I shake my head. It certainly wasn't in the instructions, but it sure did happen. I watch him chomp his apple with his mouth open and, instead of getting irritated by him, I find myself envying the fact that he just doesn't mind what his classmates think.

'I think we need to test it again tonight, don't you?' I say. 'Just to be sure.'

'Awethome!' he repeats, and I pick a bit of chewed apple out of my hair.

That evening I use Mam's laptop to look up 'lucid dreaming' – the phrase Susan had used that was also in the instructions. There are pages and pages of people describing how they do it and it usually involves lots of practice and preparation, like meditating, regular sleeping habits, room temperatures, 'dream diaries' and even special foods. I'm soon bored, so I look up 'dreaminator' to find it's the name of some pop band, but there is no mention of a device to create lucid dreams whenever you want them.

And no mention of *sharing* dreams, either.

Finally, and nervously, I type in 'dangers of lucid dreaming' and everyone seems to agree that the only danger is from nightmares, which, when you're lucid dreaming, you can wake from whenever you like.

That's all right then. The instructions said, 'perfect results may not be achieved first time,' didn't they? Obviously, that didn't apply to me: Malky Bell, Super-Dreamer!

That night, Sebastian and I fall asleep under our Dreaminators.

And they work again.

And the next night.

And the next.

CHAPTER 22

It is honestly hard for me to describe just how completely amazing it is to be awake during a dream. I'm going to give it a go, though, because unless you understand then everything that comes next will be pretty meaningless.

You know when you're dreaming, and it all seems real? It's only when you wake up, and you try to piece everything together, that you forget most of it so that it's jumbled up and a bit nonsensical, and by the time you get downstairs you've usually forgotten it, anyway.

Well, the waking dreams that Seb and I have are not like that. We remember them perfectly: as if it really happened. I can remember the people and what they said; I can remember the sounds, the smells, the tastes.

Best of all, I can make happen exactly what I want to make happen. I am in charge of the whole dream world. Whatever I want to do, I can do. It's like being prime minister, president AND king all rolled into one!

So far, there's pretty much nothing that I haven't been able to do. It's just like that thing that Mrs Farroukh said on the first day of term:

Dream your greatest dreams, children, and you can make them come true!

Only, instead of it being a thing that teachers say, it is real.

Really real. Over the course of the next few nights, Seb and I discover what works and what doesn't.

For example, Seb can share my dream, but I can't share his. I don't know why this is: it just is. If Seb comes along into my dream and *doesn't* want to share it, that's okay. He just wanders off into his own dream.

We find that reading books about stuff, or watching TV the evening before, can help create the dream we want. Seb always wants to dream about *Kobi the Cave Boy*, because it's his favourite book.

One night, Mam was watching the news on TV when I was going to bed and I watched some of it with her. My dream that night took place in a war somewhere, and even though I tried changing stuff it wasn't fun so I woke myself up. I soon fell asleep again.

Most importantly – it doesn't *always* work. The power to change stuff, to control stuff, seems to wear off the more it is used. Then we end up in just a normal dream.

So it's not like unexpected dream-stuff doesn't happen: it does, all the time.

Got a minute? Let me tell you some of our dreams.

CHAPTER 23

Ladies and gentlemen, boy and girls, I present to you . . .

Malcolm and Sebastian Bell's Top Shared Waking Dreams

This will take about a minute – I have discovered that's about anyone's limit on listening to other people's dreams.

1. Kobi the Cave Boy

I've told you about this. It's the one we do most, and the one that works the best, though I'm getting a bit bored with it. We live in a cave, and go hunting, but all the animals run away and we can't catch anything so we have to steal meat from another tribe, with adventures along the way. The dream landscape is usually a cross between the pictures in the book and Tynemouth beach. Seb reckons he is friends with Kobi and his family. I suggested that we bring a car into the Stone Age dream (I've done that before, and I can drive really well), but

Seb said no, it wouldn't be 'real', and because it was his idea I kind of let him have his way, which is nice of me. He doesn't seem to mind the fish-shaped airship that is often there. We both think it's quite cool.

2. The Battle of the *Santa Ana*

The *Santa Ana* was a ship in the Spanish Armada, a navy that England fought against hundreds of years ago, and Seb and I were both sailors during a massive gun battle where the cannonballs were huge Christmas puddings. It was quite hard to control. The more people and things (like ships) there are in a dream, the more opportunities there are for strange dream-stuff to happen, which has to be controlled. For example, the main English ship that we were fighting was being captained by Fit Billy, but my crew started playing keepie-uppies with our Christmas-pudding cannonballs, so I had to change that or we'd have nothing to fight with.

3. Scoring the winning goal at the Champions League Final

Okay, so there's me and Seb (sometimes – he's usually in goal) and assorted opponents: famous people, kids at school . . .

That's a minute.
See what I mean? I could go on for ages, but I won't.

I could tell you about the time I shrank to the size of a garden gnome; or when Seb and I could breathe and talk underwater; or when we were both climbing a snowy mountain dressed in beach clothes and Seb had an enormous hat . . .

But you see nobody's all *that* interested, because everybody's had crazy dreams.

The fact that I can choose what happens in our dreams, change them and repeat them as I like isn't interesting to anyone because no one believes me. No one, that is, except Susan Tenzin.

I have had a couple more goes at explaining it all to Mam, but she just thinks I'm either:

a) joking
b) being brilliantly imaginative and creative and that I 'should write some of these adventures down, Malky: you could be a famous author!', or, more recently . . .
c) lying. 'And you're encouraging Seb as well, Malky. Tone it down, eh? People'll think you're nuts.'

So it's all been more or less my and Seb's secret-that's-not-a secret . . . although I wasn't counting on Susan Tenzin's granny getting involved.

CHAPTER 24

We're a couple of weeks into the new term now, and, if Susan Tenzin passes me on the way to school in her rattly old car, she *always* stops and offers me a lift. It's virtually impossible to say no, even though the journey is terrifying. It involves a lot of her grandmother swerving, braking sharply and saying a word that sounds like '*kyakpaa*' – probably 'you idiot' or something.

Other kids such as Mason, Callum and Kez Becker have noticed that Susan and I sometimes talk to each other and Mason once made a snide crack about me joining the school orchestra. That's why I always ask Mola to stop the car at the bottom of the road so I can get out and walk the last bit to school instead of me and Susan getting out at the school gates together as if we were best friends. I don't think she minds. She always smiles, anyway.

Anyway, this morning I hear the car chugging towards me from behind, and there's no escape. It coughs to a halt at almost the same spot they first picked me up, and Mola leans over to shout out of the passenger window.

'Hey! Hey! Dream-boy! Get in!'

Dream-boy? What the . . . ?

Mola waves a finger at me as I approach the car. 'No, no! You get in the front seat! Special treatment for a special boy!'

Honestly, she's grinning so hard that her eyes have disappeared into the creases of her face. From the back seat, Susan gives me an apologetic look. 'I told her about your waking dreams, Malcolm. She's quite excited.'

'Excited? Yes! You're very special! Here, I got something for you.' She reaches over to open the glove compartment, causing the car to swerve violently and narrowly miss a cyclist. I'm not sure how to react to all this. On the one hand, everyone likes being told they are very special. On the other hand, I don't like Susan going around telling just anyone.

'Mola! Be careful!' says Susan. 'Sorry, Malcolm!'

Mola gives me a Tupperware box. 'Go on! Eat it!' she says. I pop open the lid, and the smell is familiar but I can't place it. Inside are pieces of a pale, solid-looking cake with nuts.

'Thank you,' I say, a bit perplexed.

Susan leans over from the back seat and says. 'It's butter cake. We call it *tu*. It's a Tibetan thing. You're very honoured.'

The smell is a bit like the rancid yak's butter (which I eventually threw out after some of it melted on to an old school sweatshirt) only . . . not as rancid, I suppose. I take a small bite, but Mola's not impressed.

'No! Take a big bite! *Biiiig* bite!' She cackles and beeps the car horn for no reason that I can tell. So I do. It's delicious. Sharp, buttery, milky.

'That's lush, that is!' I say, and Mola beams with pleasure.

'You see, people who waking-dream without effort are very rare. Very rare! I would say they have a special gift! They are blessed. *Outta my way – kyakpaa!* Me, I manage it only sometimes. It is a great pleasure to meet a waking dreamer and see him eating my *tu*. Now, Dream-boy, you tell me what you dreamed of last night and I tell you mine!'

So, a bit reluctantly, I tell her about the Stone Age dream that I had, and how I had gone hunting with Kobi the Cave Boy. I miss out the bit about Seb actually sharing my dream because it still sounds too weird, but Mola hoots with delight and urges me to eat more cake.

I eat another piece, and I'm pretty full by the time we pull up near the school. I have my fingers on the door handle to get out when she says, 'Wait! I have not told you mine yet!' and I sit back. Mola turns off the engine, folds her hands in her lap and closes her eyes for a moment.

'I dreamed of nothing,' she says at last.

This puzzles me. 'Oh,' I say. 'Bad luck.'

She turns to smile at me. 'No. It is good.' Then she closes her eyes again and that kind of closes the conversation as well. It's embarrassing, but it only lasts a second or two.

'You be careful, Dream-boy,' she says when she opens her eyes again. She leans across from the driver's seat and quickly taps me on the forehead with her wrinkled forefinger and giggles at my alarmed face. Then her expression changes again instantly in that way she has and she stares furiously into my eyes. 'Inside your head is bigger than outside, Dream-boy. It is easy to get lost in there.'

Out of the car at last, and feeling a bit startled, I say to Susan, 'What was all that about the inside of my head? And who wants to dream of *nothing*?'

She hooks a lock of her dark hair behind her ear as she looks upwards and thinks for a moment. 'It is a Buddhist thing. Shun-yata, it's called. It is one of the goals of meditation. It's not so much "nothing" as "everything". That is . . . I think.'

'Huh,' I say. 'Sounds boring. I think I'd sooner be on a mammoth hunt.'

Susan nods in reply, managing to look as if she is both agreeing and disagreeing.

It's a thing she has. It's less annoying than you might think.

CHAPTER 25

Over those mornings, and between the moments of terror at Mola's driving, I learn a lot about Susan, mainly because she never really shuts up. She has been in international schools in Singapore and Dubai. She talks to me about music (she's in the school orchestra, natch – the thing in the case is a piccolo); about the prime minister (her mum has met him); about stuff going on in countries that I've never even heard of.

To be honest, I'm getting a bit sick of it and I'm starting to think she does it just to make me feel stupid. (I once responded by telling her I'd binge-watched four episodes of *Celebtastic* back to back, and had she seen the one where Jamie Bates the TV reporter got pushed into the pool, and she just gave me this blank smile and said, 'Oh, that's nice.' I honestly don't think she'd even heard of *Celebtastic*. She probably doesn't even have a TV.)

Mola doesn't mention her empty dreams again and I'm sort of relieved. I was a bit embarrassed last time. It felt a bit like saying to someone that you enjoy reading comics and them saying they prefer to read Shakespeare. Or like Susan never watching *Celebtastic*, I suppose. She tells me her mum works at the university and I say that Mam used to work there as well.

'Oh really? Which department?' she says.

'Catering. Not any more, though. What about yours?'

'Politics. She is a senior lecturer.'

Clever then. It figures.

'What about your dad?'

'Oh, he is fine,' Susan replies, which seems like a strange answer to my question and I turn my head to her. She immediately looks out of the car window and says something that sounds rehearsed. 'My daddy is still in China, but we hope that, all being well, he will soon be able to join us here in the United Kingdom.'

The mood in the car has shifted in a way that I don't really understand.

'When did you last see him?' I ask. 'Is he working there?'

Susan's still staring out of the window and she swallows hard. 'No. He, erm . . .'

Suddenly the car swerves to the kerb and shudders to a halt. 'Visa!' barks Mola over her shoulder. 'He needs a visa and that's it. Now we are here. Get out.'

It's like the car has been filled with a huge, spiky ball of awkward and I scramble out gratefully, followed by Susan, just as Kez Becker crosses the road in front of us.

We're sort of forced together going through the gate. Susan takes a deep breath through her nose.

'Are you okay . . . ?' I begin.

'Yes. Yes. See you later,' says Susan, quickly. 'And . . . and you too, Kezia.'

Kez was going to ignore us, but she can't now. 'Why me?' she grunts.

'COMMS taskforce! Mrs Farroukh's announcing our duties.'

COMMS! I hadn't exactly forgotten about it, but I was trying not to remember. Kez just rolls her eyes and lumbers off. Susan's about to go in the same direction when she stops and turns back to me.

'Three years,' she says and I give her a puzzled look. 'You asked. It is three years since I saw my daddy. My "dad".' Then she turns abruptly and marches off, leaving me wondering what the heck I said wrong.

It's lunchtime. Mrs Farroukh's at the front of the classroom, guarding the biscuits ('Only two each, please, Malcolm!'). Kez isn't there and I can't say I'm surprised. She'll have wriggled her way out of this somehow, probably with the help of her dad calling the school or something. Two students from the sixth-form college up the road do most of the talking, and hand out a list of 'COMMS tasks'.

Anyway, long story short: Susan Tenzin and I are

visiting some old geezer on Collingwood Terrace. I put my hand up.

'Yes, Malcolm?' says Mrs Farroukh.

'How long do we have . . . that is . . . how long do we stay?' I was going to say *have to stay* but it was halfway out of my mouth when I realised that might sound like I have the wrong attitude. It makes no difference: Mrs Farroukh's on to me and she purses her lips.

'I think, Malcolm, a rule of thumb will be long enough to have a leisurely cup of tea. Is that too onerous for you?'

I don't know what 'onerous' means, but I shake my head and say, 'No, miss,' and she seems satisfied.

'Good. Mr McKinley will be very pleased to see you. To see you *both*,' she adds, aiming a sickening smile at Susan Tenzin.

I look down the list:

Mr Kenneth McKinley
12 Collingwood Terrace

It's been staring me in the face since the sheets were handed round. How come I didn't see it? But, when Mrs Farroukh actually says his name, I think I almost jump out of my seat.

Mr McKinley.

McKinley. That's the name on the box I stole!

Someone is saying my name and I look up.

'Malcolm! Do pay attention. He'll be expecting you both tomorrow morning. Is that all clear?'

Am I imagining it? Is there a sly look in Mrs Farroukh's eye?

I look again at the sheet. Collingwood Terrace. Mrs Farroukh has even printed off a little map and a Street View picture. The backs of the houses lead to the lane where I was with Kez Becker when I took the Dreaminators. A kind of sick feeling comes over me.

I am being sent to visit the very person I stole from.

CHAPTER 26

That night, Seb is excited. We've been getting good at the Stone Age dream, and Seb wants to ride on the back of a 'mammuf', but I'm just not in the mood. I'm too worried about tomorrow.

Mam has been tidying and has taken the box the Dreaminators came in from under my bed and put in on the chair. I sit on the edge of my bed and stare at it again: the big, colourful letters, and the picture of the man peering over the top of his glasses.

That night I hardly sleep. I definitely don't dream. All I can think of as I lie there in the dark is the visit to Kenneth McKinley tomorrow morning.

Our house is tiny and the walls are thin and I can hear Mam on the phone downstairs. Fit Billy's gone home. I know she's talking to Dad. I usually try not to listen when they have their 'discussions', but then I hear her say the word 'dreams' and my ears kind of tune in, like a webpage loading on a slow connection.

'Sinister? Spooky? We're talking about dreams here, Tom, nothing more . . .

'. . . For heaven's sake, Tom, can you hear yourself? They're *mobiles*, you know? No, not like that. Turning ones. Like you hang above a cot . . .

'. . . Of course it's rubbish, Tom. *Harmless* rubbish . . .'

There's a longish pause, and I can tell she's pacing round the living room, like she does when she's angry. I hear the creak of the floorboard under the rug in the middle of the room.

'. . . No, you listen to me, Tom. Whatever is causing it, they're sleeping well, they're going to bed on time without any argument, and they haven't had a fight for ages, not even an argument. They're laughing and joking as if they actually *like* each other, which is a first . . .

'. . . No, Tom, you gave up the right to say how I bring them up three years ago . . .

'. . . Yeah, well, tough luck, Tom. With them two, what I say goes, and I say . . . what? Billy next door? Don't bring *him* into it . . .'

Three years ago, Mam said. That's how long it is since Dad left. Susan said the same thing: it's three years since she's even *seen* her dad. At least I've seen mine. Not much, but still . . .

Eventually, I pull the pillow over my head to block out my thoughts and Mam and Dad's bickering and I fall into a sweaty sleep.

NOW

CHAPTER 27

'The next forty-eight hours are critical,' the doctor had told Dad, and that – or variations of it – are what Dad keeps repeating to me as we drive home from the hospital. Forty-eight hours, two days . . .

'I know, Dad,' I say, as gently as I can.

I haven't seen my dad, apart from on FaceTime, for months. He's 'trying to get his life together,' says Mam, who does her best not to be mean about him to me and Seb, but I know it upsets her as well.

He drove the hour from Middlesbrough, where he lives now, as soon as he heard that Seb was in hospital. His girlfriend Melanie isn't with him, which I'm quite pleased about. I mean, she's okay – I just prefer Dad without her. He's got a beard now with grey bits in it, and new jeans and expensive glasses. (To be honest, they just look like ordinary glasses to me, but I heard Mam on the phone to Uncle Pete saying, 'bloody designer glasses,' so I guess they are.)

Mam has stayed with Seb in the hospital. The staff

brought in a wheeled bed for her to sleep on tonight so she could be next to him.

Dad is changing the car's gears with too much force, jamming the stick into place angrily. His mouth is clamped into a firm line like he's trying his hardest not to cry. He used to cry a lot when he was living with us, but that's when he was poorly. He's a lot better now.

'The worst thing is the not knowing,' he says.

Not knowing is hard. Hard? It's agony. I *tried* to explain everything about our dreams, about our adventures in the Stone Age, to Dr Nisha. It didn't go well.

Dr Nisha had sat down next to me and put her pen and clipboard and iPad down as a sign that she was giving me all of her attention. She said to Mam and Dad, 'I'd like a word with Malcolm alone, if I may?' and they went to get something to eat.

We were in the beige room with the hard sofas and the Narnia mural, which I'd been staring at for ages and decided that I didn't like.

'So, Malcolm,' she began, 'you share a room with your brother, right?'

I nodded.

'And you were the one that discovered that he would not wake?'

I nodded again.

'Roughly what time was this?'

I had told her this before, but I repeated it. 'About six o'clock. This morning.'

'All right. And what were you doing immediately before this all happened?' Her tone was soft and gentle. I looked at her eyes and they were large and trusting. Should I tell her? Should I bother?

I's not like I hadn't given this any thought. In fact, I had barely thought of anything else. What *would* I say? How about the truth?

The truth is the truth. The truth is what happened. Telling the truth might – *might* – help Seb. I don't know what these doctors can do, do I? So I decided that I would tell her exactly what I was doing just before it all happened.

'I was . . . I was trying to steal meat . . . And they were all waving their spears at us and –' this sounds stupid, I know it – 'at Kobi.' I looked at Nisha and added, 'I was dreaming.'

Her patient smile became a full one. 'All right, Malky, I don't mean . . .'

'And Seb was there too. And he was captured by the big people, and . . .'

'Yes, yes. It sounds like quite a dream.'

'But we were in the *same* dream, do you understand?' I waited to make sure I had her full attention, then I said, 'And he's still there. I think.'

Dr Nisha lowered her eyelids and looked at me

sideways. 'No, Malcolm. I'm not sure I *do* understand. But I hardly need to remind you that this is very important. I need you to be serious.'

I fought the urge to let my voice get higher and louder, in my agitated way. I took a deep breath.

'I *am* being serious. Honestly. Seb and I can . . . we can share our dreams. That is, we . . . we experience the same dream at the same time. You see . . .'

'Hang on – what?' Dr Nisha had stopped leaning towards me and was sitting back, arms folded.

'Our dreams. We agree beforehand: we read and watch stuff to make sure it's right and then we fall asleep together under our Dreaminators and then . . .'

Mam and Dad came back in with baguettes from the shop downstairs. Mam's eyes were red from crying and I stopped because I knew what Dad's views are on the Dreaminator. Unfortunately, he heard the last of what I was saying.

'Oh, I'm sorry, doctor. Is he on about that flamin' dream thing again?' He shook his head, angrily, like a dog dodging a wasp. 'It's a toy, for heaven's sake. A child's mobile that hangs above his bed and he reckons . . .' He tailed off and turned to me, a pleading look on his tired face. 'Malky, mate. Dr Nisha's very busy and this is very serious. She's got no time to listen to this.'

'*Dad!*' I protested, and this time my voice did actually go higher and louder. 'I was there!'

'Malky, if I hear one word . . .'

'Mr Bell. Please.' Dr Nisha stood up. 'Malcolm has suffered quite an upset. This, this . . . "dreaminator" is not something I have ever heard of, and I certainly don't think it's possible for it to work as Malcolm describes. But . . .'

She paused. Her back was to me, so I couldn't see her face. For all I know, she was doing that grown-up thing when your facial expression says something different to your words, by winking or something. I don't know.

'. . . why don't you bring this device in for me to have a look at? I can examine it and determine whether or not it may have played a part in Sebastian's condition. We are feeling our way in the dark a little here. Any help, any further information might be useful. And it might put Malcolm's mind at rest. I think he feels as though this is somehow his fault.'

'Because it *is*!' I wailed.

It was like I had climbed to the top of a hill, then tumbled all the way back down again. For the first time ever, I had told someone the whole truth, and they hadn't tried to shut me up. And then Mam and Dad came back in and . . . pushed me back down the hill.

It was also the first time in ages they'd actually agreed on something.

They'd agreed that I was talking nonsense. That's a shame because right now I need people to believe me.

CHAPTER 28

Before Dad drove me home, I went into Seb's room along the wide corridor. He was fast asleep, connected by wires to a machine that was making no noise but had little flashing numbers on a panel with switches and stuff. Mam and Dad were outside in the corridor, talking to yet another doctor.

He looked okay, lying on his back, mouth half open. His green goalie top was folded on a shelf next to him. The nurse who was with him had closed the blinds, and it was cool and shady. When I got closer, I could see his eyelids twitching, and occasionally he parted his lips as if he was muttering something, but when I put my ear to his mouth I couldn't hear anything. He was definitely dreaming.

'Seb! Seb!' I said, but the nurse gently told me, 'Shush. The doctors think it might be better to let him sleep. If that's what his body needs.'

'He's been asleep for *hours*,' I said, but I didn't try to wake him again. Instead, I sat on the chair and took his hand and told him quietly, 'Wake up, Lil-Bro, wake up.'

Then I lowered my head to rest it on his hand and I stayed there for a few minutes and the nurse left the room.

It's daft: I half expected – or perhaps hoped – that Seb would open one eye and say, 'Hey – we fooled them!' Of course, he didn't. He just lay there, occasionally twitching part of his face, or the hand I was holding.

I looked down at his hand and saw something I had not noticed before. A slightly red patch around his wrist, like a rash. His other arm had it as well. Red, and a bit sore-looking.

The marks were in exactly the place where the huge man had tied the rough woven rope.

I let go of Seb's hand and staggered back, knocking over the chair, which clattered to the floor and caused Dr Nisha to open the door.

'Is everyth— Malcolm, what's the matter?'

I pointed. 'His . . . his wrists. Look!'

She took Seb's left wrist in her hand and examined it. Then she switched on a bedside light. 'Nurse! Bring me a magnifying light, please.'

She shook her head. 'This could be something or nothing. Whatever it is, it does not appear to be severe, but we'll certainly keep a close eye on it. Malcolm, you look like you want to say something.'

'It . . . it's where Seb was tied up. By the wrists. With rope.'

'And when did this happen?'

'In . . . in our . . .'

'Don't you dare say "in our dream", Malky,' said Dad behind her, and so I never finished my sentence.

Back home, I watch Dad snatch the Dreaminators from their hooks above our beds.

'I'm taking these back to the hospital, although I've no idea why,' he said, quietly. 'You're lucky I'm going back, anyway.'

He heads down, then he stops on the stairs for a moment, thinking. He turns and comes back up. He gives me a brave, mirthless smile and his voice is almost a whisper.

'Malky, son. I know as well as anyone the dangers of messing with your mind, do you understand?'

I nod. He forces me to wait before he nods back, slowly.

'I paid a hell of a price. It cost me your mam, your brother, you. I'm still paying it.' He paused again and I thought there was more to come, but he was done. 'I'm back in a couple of hours, Malky. Don't go anywhere. Keep your phone on.'

I stay sitting on my bed, still unmade from this morning. Seb's pillow is indented where his head was. Then I pick up the Dreaminator box.

Kenneth McKinley? I cast my mind back to the first time I met him. It was only three days ago, but feels like much, much longer – perhaps because so much happened in a single day.

THREE DAYS AGO

CHAPTER 29

It's Saturday morning on the Tynemouth seafront. Above King Edward's Bay, seagulls are straining at the wind and screeching at the rough grey-and-white waves. Sometimes there are surfers, but there are none today.

I slept badly. Today is the day when I have to visit the man whose face is on the front of the Dreaminator box, and whose shed I burgled.

Except I didn't burgle it, or rob it, or anything, okay? I just trespassed and ended up with some items that I can't give back now without admitting that it was me.

Mam's had to sign some form for the school letting me visit this McKinley man and she thinks it's great, like I've been 'selected' and it's a great honour, and of course I can't tell her the truth. She makes me brush my hair twice and Fit Billy, who has recently started to have breakfast with us, says it's too neat and ruffles it up for me again, making Mam tut and laugh.

So anyway I'm late and Susan Tenzin is already waiting at the address on Collingwood Terrace that looks out over the mouth of the Tyne and, in the distance, the crumbling ruins of the old clifftop priory.

'So. In and out, yeah?' I say, trying not to pant from running.

Susan holds up a bag. 'Good morning, Malcolm. Enough time for tea and butter cake, though.' The hot night has become a cool autumn day, and she looks like she's dressed to go somewhere posh. The skirt and knee-socks are there, with blinding-white trainers and a neat navy-blue jacket, buttoned up. Even though Mam's made me put on my best jeans and a clean hoodie, I immediately feel inferior.

I have an old baseball cap on as well, because I'm worried in case someone in the house recognises me.

'He's expecting us,' Susan says. 'He has a carer who lives with him. Mrs Farroukh's already been round too, to check him out.'

A carer? That'll be the woman who chased me the day I stole the Dreaminators. I look up at the tall terraced house and the huge black door with peeling paint. Susan mounts the steps to the front door. I am at the bottom and still wary. 'So, if old Farroukh's already been round, why didn't she just, you know, visit him herself?'

Susan replies over her shoulder. 'She did, but Community Outreach is a valuable opportunity for Marden Middle School students to foster links with elderly people in the area,' she says. She's obviously memorised it. 'You know what Mrs Farroukh's like. Thinks we all live in a bubble of social media and should get out and meet people in our locality. I cannot actually say I disagree.'

I pull a face behind Susan's back. She pushes the doorbell: a round button in the middle of an ornate stone carving on the side pillar. Behind the door, I can hear footsteps, and the door opens wide to reveal . . .

A large, middle-aged woman with big hooped earrings, and short-cropped Afro hair. I know from her outline that this is the woman who followed the dog out of the yard and down the lane.

Will she recognise me? My heart is thumping, and I don't meet her eye, tipping the brim of my cap down low. I try to remind myself yet again that it was twilight when it all happened, and I had my back to her as I ran away, but still . . .

'Hi!' she says. It sounds like she's smiling, but I'm trying not to look up. 'You must be Susan? And . . .'

Her eyes flick to me. Susan says, 'This is Malcolm. He's part of the project as well.'

I still don't lift up my face.

'I'm Andrina. I'm Mr McKinley's carer. Call me Andi.' She's still sounding pleased to see us. She beckons us into the high, wide hallway with a highly polished tile floor and a wide staircase. She stops at the first doorway and points to a bottle on a small table.

'Hand-san, please. Mr McKinley's ninety and he's had a nasty cold recently.'

As we're doing it, she takes out a device from her smock pocket and holds it up. Meanwhile, I'm looking around for the dog, and so far no sign.

'Cap off, please, Malcolm. I need to take your temperature.'

Slowly and reluctantly, I remove the cap, but my face is still cast downwards. 'Come on,' she says. 'Don't be shy!' She reaches out and gently holds my chin to make me face her and puts the thermometer to my forehead. As she does so, she looks closely at me.

Now if you'd asked me a few weeks ago if I thought that anyone could be psychic – you know, read minds and stuff – then I'd have said, 'Obviously not.' But since I began sharing dreams with Seb you could say I'm not so sure. And now, with this woman's face centimetres from mine? I'm so convinced that I know what she is thinking that it is like she is talking to me.

I know it was you that night, you little tyke. I'd recognise that haystack of hair anywhere. And so you can make amends by visiting a dying old man and listening to his rambling stories.

She looks at the thermometer, then at me and shakes her head, tutting.

'Oh lordy!' she says, and pauses, looking grave. Then her smile comes back. 'Only joking! You're fine. Come on in. He's looking forward to meeting you. Shoes off, please.' She's being jolly, but there's something in the narrow-eyed look that she throws at me that puts me right on edge.

From behind the thick door I can hear classical music: the sort played by an orchestra, although it doesn't sound very tuneful – not that I'm an expert. My heart is still thumping like crazy.

We pause, and she beckons us forward.

'Come on in. You're in luck: he's having a good day today. Though I warn you . . .' She pauses, and we wait expectantly. 'Even on good days, he's quite tired, and that can make him a bit short-tempered.'

Oh great. A tired, grumpy old man.

Who, it'll turn out, will change my life.

And not necessarily in a good way.

CHAPTER 30

The room is huge and over-warm, with a high ceiling and a big bay window looking on to public gardens and, beyond that, the priory and the River Tyne. Two of the walls are lined from ceiling to floor with crammed bookshelves, spilling over with papers and folders and books jammed in any old way; the others have wallpaper with a bright but faded symmetrical pattern. There's a long sideboard and an equally long buttoned sofa in faded green.

Looking up, I see dozens of huge silk scarves in various colours and patterns hanging from the ceiling, and between them dangle pendants of all kinds: a bamboo wind chime, two large, round glass discs winking in the light, and a mass of blue butterflies linked together with thread that I can hardly see. The whole effect is a bit like being in a magical, multicoloured antique shop.

A high-backed armchair faces the window.

Despite the thick, warm air, through the soles of my socks the tiled floor feels cold. We hesitate in the open doorway. The music is much louder in here: classical music of violins and horns – the kind of stuff that Susan probably likes.

'Well, come in if you're comin' in and closhe the door behin' you! I cannit abide a draught!'

The voice is slurred and muffled and comes from the direction of the armchair. When I approach, I see a bunched-up tartan blanket with someone sitting under it, low down and slightly hunched over. Next to the chair is a large silver cylinder, upright on a trolley. A rubber tube comes from it to a plastic mask that is fitted to the old man's face.

When Susan and I get near, he squirms in his chair to sit up straighter. It's only then that I realise that he's not under a blanket, but actually wearing a huge blue-and-green tartan cardigan. He removes the oxygen mask from his face and uses a skinny, shaky hand to smooth down his white hair, of which there is a lot. His thin face has more lines than anyone I've ever seen, and he peers at us suspiciously through the purple spectacles perched on his large, veiny nose. It's the face from the Dreaminator box, for sure, only much older and definitely not grinning.

'Not too close!' says Andi as we get nearer, but he waves his hand to dismiss her.

'Och, ignore her! Come's closhe as you like. Y'don't have lyshe, do you?'

Lice? I feel myself reddening. Seb and I did have nits last term.

'No, but . . .'

Susan interrupts. 'No, Mr McKinley. We *definitely* don't have lice.'

'They're fine, Kenneth. Really. Be nice.' Andi is unrolling something from a long box.

'Och, very well. You'd better set down on Andi's paper. What thash for, I have no idea. You're not thinking of *shoiling* yourshelves, are you?'

'Just keeping you alive, Kenneth,' says Andi with a smile, as she tears off a long sheet of soft, wide paper from her roll and places it on the seat of the sofa for us. We sit down cautiously. The old man responds with a gargling growl in his throat as if he thinks her efforts to keep him alive are a waste of everyone's time.

As well as the music, I now detect another noise: a clacking sound that comes from the old man when he speaks.

'You'll wait, I hope, until we get to the end of thish movement? Mr Bruckner, I find, is not a composer that can be hurried.' And there it is again: *clack-clack.*

His eyes are closed, but his hands are moving in time with the strange music, as if he is conducting an invisible band. Andi crosses the room to an old-style record player where a black vinyl disc is revolving and, when she pushes a button, the music stops abruptly.

The old man opens his eyes at the sudden silence. What happens next is an amazing transformation. It is almost as if Mr McKinley becomes younger before our eyes. He doesn't, of course, but as he talks it is as if he is warming up. He slurs less, and straightens up, raising his wrinkled neck from out of his slumped shoulders, like a tortoise.

'Come now, Andi. That surely wasn't necessary?' he says.

'Mr Bruckner can wait, Kenneth. You have visitors,' says Andi. 'Susan Tenzin and Malcolm . . . ?'

'Bell.'

'Malcolm Bell. And Susan has brought cake.'

The old man rattles the phlegm in his throat and it's as if his mind clears at the same time. His eyes, which are almost hidden beneath a hedge of white eyebrow, widen a little. 'Och, yes. I've been expecting you. Welcome to my wee abode. Andi – we'll take tea right here, I think.' Then that noise: *clack-clack*.

Mr McKinley has the face of someone who has recently been on a strict diet. My Aunty Gina did it once and she looked awful. His jowls hang thinly and there's a long strip of loose flesh starting under his chin and swooping down until it is concealed by a black silk cravat tucked into his cardigan top. His trousers, shiny with age, seem far too big for his skinny legs.

His long hands are thin and knuckly and crisscrossed

with blue veins, with one big, showy gold ring with a large purple stone. It swivels a bit loosely on his finger. I look at him, he moves his jaw a little, and the noise comes once more: *clack-clack.*

He clears his throat again and says, 'Och, well: this is nice. I'm so glad you're not *garrulous.* I just can't abide garrulous people. Far better to keep your mouth shut, and have people think you're stupid, than to open it and remove all doubt is what I always say! Don't you agree, Malcolm? Good Scots name that, by the way!'

I don't get this, but I smile and nod, anyway, and he smiles back: a white grin showing teeth that must be a least sixty years younger than him. When the clacking noise happens again, I realise that his teeth are false ones, and liable to dislodge from time to time, making the noise. His voice is full of phlegm, his accent singsongy and definitely Scottish. It's like listening to someone gargling with pebbles.

He turns to Susan as Andi comes back into the room, wheeling a trolley clinking with teacups and a plate of butter cake.

'Tell me, Susan,' he says. 'Can you enlighten me a wee bit further about who you are? Why are you here?'

He smiles awkwardly. It really is like the grouchy man of a minute ago has been replaced by someone doing his best to act charmingly. I think of the words in the

Dreaminator package: 'You may know me from my appearances on stage, radio and television . . .' This is definitely someone who is used to putting on an act.

While Susan gives him the spiel about Community Outreach Marden Middle School, I look round the extraordinary room with the colourful decorations hanging limply in the warm air. There is a sharp smell of ointment of some sort, disinfectant, wood polish, and . . . old tobacco? But now there's another smell: a sour, cabbagey odour that gradually wraps round us. It gets worse over the course of about ten seconds.

Susan pauses in her little speech to cough as the stink reaches her.

'Dearie me,' says Mr McKinley at last. 'I'm afraid that rather, ah . . . arresting aroma is emanating from Dennis. Dennis, you're a disgusting old beast . . .'

Dennis? Surely not . . . ?

Surely yes. At the mention of his name, a huge old black-and-ginger dog heaves itself to its feet from its position under a heavily draped table and limps forward, one of its front paws wrapped in a purple bandage. It stops and raises its greying muzzle towards me.

'He sleeps most of the time these days, just like me,' Mr McKinley says. 'Still a good guard dog, though, aren't you, old son? Saw off a bunch of prowlers from our backyard not so long ago, didn't you? Paid a price for it, though. One of the wee scunners trapped his paw in the back door. Nearly tore his claw off. Still, it's almost better now.'

The evening with Kez Becker floods back. Meanwhile, Dennis has begun a low growl. There's no doubt he remembers me from the backyard that night.

I stand very still. Surely it must be obvious to everyone what I've done?

I swallow hard.

CHAPTER 31

'Dennis!' says Mr McKinley, and I look up, startled. 'Stop that. These are my guests.'

Still Dennis growls on, his top lip curled back, his amber eyes fixed on me.

'Andi,' Mr McKinley says, 'take Dennis out, would you? And, Malcolm, would you render open the casement, please?' He sees my blank look and translates. 'Open the window, would you, laddie?'

Andi leaves, leading Dennis behind her.

Feeling a little wobbly, I cross the room and lift the stiff sash window to let out Dennis's stink. The breeze that enters wafts through the silks scarves and makes the wind chime hanging from the ceiling tinkle. I'm still half expecting to hear someone shout, 'Stop, thief!' or, 'That's the boy who hurt Dennis!' No one does, of course: there's only the three of us in the room.

I take a longer route back to my chair. On one wall is a collection of black-and-white photographs of a younger Mr McKinley, all posing with someone else. I can't be sure, but in one it looks like he is shaking hands with the Queen when she was much younger; in another he is standing with a group of four young men in matching suits and holding a sign saying FAB. Below these, on a small wooden table, is a framed photograph, in colour, of him and a boy of about my age, their hands round each other's shoulders, buddy-style, both of them with identical grins.

Mr McKinley has seen me looking. 'That's my son. He must have been about your age when that was taken.'

I point to the picture of the Queen. 'And is that . . . ?'

'Aye. That is indeed Her Majesty. Private audience. Balmoral, 1968.' He clears his throat loudly. 'Now, tell me something. Have either of you ever heard of me?'

Susan shakes her head: 'No.' I say the same although in my case it's not the truth. My heart leaps a bit. I sit back down. Is he actually going to tell us all about it?

Or does he know what I've done?

'Kenneth McKinley. The Mystic o' the Highlands they called me. You're quite sure you don't know who I am? How old are you, Malcolm?'

'Eleven,' I say. 'Nearly twelve.'

He closes his eyes as though he's doing a quick mental calculation. 'That would make sense. You see it was all a long time ago. Disappointing, I suppose, but not entirely surprising. You're not journalists or anything?'

'Of course not. We're children,' says Susan.

'Och, you can never tell these days,' he says. 'I've trusted people in the past and they've written some wicked lies.'

Behind us, Andi – who has just come back into the room, now without Dennis – pipes up, 'Kenneth. They're from the local school. I told you, do you remember? They've come along to see you as part of a community programme.'

'Oh aye. You said that just now, didn't you?' He falls silent and closes his eyes. This goes on for so long that I wonder if he has fallen asleep and I nudge Susan. But then he raises his head again. 'Andi! More tea, I think. Please.'

He waits until she has gone out, then turns his head and restarts his throat.

'I've had a wee think. Roll me a cigarette and let's get on with this.'

'Ro . . . roll you a *cigarette?*' I am astounded. Behind her glasses, Susan's eyes widen in surprise.

'Yes. These fingers won't do the business any more. Arthritis.' He holds up his gnarled old hands. He jerks his thumb behind him to a flat, furry bag hanging by a leather strap from the back of his chair. 'You'll find a packet of tobacco in my sporran. Andi's not allowed to make me one. Apparently, it's detrimental to my health, as if I give a rat's doodle about that in my state! There's a machine there as well. I'll talk you through it.'

I open the pouch – his sporran – and notice that next to it, attached to the leather belt, is a knife about fifteen centimetres long, in a polished leather sheath. The handle of the dagger is carved with a pattern that reminds me of the tattoo on Fit Billy's arm. The old man sees me out of the side of his eye. 'I can read your mind, laddie,' he croaks.

He *can*? Oh no. I hold my breath for the accusation that's about to come.

'And the answer is yes,' he continues. 'It's sharp all right. Careful with my *dirk*!'

I breathe out. For a few minutes, I fiddle with the cigarette equipment on my knee, with Mr McKinley saying things like, 'No – too much baccy, laddie. No, not like that!' until eventually Susan says, 'Let *me* have a go.'

Thirty seconds later, an almost-perfect cigarette pops out from between the little machine's rollers. Mr McKinley says, 'Grand job, lass!' and I am feeling weirdly angry towards her, as if she has shown me up.

Little Miss Perfect rolls a perfect little cigarette.

Mr McKinley wriggles himself upright again. 'Now hand me the lighter and open the window a bit more. As for you two: stay away from the smoke. It's not good for you. Put the music back on, would you? A bit quieter. I've got something you may be interested to hear.'

CHAPTER 32

Old Kenneth McKinley takes a shallow puff of the cigarette that Susan made, blowing the smoke out straight away, and closes his eyes again. Then he raises his head and looks first at us, then at the lengthening column of white ash on the end of the cigarette.

I go to the record player and somehow find the 'on' button. The black disc revolves, the arm-thingy descends, and the strange, discordant music begins again. Mr McKinley waits until I'm sitting down.

'I don't actually smoke it, you know,' he says. 'My chest cannit take it. I just like the smell. It helps me to think.' True to his word, he doesn't place the cigarette in his mouth again, but holds it in his fingers, allowing the smoke to curl up to the stained ceiling.

Then he starts speaking, and it is exactly as though he is giving a speech. Something he has said before.

'There was a time – not so long ago, either – when the world seemed as though it was open to new ideas.' He pauses, then fires us a look over his round glasses. 'Are you listening?'

'Yes,' Susan and I say in unison, and we really are. There is something about his way of talking that forces you to pay attention.

'Well, that was the world I grew up in. Everything was changing; everything was new. Jet aeroplanes, heart transplants, space travel, foreign holidays, pocket calculators, central heating, colour television, cures for this disease and that disease, computers, oh – the excitement about computers!'

Mr McKinley wafts the cigarette under his nose and resumes his little speech.

'After the horror of the war with Hitler, we thought we were creating the perfect world! And all the while we were ignoring what was right in front of us. What was right *within* us. *Inside us!* Hmm? And look at us now, eh? We've become more interested in staying alive for as long as we can than in actually living the life we have.'

I shift on the couch and the paper under my bottom crackles. This has all the signs of a speech that could go on for a long time, but I don't care. I think I know where this is going, and I want him to get to the Dreaminators. Susan has leaned forward and is nodding along enthusiastically.

'The limits of the conscious mind, my wee friends, have never been discovered. As for the *un*-conscious . . . well, that might as well be limitless.' He sighs. 'But no one wants to know. Not these days.'

He flicks the cigarette, with good aim, out of the window.

'*We* would like to know, Mr McKinley!' says Susan. From anyone else, something like that would sound too keen, creepy even. But it's obvious that Susan is being sincere. It's the mention of the conscious and unconscious minds, I think: it'll have something to do with her meditation.

At that point, Andi bustles back in and starts sniffing and tutting and flapping a tea towel towards the open window.

'Oh, Kenneth!' she says, crossly. 'You must think I was born yesterday! It's bad enough for yourself, but worse for these two, and I'm entitled to work in a smoke-free environment! Did he ask you to do it?' she says to me and Susan.

'No,' I say, automatically lying.

'Yes,' says Susan, and I think her response is just as unthinking. Mr McKinley's teeth go *clack-clack* and he looks annoyed at being interrupted.

I don't want to go. I want to find out more, but Andi is fussing with the tea tray and says, 'You should take this leftover cake home with you.' Susan gets to her feet and looks at her neat little wristwatch.

'I think we've taken up quite enough of your time,' she says in her prim, grown-up way. 'It has been delightful.' I'm desperately trying to tell her *no* with my face, my eyes, but she's not looking at me.

Just then, there's a loud bell and I'm so tense I actually jump, making Susan turn in surprise.

Mr McKinley stretches out his skinny arm to an ancient telephone next to him on the table. It's one of those with a handset resting on top of a box-thing and he picks it up and holds it to his ear.

'That'll be you, will it, Uri?' he says, a warm smile spreading over his face. 'Hold one moment.' Mr McKinley presses the handset to his chest and looks at us. 'It's my son, Uri. It's been wonderful to meet you. Thank you for coming. We'll continue this another time, shall we? Goodbye.'

He turns back to his phone call and starts chatting while we head to the living-room door. Just like that, it's over.

CHAPTER 33

I'm raging inside at Susan for being so keen to leave. I hear a growl coming from down the corridor, and old Dennis's claws clicking unevenly on the tiled floor as he limps towards me. Andi's behind him, calling, 'Dennis! Dennis! No!' She grabs hold of his collar and starts to drag him back towards the kitchen as he lets off another gas attack that sounds like a bicycle puncture. 'Oh, Dennis, that's foul. Can you see yourselves out, kids? I've got to deal with this dog.'

Andi drags Dennis down the hall and back into the kitchen. She has left the tray of tea things on a hall table and I remember I was going to take the leftover butter cake back for Sebastian. A few weeks ago, I probably wouldn't have bothered, but he's been okay recently.

'Wait for me,' I say to Susan. 'I'll just be a minute.'

I turn back and the front door bangs shut behind me. I'm on my own. Well, not exactly on my own, only that Kenneth is on the phone to his son in the living room, while Andi has turned on a noisy blender in the kitchen. No one knows I'm here and it's a slightly odd feeling.

A long, tiled hallway stretches to the back of the house where the tea tray is, and it takes me past a room on the left with the door slightly ajar.

Don't judge me. I just want to have a look inside. Just a peep, you understand. It's not as if the door is shut, either, so it can't exactly be super-private, can it?

No one knows I am here. I push the door and it makes a soft *shushing* noise as it scrapes over the thick carpet in the room. I can see the bottom corner of a bed. I poke my head round the door and take in the rest. It's just an old man's bedroom. There are slippers on the floor, a pair of trousers folded over a chair, a dressing table with a hairbrush and comb. And there, twisting above the bed in the slight breeze from the open window, is a Dreaminator.

It's bigger than the ones in our bedroom, but there's no mistaking what it is. I walk closer to get a better look and my eyes widen.

Kenneth McKinley's Dreaminator is a thing of wonder, and as different from mine as a Rolls Royce is from Mola's beaten-up old SUV. Where mine has a hollow plastic hoop, and a cheap-looking pyramid 'roof', with wires and strings attached, this is made of pale, weathered bamboo, bent into shape with no visible joins. Set into the wood are tiny flakes of glittering pyrite. There are little carved eagles, flowers, mysterious symbols and writing of a kind I don't recognise.

And there, on one of the pyramid's sides, three letters: URI.

Wasn't that the name he said when he answered the phone? His son?

Inside the hoop, fine threads that look like pure gold are woven in a tight, intricate formation of circles repeated again and again, with beads and jewels sewn into the mesh. Hanging down are long strings, wound round with more gold thread, some with fine black feathers attached, and with large bluish crystals at the end. Even the battery housing is carved and inlaid with more stones.

It really might be the most beautiful thing I have ever seen.

'Can I help you?'

I yelp and spin round to see Andi in the doorway.

'Is this a habit of yours?' she asks.

My mouth flaps but no sound passes my throat, which has suddenly become desert-dry.

CHAPTER 34

'Letting yourself into places,' continues Andi. 'Snooping around.' She stops and leans against the doorpost, blocking my exit. At last she says, 'You may already have guessed, but . . . I know it was you that night. I have no proof, of course, but I know.'

'I . . . I . . . I was looking for the kitchen. Erm . . . butter cake. I left it.'

And folds her arms and looks at me for the longest time. 'I see,' she says, not taking her eyes from my face. 'This is Kenneth's bedroom. You'd better wait by the front door. I'll bring the cake to you.'

I'm about to squeeze past her and head for the front door, but she closes the bedroom door behind her with her foot.

'Actually, before you go, tell me one thing, Malcolm,' she says. 'What *were* you doing that night?'

It seems pointless to lie – you know, brazen it out. She's even being gentle. So I try to look apologetic and say, 'It was a dare. Pretend to be a robber sort of thing.'

She bites her cheek, seeming to literally chew over my answer. Then she nods. 'You could get into a lot of trouble doing that, you realise. People don't like it. You know I reported it to your school?'

'I know. I'm sorry.' This, of course, is the point at which I should apologise for taking the Dreaminators, but slowly something begins to dawn on me: *she seems satisfied.* I mean, if she knew I'd taken them, she'd say something like, 'And is there anything else you want to own up to?' but she doesn't.

She doesn't even know they're gone.

Instead, she goes *hmmp* and says, 'He likes you. I can tell. That is, as much as he likes anyone. I think you remind him of his son.'

I'm a bit embarrassed so I just say, 'Oh? The one who's just phoned?' and she gives a little sigh.

'He's a complicated man is Kenneth. He thinks deeply. Too deeply, if you ask me.' Her eyes flick to the Dreaminator above the bed and then back to me. 'And he's known a lot of sadness. It can all make him very confused. But, if you wanted to come back, I think you'd make a lonely old man a bit happier in his final days.'

'His . . . his final . . . ?'

She shrugs. 'Who knows? Now go and wait by the front door.'

Andi returns a moment later and hands me a plastic

box of cake with a slow nod and a warm smile. Before the door closes, she says, 'Will we see you again?'

She doesn't really say it like a question, and there's only one answer required.

'Yes.'

CHAPTER 35

'Good heavens!' says Susan, as we walk down the road, which might be the first time I've ever heard someone say that in real life. 'Wasn't that just . . . wonderful, Malky! I absolutely reek of smoke, but I don't care!'

'Aye, I s'pose,' I mumble, but all I'm thinking of is the Dreaminator above Mr McKinley's bed. 'Why'd you wanna leave so soon, anyway?' I'm still cross with her for that.

'Oh, but I thought you looked a little bored at all that talk of unconscious minds and so on.'

Bored? I was anything but bored! If my face was blank, it was because I was fascinated.

I say nothing, but my silence isn't going to last for long. Susan's still babbling on, just like someone's parent. We've gone past Prior's Park and reached the road by the little bay when she says, 'Do you want to go back another time? Mrs Farroukh would like it, I think.'

Obviously, I do. I grunt in response. You know, a sort of, 'Hmp, aye.' The kind of reply that drives adults nuts, then I go back to swimming in the whirlpool of my head again.

Old Mr McKinley's Dreaminator . . .

Andi saying 'his final days . . .'

'Are you all right, Malky? You are rather quiet.'

'Aye, fine.'

Should I tell her? I find myself wanting to talk to her – not just about my dreams, but also to ask her about her dad, tell her about mine . . .

Should I let this strange adult-girl into my head?

The problem is, she's just too flippin' annoying. Little Miss Perfect. Not my kind of friend at all. Too posh for me.

And she's talking again.

'Do you have any plans for your Saturday night?'

Where it comes from I don't know, but I hear myself take a deep breath and reply, 'Yeah, Seb and me are going to the Stone Age!'

Susan knows nothing at all about me sharing my dreams with Sebastian. And yet there was something about our encounter with Kenneth McKinley, and my 'confession' to Andi, that has made me bolder.

'Seb? Your brother?' She frowns.

Dammit. Think, Malky, think. Just tell her it's some daft game we play.

Then there's another voice in my head, contradicting me.

Why don't you just tell her the truth, Malky? Everything might be fine, you know?

And so we sit on a bench, looking at the little sailing-club dinghies skittering in the grey sea, and first I get her to promise that she won't tell *anyone* at school. The way she looks at me when she promises is reassuring. Her small dark eyes widen behind her glasses and she nods earnestly, hooking her hair behind both ears as if she's preparing for something important. I'm building up to telling her about the Dreaminators, I think because – for the first time – I realise that I'm not under suspicion.

I can tell her, surely? She won't snitch . . . surely? First I'll tell her about Seb and me sharing our dreams. Only then, depending on her reaction, will I tell her about the Dreaminators, and the one I saw hanging in Mr McKinley's bedroom.

Good plan, Malky.

Then I start. Susan goes quiet. For perhaps the only time since I've known her, she doesn't offer an opinion or interrupt me, or sound clever or superior. She just lets me speak. When I tell her about Seb being in my dreams, she leans forward and tilts her head like it's the most fascinating thing she has ever heard, and she doesn't scoff and accuse me of making it all up.

She giggles occasionally and it reminds me of the teacups tinkling on Andi's tray. She likes the *Santa Ana* ship story. I exaggerate it a bit, and she laughs some more, putting her hand over her mouth. When I get to the bit with the Christmas puddings, her hand goes down, she grins widely and laughs out loud and I realise I have never seen her teeth before: she always smiles with her mouth closed.

(Her teeth are small and white and even and no doubt very, *very* clean. In case you were wondering.)

Then, after a few seconds, she stops laughing. She shifts round and puts both of her hands on my forearm – a sort of gesture of concern, I guess. I've seen adults do it. 'But, Malky,' she says, suddenly looking serious, 'I don't think this is altogether safe.'

Altogether safe? Who speaks like that? I immediately start to regret my decision to share this stuff with Susan.

'Safe?' I repeat, suddenly feeling annoyed and yanking my arm from her grip. 'Why wouldn't it be safe? I mean . . . we're not doing it for *real*.'

This has put me off my stride, I can say that. I was building up to the Dreaminators, and suddenly she's gone all superior. She clasps her hands in her lap. She closes her eyes for a moment, then says, quietly, 'It's a dream, Malky. But that doesn't mean it isn't real.'

'Eh? Of course it does!'

'How do you know that? My Mola even questions whether *this* is real.' She waves her hand around, and taps the wooden fence with her fist, and looks out to sea. 'Everything. It all could be a dream. An illusion. It is like Mr McKinley was saying. Exploring these things could be . . . dangerous, I suppose. They can mess with your head. Think about it. I mean *really* think about it, Malky.'

The way she says *really* suggests that I don't ever think about things properly, and I don't like it.

We sit in silence for a moment and when the church clock chimes up on Front Street she says, 'Lunchtime, methinks!'

I mean, really. Who says *methinks*?

We walk without saying anything until we're at the top of the beach path joining Front Street that runs through Tynemouth village. On the corner at the top of the path is a newish building, which is Becker & Sons, the funeral directors. It's painted white and blue, with big display windows, and I think they try to make it look friendly and modern, but they have things like gravestones in the windows and those little statues of angels that go on top of graves, so I still get creeped out by it.

Just as Susan and I get there, Kez Becker comes out of a side door. She lives with her mum and dad and older brothers in the flat above the shop. I keep my head down, but I've never been good at blending in.

'Oi, oi, Blondie Bell!' she says, like she's trying out a new nickname. She swaggers towards us, hands deep in her pockets.

I force a smile and murmur, 'Oh no, here we go.'

CHAPTER 36

'Hello, Kezia. How are you?' Susan says, sounding like an adult again.

Kez looks right through her as if she isn't there and then says to me, 'I see you're developing a better class of friends, Bell.' She pronounces 'class' with a long 'a' – *clahss* – like Susan does. It's a deliberate dig. I answer this with a shrug.

Susan blinks with surprise at this unprovoked attack. Kez has spotted Susan's discomfort like a lioness spots a nervous gazelle.

'Y'know, Kez, I'm in a hurry so . . .' I say, and start to move off. Kez steps casually in front of us, blocking our path, but making it look natural.

'Oh, I say! Are you *indeed*! Are you going to a luncheon pah-teh!'

I don't know why I do the next thing: a thing that changes everything. Well, actually I do: self-preservation.

I laugh.

I know, I know. You're going to hate me, aren't you? But you don't know Kez Becker. It's best staying on her right side and sometimes, in order to do that, you have to make harsh choices. And so I laugh at Kez's ridiculous posh-voice mockery of Susan. Then, to make it worse, I add something of my own.

'Followed by a piccolo lesson?' And as the words pass my lips I feel wretched and guilty and immediately want to take them back, but it's too late: I have sided with Kez. Quickly, I add a forced 'ha ha!' as insurance because I know that in a few seconds I'll have to say, 'It was a joke, Susan!'

Susan stops, right there in the street, and, ignoring Kez completely, turns full-on to me, blinking in hurt and surprise. She is actually stammering, she's so upset. Her mouth quivers. 'You . . . you know your problem, Malky Bell?'

I find myself going on the offensive, even though I realise I have hurt her. 'No, Susan Tenzin. What is my problem?' My tone is sullen and defiant.

'You're a snob.'

Well, that takes me by surprise.

'I'm a snob? What – says the posh girl who plays the piccolo, who has a massive garden?'

'Exactly. You have just proved it. You look down on me because of my background, because of who I am, and because of how I speak! None of that has *anything* to do with who I am, but you have decided you are better than me. Isn't that exactly what being a snob is?'

I was angry at Susan, but I hadn't wanted to upset her. 'I don't think I'm better than you.'

'Yes, you jolly well do! You make jokes about my accent, you think that I live in a nice house and that I assume you are inferior, when all I have done is try to be friendly. You're even ashamed to be seen getting out of my car. You have no idea, Malky, how many people at school are like you. *Ooh, look at her, little Miss Perfect!* Talk about judging people! So what do I do? I do what my daddy says: I keep my head down, I work hard and I join things. Orchestra, library club, COMMS – anything. I thought you were different, Malky. I really did. I thought we were *friends*. But you are not: you are just as snobbish as all the rest and I hate you!'

Her volume has not increased while saying this, and in fact the last bit is almost whispered. But I can see her eyes are wet. I wish I could take back what I said. I really didn't mean to *hurt* her.

Just five minutes earlier I loved the way she hung on to every word I said.

'I . . . I was only joking,' I murmur.

'There is something you are keeping quiet, Malky Bell. I thought you were going to tell me back then, I thought you trusted me, but you know what? I am not even interested any more. And as for your dreams? You are not the only one that can do it, you know. You are not all that special.'

I don't have a chance to apologise, because she turns and runs across the road and down the back lane in the direction of her street.

Kez and I watch her go. Then Kez tuts.

'Posh lasses, man Bell. Nowt but trouble. What was all that about dreams, anyway?'

'Oh, nothing. She's nuts.'

I'm about to walk away when Kez says, 'Hold on. Have you thought any more about my Halloween Challenge? Only I've come up with some refinements, and . . .' I interrupt her.

'No, Kez. I haven't. I think it's a horrible idea!'

Where was that courage two minutes ago when I should have stood up for Susan Tenzin?

Kez takes a step closer and takes her hands out of her pockets. 'You're just chicken, aren't you, Bell?' She starts to flap her arms, chicken-style, when there's the deep grumble of a motorbike engine behind us and we both leap out of the way. The motorbike pulls to a sudden halt between us and the rider lifts up the visor helmet.

Kez's dad nods at me, then says, 'There you are, Kezia! Your mum's calling you. I'm going up the coast.' He waits. Kezia doesn't move. 'Now, Kez. Off you go. Chop chop.'

It's the distraction I need. As Kez's dad twists his wrist and the bike moves off, growling, along Front Street, I walk away quickly in the same direction that Susan went.

Kez is left standing in front of the shop window, looking furious, with a stone angel peeping over her shoulder.

Then her expression changes to a smirk and she makes the chicken-arms again.

I trudge home. *Nice one, Malky*, I think, bitterly. I seem to be losing control of everything in my life and it is not even lunchtime.

Roll on bedtime, I say.

CHAPTER 37

That evening, Fit Billy's round again. He's made salad, which at least makes Mam happy, and she's put on make-up for some reason. She's fine without it, if you ask me.

Because he made our food, Mam says Billy can choose what to watch and of course it's something about World War Two. We can't afford Netflix and stuff, so he's brought a DVD: some comedy with a man pretending to be Adolf Hitler, which I don't really like, but Mam and Billy are laughing and even Seb looks like he's enjoying it.

Before it finishes, I say I'm going to bed, and Seb gets up to follow me.

'Are you all right, pet?' says Mam. 'You've been very quiet. You never told me about your school visit thingy.'

'I'm okay. I'll tell you tomorrow.'

Billy gets up and sits on the sofa close to Mam, because you get a better view of the screen. 'He's just tired, aren't you, pal? Go on, off you go!' Well, that's strange – Billy sending me off to bed, but I'm halfway out of the door, anyway.

As soon as we're upstairs, Seb says we should dream about killing Adolf Hitler.

'It'll be *awethome*!' he said. 'We'll be the boys who assassinate a mass murderer!' (Try saying that with no front teeth, I dare you.)

We're at the top of the stairs. I can hear the film has finished, and the *pop* of a wine cork, and now Mam and Fit Billy are talking about painting the fence between our backyards and they're laughing. (I can't imagine what's so funny about painting a fence.)

'No,' I say, firmly. 'We're not killing anyone, Seb. Not even in a dream. You know that.'

His face falls.

'Think about it. Our dreams are so real, there's hardly any difference between them and real life, yeah?' He nods. 'So, do you really want to know what it's like to kill someone? Even someone like Hitler? When you're *seven*? It's horrible. It could really mess with your head.'

I've just used the same phrase that Susan used with me, but it's different this time because Seb's my little brother.

He agrees, reluctantly. Then he comes up with the idea of attacking Adolf Hitler with our Nerf guns. It's still more ambitious than anything else we have tried. Perhaps I am getting cocky.

But it does sound fun.

*

Seb and I were supposed to see Dad this afternoon, but he texted earlier to say he couldn't make it. Mam tutted and said, 'You'd think he lived in Mexico, not Middlesbrough.'

So, when we get to our room, I FaceTime Dad on my cracked phone instead. As soon as he answers, he says, 'Are those the dream things behind you? I've heard a lot about them.'

I've listened to Mam and Dad talking on the phone and I know that Dad thinks it's all a bit strange. Seb, though, comes over to my bed and grabs the phone, excitedly. 'Yes!' he says. 'Do you want to see them?'

'Sure,' says Dad.

'Okay.' Seb gets up, switches them on, gets even more excited and before I can stop him he says, 'And, best of all, me and Malky can share each other's dreams! Can't we, Malky?'

I might have known this would happen. It's all very well me keeping quiet, knowing – because I'm much older than him – that people will react with disbelief, or scoff, or simply not understand. But Seb doesn't do that. He just says it all, straight out, while Dad's face stays blank. Seb gets one of the Dreaminator boxes and holds it up to my phone to show Dad.

'A Dreaminator?' Dad says in a mysterious sort of voice.

'Have you heard of it?' I ask. I'm about to tell him

that I met the inventor this morning, but I'm put off by his suspicious tone of voice.

'The name rings a bell,' Dad replies. 'Dunno where from, though.'

At that point, Dad's girlfriend calls for him and he has to go. I keep thinking that the word 'Dreaminator' has stirred up some memory in Dad that he doesn't want to – or can't – tell me.

CHAPTER 38

Hours later, I still can't sleep. It's a really warm night for September. I've flung the cover off and I lie there, listening to Seb snuffle.

'You awake, Malk?' he whispers.

'Mm-hm.'

'Me too. Are we going to do the dream, with the Nerf guns? Shooting Hitler?'

'If we get to sleep, yeah.'

'Cool.' He lies back. 'Will you read *Kobi* to me?'

I put the light on with a sigh. He's already sitting up now and has got the book in his hands. I prop myself up on my pillow and start reading.

**'In the shadows of the cave, the fire flickers
red,
And Kobi lies down with a rock beneath his
head . . .'**

We get halfway through the story, to the bit I know is his favourite.

'A ride upon a mammoth? What a wonderful idea!
Kobi clambers up its trunk and hangs on to its ear . . .'

But Seb's already asleep. When I close the book's cover, I see something that I've never noticed before. On the flap is small, scrawly writing:

To Seb from Dad. Be brave like Kobi x

Only it's obviously not Dad's writing. It's Seb's.

Seb, who hardly ever mentions Dad. I turn out the light and flop back on to my hot pillow, a strange feeling inside me. I think it might be protectiveness towards my brother?

It's new, and I don't like it.

And that's not all. Because, a few hours later, I'm dreaming the dream that will change everything.

CHAPTER 39

Remember: it was Seb's idea. I can at least blame him for that. He was the one who came up with the idea of attacking Adolf Hitler.

It starts in Kobi's cave. I'm getting a *bit* bored with the whole Kobi thing, to be honest, but at least I know it works and how to control it properly. It's a bit like the early levels of a video game if you forget to save your progress: you can just whizz through to get to the bit you want.

Outside the cave are plenty of other boys the same age as me, all wearing the same uniform. I'd be sure to blend in, but I am still nervous.

There's a crowd on the beach getting noisier. Beyond them, at the shoreline, are the mammoths that are usually there, but no one is bothered by them. I hear a couple of shouts go up:

'*Er is hier!*' and, '*Er kommt!*' which I know from Miss Linton's German lessons means 'He is here!' and 'He is coming!'

I look down at myself and I don't really like what I

see. I am wearing a smartly ironed brown shirt and a neckerchief like the one I had in Cubs, only it's black. My baggy shorts are held up by a shiny leather belt and on my head is what I now know is called a 'forage cap' because I looked it up on the web for my school project.

The uniform of the Hitler Youth.

The noise of the crowd has increased and more and more people are surging forward, but they are kept back by stern-looking policemen.

Then Seb turns up, dressed completely wrong. Instead of black, his neckerchief is bright green, made from the same fabric as his favourite goalie top. Still, no one seems to have noticed. I could get rid of him. He'd leave if I told him to. But I'm beginning to learn that it's best not to be too controlling in these situations, if it can be avoided. It's as if I'm allowed a certain amount of control, and it can get used up, like a battery.

I think of Mam's song, and decide to just 'let it be . . .'

'Come on, Seb – head down. Got your weapon?'

'Yep! Got yours?'

Do I? I look down – yep, there's my Nerf gun. I pat the holster attached to my belt and unhook the cover in readiness. 'Let's go!'

We push through the dense crowd as purposefully as we can. No one looks at us.

I catch a glimpse of a car, still a hundred metres away, and to get a better view I say, 'Float!' and I begin to hover a little way above the heads of the crowd and nobody takes any notice at all. The car's body is polished like a black mirror, coming slowly down the beach.

It's the longest car I have ever seen: a Mercedes-Benz, open-topped so that everyone can see the occupants of the three rows of seats – although there is only one that anyone cares about.

In the back row are two grey-uniformed soldiers, staring warily at the crowd. In front of them, in the middle row, are two more officers. And riding up front next to the driver is the man everyone is cheering. He stands, unsmiling, throwing out his stiff-armed salute to the crowd, who return it, with grins and hoots of joy.

My heart thumps in my chest. He is so familiar to me from countless pictures, and YouTube clips, and movies and TV shows, and yet here he is in front of me, his car coming along the shore straight towards me and Seb.

'Are you ready?' I ask Seb again and he nods.

'Ready, Freddie!' he says.

The two of us step calmly from the front row and raise our blue plastic guns, ready to go down in history.

Malcolm and Sebastian Bell: the British boys who shot Adolf Hitler with Nerf guns.

CHAPTER 40

The driver of the big black Mercedes sees us first, before the officers who are seated behind him, and before Hitler, who is looking out, smirking now, at the cheering crowd.

I look at the driver and a puzzled expression crosses his face. The car's not travelling fast, so he has plenty of time to brake as he gets closer. The sudden slowing of the vehicle causes Hitler to jolt forward, grab the top edge of the windscreen and look crossly first at his driver, and then ahead at me and my brother.

There can't be many people alive who have seen Adolf Hitler in real life. (I know: you're probably thinking, *Well, neither have you*, but it really feels like I have.) He's shorter than I expected and his face is fleshy and pale. The little square moustache is unmistakable, though, and his cold blue eyes are furious at this interruption to his parade.

The next few moments appear to pass in slow motion.

The driver gesticulates angrily with his arm and barks at us, but I don't understand a word: they are probably ones that Miss Linton won't ever teach us. At the same time, two of the officers from the car leap out and start coming towards Seb and me.

'Now!' I shout. 'Fire!'

Together we pull the triggers of our guns, unleashing a volley of orange sponge darts at the man they called the *Führer*. Our aim is rubbish, though: most of the darts ping off the windscreen of the car, leaving Hitler startled but clearly unharmed. A gasp goes up from the crowd.

'Look out!' I yell at Seb. Then, 'Reload!'

On my command, the guns reload automatically, and we turn and fire a burst at the soldiers coming for us. This time our aim is better: the men go down, clutching their heads in pain.

Only in a dream could sponge darts be that effective!

The atmosphere in the crowd has changed in seconds. They watch in amazement as Seb and I run closer to the car, firing our toy guns at the uniformed officers, who have extracted their own pistols, but seem uncertain of how to proceed against two boys. One of them looks at Hitler as if for guidance, but Hitler continues to glare at us in silent astonishment.

This is even more fun than I had expected! I glance over to Seb: he has already downed the SS officer in a burst of orange missiles and is ready for another go at Hitler.

I raise my gun, tasking careful aim at Hitler's moustache.

'Okay, Adolf – get ready for one right in your gob!'
I shout.

My finger is squeezing the trigger when, from behind me, a large arm in a grey sleeve thumps down on the barrel of my gun, causing the ground in front of me to be peppered with orange foam. My assailant's other arm grabs me in a chokehold and yanks the Nerf gun from my grasp, throwing it to one side.

I am caught, and immediately think about the Emergency Escape procedure. But before I can say anything I hear Seb scream from the other side of the huge motor.

'Get off me!'

A huge soldier drags him, hand clamped over his mouth, his feet kicking up sand, until we are standing together facing the big black car, as Adolf Hitler climbs down and walks towards us slowly, his hands clasped behind his back, a cold half-smile on his damp lips. Following a pace behind is a stern-looking female SS officer, her cap pulled low, shielding her face. She is wearing the familiar black uniform, complete with the red-and-white armband featuring the hated Nazi symbol of the swastika.

She speaks first. 'Silence! *Ach so!* Ve have a pair of Englishers, *ja*? In the uniform off the *wunderbar* Hitler Youth!' She indicates me. 'Do you see, *mein Führer*?'

Hitler nods solemnly, looking me up and down.

'*Ja*, Kapitän Becker. *Jawohl!*'

This is good stuff. These people are talking *exactly* like the Nazi officers in Fit Billy's film. For the full effect, the woman officer should click her heels together . . .

And she does. Then she takes off her cap, and angrily tosses her purple dip-dyed hair. I splutter with laughter when I realise she looks *exactly* like Kez Becker, and Hitler glares at me.

Seb cocks his head to one side and sticks out his tongue at *Der Führer*. 'I'm not scared of you! You're a big bully with silly hair and a stupid moustache and . . . and a rid-ridinkulous salute! Look!' Seb imitates the Nazi salute and then waggles his fingers wildly, adding a big, wet raspberry through his missing teeth for good measure.

Hitler pale face turns pink. He purses his lips and narrows his eyes into an expression of pure fury and he barks a command.

The female officer leans forward and points to the letters SS on her collar.

'Ha, my little friend! Do you know what these letters stand for?'

Thanks to Fit Billy's obsession with World War Two, I do. They stand for *Schutzstaffel* – Hitler's dreaded Nazi paramilitary police force. But I don't know if Seb knows. (Nor do I like the way things are going. Bravery and excitement are all very well, but I am getting very close to calling it quits with the Emergency Escape.)

Seb peers at the letters and adopts an innocent expression. 'SS?' he says, and then he pauses for comic effect. 'Are you a member of the Secret Seven?'

It takes a second or two for the SS officer to register what Seb has said, then she screams the German word for 'no', '*Nein!*'

'Nope. I've read the books,' says Seb. 'I'm pretty sure there's only seven.'

'Insolence!' she hisses. '*Mein Führer!* We must make an example of these English boys!'

Hitler nods solemnly and waves his hand casually as if to say, *Get on with it then!*

'Very well. Bring it out.'

The officer strides to the rear of the big Mercedes and pops open the boot. Nothing happens for a moment, then a long crocodile flops on to the ground and uncurls itself, turning its head until it faces me.

I recognise it immediately and a chill goes through me from my skull to my toes.

Cuthbert.

This is *not* in the plan.

CHAPTER 41

I stare at the crocodile from my childhood nightmares.

This is not meant to happen!

On the other hand, I'm quite looking forward to seeing the expression of Hitler's face when this massive crocodile turns into a furry toy in front of him. A murmur goes round the crowd, and Hitler turns away as though he does not want to witness what comes next.

It's okay, Malky. You know what to do. Remember last time?

The last time I had seen Cuthbert had been the very first Dreaminator dream: the one in the classroom, when he had emerged from beneath the desk I was standing on. Just as I had done then, I extend my hand and say, Cuthbert!', then, 'Stop!'

It doesn't work.

Instead of turning into a cuddly toy before my eyes, the beast rises a little on its stumpy legs and starts coming towards me.

Hitler turns to his officers and laughs. Then he faces me. 'It's not vorking, is it, little English boy? You think you are so cleffer. You forget: I am Adolf Hitler, one of the most evil men who has ever lift! Ha ha ha ha! Kutbert – attack him!'

I try again. 'Cuthbert! Stop! Stop!'

Still he advances. I don't understand: my powers of dream-control should have lasted much longer than this. But I am taking no more risks.

'Emergency Escape!' I yell to Seb. 'Ready?'

'Aye aye, sir!'

SNAP!

In a flash, the croc's jaws clamp down on my extended arm in an agonising grip, tearing at my flesh as it tries to wrench my arm off.

'Wake up!' I shout, 'WAKE UP!'

Nothing happens.

CHAPTER 42

'Wake up!' I shout again.

I take a huge lungful of air. Then I tighten my mouth and throat shut and try to breathe out. My cheeks bulge. I strain harder, urging my ears to pop with the effort.

Meanwhile, the crocodile chews down deeper, his teeth inching further up my arm towards my shoulder. With my other hand, I pinch my nose and blow hard, feeling my eyes and cheeks bulge until I release the air with a loud *paaaah!*

Then I open my eyes.

I'm in bed, panting hard, still imagining that my arm is being eaten by a crocodile. I know now that, if I close my eyes, the images from the dream will come back to me for a few seconds before fading away. So I do, just to test it.

And there's the croc, jaws clamped on my wrist, and a shooting pain goes up my arm until I open my eyes again and the croc has gone.

I am awake, in my own bed. I turn my head and there is Seb, fast asleep in his.

Except my arm is still hurting. Not *badly*. Not a-crocodile-is-biting-my-arm-off agony, but it's definitely sore. I wait a moment until my breathing returns to normal, and look up at the Dreaminator above me.

No more nightmares! the instructions said. Even when I was little, and before Mam and I had renamed the crocodile Cuthbert, the thing had never actually bitten me. I swing my legs out from under my duvet and shuffle out of bed.

I turn the bathroom light on and have a wee, and I roll up my pyjama sleeve to look at my arm. The pain is lessening, but it's still there and . . . am I imagining this? I look closer.

Surely not.

There is a line of indentations, little pink marks, where the croc chomped down. *Exactly* where its teeth were. Turning my arm from side to side, I can see the marks clearly. Then I hear a noise on the landing outside and the rattle of the bathroom doorknob. It'll be Seb coming for a drink of water.

I'm facing the mirror, which reflects the bathroom door behind me.

The door opens slowly, creaking a little. I look in the mirror and get ready to say hi to Seb, but there's no one there. That's odd: it looks like the door is opening by itself.

I don't want to turn round. I don't want to see what

is opening the door, because it has to be at ground level, but I force myself to look . . .

. . . and he's there, on the ground, raised up on his squat legs. He's half in and half out of the bathroom door. The massive crocodile takes two tottering steps towards me across the tiles and I scream, 'No!' as it opens its jaws wide, and slowly closes them again.

Then from within the beast comes a grating, hollow growl, like an empty metal bin being dragged across rocks. The croc's mouth opens slightly and it sneers in a deep, upper-class drawl like a British army officer in one of Fit Billy's war movies.

'I say. Look who it is. Hello, Malcolm!'

How can this be? In my terror, I scream out for Mam, and back myself up against the sink as the croc inches forward.

'Mam! Seb! *Maaaam!*'

Cuthbert's at my feet now, and I hoist my bum on to the edge of the sink to raise myself off the ground. I kick out at the advancing beast and I can see the shine on his teeth as he slowly closes his mouth and lowers himself on to his belly, bending his back half until he has cleared the door, then using the weight of his knobbled tail to slam the bathroom door shut, completely blocking my escape. He is clearly willing to take as long as he likes.

'Mam!' I shout again. '*Maaaam!* Help!'

'Aw – calling for mummy, are we?' Cuthbert sneers. 'It won't do you any good, you know.'

The croc blinks at me patiently, and runs its tongue round its teeth like it's sizing up its next meal. I scrabble further up the edge of the sink and search with my hands for things to throw. A nailbrush pings off its snout, a glass, a toothbrush, then I glance at the tube of toothpaste in my hand. The name looks strange.

CLOGAET

Then the letters seem to move.

LOGTACE

Wait. What? Why doesn't it say COLGATE?

Something comes back into my head. I remember reading the instructions for the Dreaminator.

Numbers on clocks and printed words are usually jumbled or indistinct during dreams.

Crocodiles don't talk, or blink for that matter. They don't have tongues, either, not the sort you can stick out, anyway.

This just *cannot* be happening.

I am still dreaming.

'Wake up!' I shout. *'Waaaake uuuup!* Wake up! Oh, please wake up!' As Cuthbert lunges forward for an attack, I kick out wildly, desperately, sobbing and shouting and trying my hardest to recapture the breath that seems to have been forced from my lungs.

And I'm back in bed, with my duvet twisted round my legs, thrashing out at . . .

. . . nothing.

CHAPTER 43

Seb is awake, standing over me, shaking my shoulders. 'Oh, you're back! What happened to you? I couldn't wake you! What happened, Malky?'

I cannot answer him. I dare not close my eyes. I lie there on my back, my chest heaving, and I feel a bead of sweat trickle off my forehead.

'Is . . . is this a dream?' I ask. I can't see Seb's face in the dark, just his shadowy form next to my bed, outlined by the light from the blue crystals hanging above us.

'A *dream*? Course not. What's the matter with you? I was in the dream with Hitler, yeah?'

I nod and wipe the sweat off my brow with my pyjama sleeve. Seb says, 'Okay, so I woke up and you were here, but you were still asleep. Your face was twitching. I've been trying to wake you. I nearly called Mam.'

My breathing's returning to normal. 'Wow. That was intense. I thought I was awake. That is, I . . . I thought I had woken up. But I hadn't and . . . and . . .'

It sounds stupid.

Seb falls back into his bed. Then I hear his chuckle. 'Did you *see* Hitler's face?'

He rolls over and is asleep in minutes, while I just lie there. The pain in my arm is still there. If I run my fingers along the row of teeth-marks, I can still feel the indentations. Very slightly. But they are there.

Mam's at the bedroom door now. 'You okay, love?' she whispers. 'I heard you shout.'

I shouted?

'Cuthbert back?' she asks.

'Yeah.'

She comes into the room, squeezing between our two beds, and sits down on the edge of mine. She reaches out to stroke my hair. 'Eee, pet. You're sweating like mad. Bad one, was it?'

I nod, and she keeps stroking my head, gently. In the dark, I see her eyes move upwards until she's staring at the Dreaminator, then she looks down at me.

Make Your Dreams Come True! the box said. It didn't mention nightmares.

I roll over so that she can't see that my eyes are wide open. I don't want to fall back asleep: I'm scared. My arm still hurts.

Then she sings the song, really quietly so as not to wake Seb. I haven't heard it for years, and I still don't know all of the words.

'*Let it be, let it be . . .*'

After a while, Mam reaches up and turns off the Dreaminator and goes back to bed.

I fall asleep, but I don't dream of anything, I don't think.

If I had stopped there, things might not have got much worse. But I didn't, did I?

And they did get worse: much worse.

CHAPTER 44

Over the next couple of days, I lose count of the number of times someone asks me, 'Are you okay, Malky?'

Look, have you ever been on a really fast roller coaster? Mam took me and Seb to Thorpe Park two years ago, and there was this ride called TerrorSpeed that Seb was too small for, so I went on my own while he and Mam watched and it was great, but . . .

When I came off, I was in a bit of a daze. Not dizzy, like staggering and so on. Just . . . spacey. It wasn't for long – just a minute or so when I felt as if I was walking on cotton wool.

Well, that's what this is like, only it's going on all the time. I keep running my fingers over the indentations in my arm left by Cuthbert's teeth. They don't hurt any more, and you can hardly see them, but they are there.

Mam sees me fiddling. 'What's up with your arm, Malky?'

I've been bitten by an imaginary crocodile, Mam.

I pull my sleeve back down. 'Nothing. Just a bit itchy.'

I can't even talk to Susan about it because of our argument. Besides, she's been away on a trip to some school orchestra competition in Leeds.

And then comes another dream, and this one is . . . well, I'd better just tell you. Bear with me. It's funny.

Sort of.

I'm in the lunch hall again. It looks normal. It sounds and smells normal as well. I'm not taking any risks, though. I go up to Mason Todd who eyes me warily – as he might, I suppose. I've hardly spoken to him in real life for weeks.

'Hey, Mason,' I say. 'Am I dreaming?'

He looks me up and down, as though I'm a stranger. 'Of course you are!' Then he adds, 'Weirdo.' He goes back to talking to Tilly Sykes who snorts with laughter at something he murmurs.

This is the awesome thing about being in a dream, you see. I wouldn't normally do what I do next. And, before I do it, I carry out another 'reality check' just in case Mason's lying. The old digital clock above the serving hatch is flashing numbers randomly – another sure sign that I'm in Dreamland.

'Hey, Mason!' I call out, loud enough for everyone nearby to hear, even though the lunch hall is pretty noisy. He turns round. 'Is it true you and Tilly are secretly dating?'

They both turn bright red. 'No!' he says.

'Well, that's what I've heard, but she doesn't dare tell you that she's also in love with Jonah Bell, except *he's* in love with Kez Becker!'

I'm making this all up, obviously, just because in a dream I can! People start to snigger, then I feel a tap on my shoulder. Turning round, I see Jonah Bell and his expression is furious. 'Did you say something?' he growls.

I'm fearless and loving every second.

'Yes I did, you big lump,' I say, right in his face. 'You're stupid and the only reason anyone hangs out with you is that they're even stupider than you!'

People are starting to laugh now, and the feeling of power is terrific. I can say exactly what I want, to whoever I like! I push between some Year Fives on their bench and use it as a step up on to the table, kicking aside some plates and cutlery as I do so. They fall to the ground with a loud clatter and smash, so that everyone who hasn't yet noticed the commotion turns round to see where the noise is coming from.

That's when I see Susan Tenzin on the other side of the hall, with a gaggle of her orchestra friends. Her hand is held to her mouth in horror. I'm still stinging from her calling me a snob the other day, so now is the chance to get even in a safe way.

'See this?' I yell at her. 'Do you and your perfect friends have enough to laugh at now?'

Out of the corner of my eye, I see Mr Springham get to his feet over in the corner where the staff sit.

'You don't scare *me-ee*!' I say in a singsong voice to Mr Springham, pointing at him and dancing a little jig on the table, dislodging more plates. People have stopped laughing now and are sitting open-mouthed in amazement.

I remember Seb's insults to Adolf Hitler, and I reckon I'll have a go myself.

'You've hated me since I came into the school, haven't you? Well, the feeling's mutual, you . . . you great baldie spud-head with your too-tight shirts and your wobbly bum!'

This gets a proper gasp. It is just like being onstage as I look down at the faces gazing up at me.

'Enough! Get down now!' shouts Mr Springham. He's only a couple of tables away and from the table I pick up a bowl of school trifle. I mean to throw the trifle and bowl so that it lands perfectly on his head: upside down, like it would in a cartoon, but it slips from my fingers and I watch – almost in slow motion – as the whole thing sails through the air and he bats it away with his arm. The trifle splats up his sleeve and some splashes the side of his face. It's not a direct hit, which is a bit disappointing for a dream, but I'm having too much fun to care.

This time the crowd groans in amazement: a loud, '*Oooooh!*'

It only holds him back for a second or two. He's nearly

on me now, so I stop my jigging and hold my hands out to the side like a life-size statue.

'Float!' I say. 'Float up!'

I wait for the feeling of the wire pulling me upwards. It's slow in coming so I lift my heels off the table. 'Float,' I say again, then louder, '*Float!*'

Mr Springham is alongside me now. He wipes trifle from his face with his hand and folds his arms in mock patience. My failure to float is annoying. I'm not used to the dream-controlling wearing off so soon.

Mr Springham's voice is normally deep and loud. Now it's chillingly quiet.

'Malcom Bell,' he hisses, 'get down from there this minute.'

I look round at the double doors of the lunch hall and say again, 'The crocodile will be here soon – but have no fear! Cuthbert! Come now!'

But there's no crocodile. I'm getting a bit desperate now. 'Float! Float, man!' I want to hover high above these people, above Mr Springham.

I'm flapping my arms now, and I hear someone say, 'He's trying to fly!'

Someone else starts to laugh, 'Malky Bell's lost it completely!' while other people join in the laughter and begin to imitate my arms flapping.

So I stop. I lower my arms. The hall falls quiet and I take a few deep breaths. I look round at everyone looking up at me, some of them with loaded forks paused halfway to their mouths; and at Mr Springham, unusually calm with his arms crossed and a blob of custard hanging from his ear like cheap yellow jewellery.

I don't know how long I'm there. Several seconds? A minute? It's hard to tell when you're dreaming, isn't it?

I *am* dreaming . . . Aren't I?

More seconds pass.

'Wake up!' I shout. I long to wake up in my bed. I hold my breath and puff out my cheeks and go *paaaah!* A murmur starts up in the hall. Mr Springham holds up his hand to shush everyone.

At the end of the queue of people waiting with their trays I see Susan. When our eyes meet, her face fills with sadness and she slowly shakes her head.

Now I feel sick, because I'm not dreaming, am I? I have just done this for real.

I have just thrown a bowl of trifle at the school's scariest teacher after calling him a baldie spud-head. I have danced on the table and tried to summon a crocodile called Cuthbert.

I try one more go. 'Earth – swallow me whole now,' I pray quietly with my eyes shut. It doesn't, of course. I'm still there, on the school dining table, and Mr Springham is still waiting for me. If this really was a dream, he'd probably have steam coming out of his ears.

But that doesn't happen in real life, does it?

CHAPTER 45

An hour later, I'm in Mrs Farroukh's office.

There's me, Mrs Farroukh and Mr Springham (in a fresh shirt, no trifle bits and what little hair he has is wet, like he's rinsed it).

I'm being asked to explain, but the only explanation available is, 'I thought I was having a dream,' and I can't say that because that's mad, isn't it?

I was given 'time-out' in the Quiet Room while Mam was called, but she can't leave work.

I've worked one bit out. Mason Todd was being sarcastic when he said, 'Yes, you're dreaming' when I asked him – no surprise there. And I glanced at the clock above the serving hatch as I was marched out of the lunch hall by Mr Springham. It was still flickering and changing like . . . well, a broken clock.

What *happened*?

I was in the lunch queue and then *I thought I was in a dream.* Something made my brain slip. I think about it. I'm wearing an old school sweatshirt that escaped the wash and I cast my mind back. When I was in the lunch queue . . . I remember glancing down at the sleeve of my sweatshirt, and realising it had some yak's butter on the sleeve. I sniffed it and then . . . boom! *That* was when I thought I was dreaming.

I must be going mad, and that is terrifying.

I look up. They are both staring at me.

'Sorry' hardly seems to cover it. They'll want an explanation. An explanation that I don't really have without sounding like I have completely lost it.

Which perhaps I have. Didn't Susan warn me, that time we sat on the bench, looking at the boats? 'These things can mess with your head, Malky.'

How could I get it so wrong?

'Do you have anything to say?' asks Mrs Farroukh.

'Um,' I say. 'I don't know.'

Mr Springham sighs.

'Perhaps we could recap the events,' says Mrs Farroukh. 'Mr Springham?'

Mr Springham recounts the episode from his point of view. It's not like he's exaggerating or anything: he's just telling the truth, and it's bad enough. He doesn't even know about the bit when I called Jonah Bell a stupid lump or whatever it was I said. I'll be paying for that later, I just know it.

And, all the time, I'm still half hoping that I'll wake up. It's as if a thick fog has taken over the space where my brain is supposed to be, and I'm expecting a sea breeze to come along to blow it away and wake me up. I would love this to be a dream, but it isn't.

Mrs Farroukh takes over, and now we're on more familiar ground. It's stuff I haven't heard in a little while, but it's still the same.

'Difficult time with you, Malky . . . disruptive influence . . . I had hoped for better things this term . . . this cannot go unpunished . . . appointment with Educational Counsellor . . . letting yourself down . . .'

And then she stops and both teachers sit down. Mr Springham clears his throat so that I think he's going to take over where Mrs Farroukh left off, but instead he looks at me steadily and says, very quietly, 'Is everything all right, Malky? I mean . . . at home and so on?'

This is a bit odd for me: Mr Springham being nice. I say nothing, so he continues. 'Look, I know we haven't always got on so well, but I'm concerned, *we're* concerned . . .'

That's when there's a knock at Mrs Farroukh's door. Impatiently, Mr Springham barks, 'What is it?' and Carol, the school receptionist, puts her head round the door.

'There is someone to see you, Mrs Farroukh. She says it is very important.'

Carol steps aside and Susan Tenzin is standing there, a meek and sad look on her face.

CHAPTER 46

'I am very surprised and disappointed, Susan,' says Mrs Farroukh, about five minutes later. 'I really thought we could expect better things than this from you. A *dare*, you say?'

Susan nods. 'I . . . I thought it might be funny. You see, everyone thinks I am so boring. "Boring Susan" they call me. To my face.' Her bottom lip starts to wobble a bit.

I have to say I haven't heard anyone call her this. But she sounds very convincing. Susan's voice cracks a little when she adds, 'It's . . . it is like I am being bullied.'

I see an exchange of glances between Mrs Farroukh and Mr Springham. A second later, I glance at Susan and, in that brief moment, she winks at me.

That's right. Susan is lying for me. *She is acting!* I can't believe it, but I have to.

She sniffs deeply, as if holding back tears. 'I did not dare do it myself. But I dared Malcolm to do it. He . . . he got carried away.'

The bullying thing is clever. Everyone knows that

teachers are terrified of bullying. There are posters up all over the school, and regular assemblies and so on. Still, I'm not sure Mr Springham and Mrs Farroukh have completely believed Susan yet.

'Is this true, Malcolm? You did this as a "dare"?'

I say nothing. 'Well, is it? Speak up!' says Mr Springham and I nod the tiniest, most shameful nod I can.

'Those things he said about you, Susan,' says Mrs Farroukh. 'How could you . . .'

'It was all planned, wasn't it, Malky? He did not mean any of it. It was just . . . banter.' She says it like she's trying out a foreign word for the first time.

Mr Springham's eyes have narrowed and his gaze flicks suspiciously between me and Susan, as though he isn't quite sure who to believe. I suppose he just can't work out why Susan would voluntarily take the blame for something she had nothing at all to do with. He says nothing, though.

Eventually, Mrs Farroukh sighs and says, 'There is no question that I will be writing to your parents this afternoon in the strongest terms. So-called dare or not, Malcolm, this is the sort of behaviour that we do not tolerate here at Marden Middle School. It goes without saying that you will both be withdrawn immediately from the COMMS project and, Susan, your roles as library monitor, orchestra captain and Green Team coordinator are suspended immediately . . .'

And so it goes on. Valerie the school counsellor gets another mention. Oh, whoopee.

Basically, though, I've got away with it.

I did pretty much the worst thing that's ever been done in this school. It's going to be talked about for years . . . and I'm being let off.

And all because of Susan Tenzin.

Of course, I wait until we're out in the corridor before I smile at her. And it makes my stomach do a little flip when she smiles back.

CHAPTER 47

Susan is free to go to her music lesson.

I am kept in 'supervised isolation' until the end of school, which basically means doing my French homework while Miss Biggs, who I've never spoken to before, does some marking and – to judge from the snorts and giggles – catches up on Facebook or whatever.

I'm supposed to be learning the perfect tense.

J'ai dormi – I slept.

J'ai rêvé – I dreamed.

Je suis devenu fou – I went mad.

I feel for the bumps on my arm again – a sort of reassurance that I am not actually losing my mind. They're not there any more, however closely I look. Did I imagine it all, just like I imagined I was in a dream?

'Malcolm,' says Miss Biggs, 'is your homework written on your arm?'

I pull my sleeve down and look again at the stain on the fabric: a large, uneven smudge. The smell is still there: faint but distinctive.

I'm wondering about this, and letting my mind drift, when I'm startled by the end-of-day bell.

It's 3.30. I'm free to go. The first thing I see when I turn my phone on is a text from Mam.

Just got an email from Mrs Farroukh. We'll talk tonight.

Not even an 'x' at the end. That's serious.

I'm walking past the library on the way out and Susan appears just as I am passing. She's been waiting for me, I can tell. I don't know what to say, apart from, 'Hi.'

We're on the Tyne path, walking home together, before either of us says anything else. It's as if Susan is waiting, but she's not impatient. She could probably wait for days. She walks close enough to me that I can smell her appley hair.

'Thank you,' I say, eventually, after the silence has become too awkward for me. She nods and waits some more. 'Why . . . why did you say all that?' I ask. 'You know, lie for me? I didn't think you lied. Buddhism rules an' that.'

'It is not a rule, Malky. It is a guideline. And I lied because I am worried for you.'

'You think I've gone mad?'

She pauses long enough for me to guess that 'Yes' is at least part of her answer. But instead, she shakes her head and says, 'No,' which is kind of her.

Then she adds a 'but', at which point we hear a voice behind us, and whatever the 'but' was going to be is left hanging.

'Hello, you two! Kenneth – look who it is!'

We both spin round to see Andi pushing old Kenneth McKinley in a wheelchair, with Dennis ambling lazily by their side.

'Kenneth. Do you see who it is?'

The old man lifts his chin from his chest and peers at us.

Andi says, 'It's the children from the weekend, Kenneth. Susan and Malcolm.'

At the mention of my name, his head straightens a bit more. He repeats what he had said the day I met him. 'Malcolm? Good Scottish name that, eh, lad?' His speech is soft and slurred.

'He's not having such a good day today, are you, Kenneth?'

The old man grunts in response and Andi leans over to zip up his thick fleecy top. I'm trying not to make eye contact with Dennis, who has flopped on to his belly at the first chance, but seems to be watching me suspiciously.

'It's nice to see you again, Mr McKinley,' says Susan, loudly.

'I'm not flamin' deaf, lassie. Ninety yearsh old, but I can hear you fine.' Seems like he's back to being a grouchy old man.

Susan, though, is not put off. She crouches down next to his wheelchair and takes one of his bony hands in both of hers, looking at his face with her head tipped to one side. She says, 'You began to tell us something the other day. Before your son – Uri – called. You were talking about the limits of the unconscious mind. I was hoping I might hear more.'

The old man shifts his eyes to look sideways at her. Then he reaches up and whips off his mauve-tinted glasses. Except that the arm of the specs gets caught on one of his big old-man's ears, making it ping back against his head. It's like he was trying to be dramatic, but didn't quite pull it off.

'I'm so glad you remember,' he says, regaining his composure and looking between the two of us. It really is as though a mist has just lifted in his head. 'Your teacher said you were curious and diligent. I was beginning to wonder. Had I got to the bit about the warning? Had I?'

A warning? What was he warning us about? We both shake our heads.

'Hmm. Aye, well, Andi – I think we should take these two home with us. Let them have a wee look at that stuff out in the shed. I mean – no one else has ever shown any interest, and there may not be . . . may not be . . .'

Whatever there may not be is lost in a coughing fit

of a violence like I have never seen before. This is not a cough from the throat, or even the chest: the poor man's *entire* thin body convulses, lifting his feet off the footrests of the wheelchair and turning him dark pink as he coughs again and again and again, louder and louder. He flaps his hands as if trying to fly.

Andi holds him by his narrow shoulders, saying, 'There, there, Kenneth . . .' After several more coughs, he stops, and I genuinely worry that he has died in front of me, but a few seconds go past and then he takes an enormous, groaning, inward breath. He leans back in his chair while Andi gets a small canister of oxygen from the shelf under the seat. She holds the mask to his face, saying, 'Okay, okay, there you go.'

And, during all of this, I have a chill passing through me.

That stuff out in the shed. Surely he can't mean . . . ?

What the heck ELSE would he mean, Malky?

No, no. There were other things in the shed. He could mean anything. Pots, a spade, tins of old paint . . .

No, he means the bag of stuff that you stole, Malky. Obviously. Because he's got one hanging over his bed. And you're going to be found out . . .

As he sucks greedily on the oxygen, Andi turns to us, a sad look on her face. 'I'm sorry, kids. That must have been frightening for you. He'll be all right in a minute.'

'What's the matter with him?' says Susan, asking exactly what I want to know.

Before she answers, Andi looks at Kenneth, who has heard this. He gives a little nod – permission, I guess, for Andi to tell us. I hardly understand a word: there's something 'pulmonary' and 'acute' and 'syndrome' and other words as well.

Susan nods sympathetically and I imitate her.

Another look is exchanged between Andi and the old man. Andi says, 'You may as well know. The outlook is not, shall we say, very optimistic.'

Kenneth removes the mask from his face. His colour has returned to normal and he smiles weakly. 'Too many birthdays, that's my problem. We all have to go one way or another, eh? But, before I do, I want to make sure my story is told once more. This time to a new generation. Andi – we'll head back now and get the bags from the shed, please.'

Oh no. That's it. Only he said 'bags'. Plural. Perhaps he's referring to something else?

Andi is looking at me closely. 'Are you all right, son? You've gone pale.'

She knows.

'Ah no, I'm fine. I was just a bit, you know . . .'

'Scared? I understand. Don't worry, he's fine now. Aren't you, Kenneth?'

'*Ahem.* Oh yes. Right as rain. Now let's go, if you

please. Are you coming, children? There's something I want to show you.'

'*Now?*' I say.

'Of course,' says Kenneth. 'Like I said, I don't have much time.'

And they lead the way to the house.

CHAPTER 48

All the way back to Kenneth McKinley's house I'm running through the possibilities in my head. Susan has taken Dennis's lead and doesn't even complain when she has to pick up his huge poo in a little black bag that Andi gives to her. Honestly – a supermarket carrier bag would be a better size. She scratches his head and calls him a 'good old boy', while he thumps his tail against her legs. I stay well out of his way to be on the safe side.

Susan and I wait with Mr McKinley and Dennis in the front room while Andi goes to the shed. I am terrified.

She's comes back, holding a paper bag. 'I've got it, Kenneth!'

She sounds cheery. Is it fake? I look at her face to check, but it's giving nothing away. Their conversation is not exactly whispered, but it is taking place quietly, as though Susan and I are not supposed to be there.

'Only one? There were two, as I recall. I'm not totally doolally yet.'

'Yes. Just this one – with the videotape.'

'And the other one? The one with the Dreaminators?'

That word! I feel a charge go through me like a little electric shock.

I glance over to where Susan is looking at the table of photos. For probably the first time since I met her, she's not paying attention to her surroundings, but seems lost in fascination.

'Couldn't see it, Kenneth.' Andi's voice is airy-don't-carey. I'm convinced now that she's putting it on. She adjusts a cushion behind his back. 'It won't have gone far. It's probably just fallen behind a shelf. I'll have to move stuff to get to it later.'

Kenneth grunts grumpily. 'I certainly hope so. They were the last two in the world so far as I know. Well, apart from the original . . .' His voice trails off and he starts coughing again after which he says nothing and closes his eyes for a moment. When he opens them, he coughs again and says, 'I'm afraid I'm very, *very* tired. I don't feel at all well, to be quite honest. Thank you for coming. Take the video with you and have a wee look at it, eh? We'll expand on it next time you come. Andi will show you out.'

'Mr McKinley?' says Susan. She has picked up a photograph from a sidetable. 'Is this you? With . . . *the Beatles*?' I look at the faded picture: a young Kenneth McKinley, with long blond hair, wearing baggy cotton clothes, among a group of other people, most of them with beards and moustaches and beads . . . I might not have recognised the Beatles, but it's the sort of thing that Susan would know.

The old man nods weakly. 'Aye. I knew them on and off for years. George especially. He was very interested in my work. I toured with them in 1962. I was visiting Paul when he wrote that song "Let It Be". I might have been the first person to hear it . . .' His voice becomes an almost-inaudible whisper, then the words turn into another coughing fit, and Andi steps in.

'Time to go, you two.'

In the hallway, there's a framed poster that Andi points to and says, 'He has quite a story for anyone who wants to listen.'

KIRKCALDY TOWN HALL
TEEN DANCE-ATHON!
23 October 1962

FEATURING
RICKY THUNDER AND
THE LIGHTNING BOLTS

plus
England's newest pop stars

THE BEATLES

And there at the bottom, in much smaller writing,

Full variety support acts

JERRY MURAD'S HARMONICATS
'Madcap Music from the USA'

KENNETH MCKINLEY
'The Mystic o' the Highlands'

She hands the bag to Susan. 'He wants you to see this.' Inside is an old video cassette – black plastic with a transparent window showing the tape inside. 'It's VHS. Have you got a machine to play it on?'

Susan nods. 'Yes. My grandmother watches old films like these. What is on it?'

Andi shrugs. 'Never seen it. I wouldn't pay too much attention. It's probably just his old mystical, hippy ramblings.'

CHAPTER 49

It isn't that long since I asked Susan if I was going mad, and she said no, then added a 'but' that was left in the air when Andi greeted us on the Tyne path. I keep thinking about it, and wondering whether I should prompt her to finish her thought. It's probably going to be along the lines of what she said before: you know, '*it can mess with your head*,' and so on.

It turns out it's all going to become a lot clearer, but not necessarily in a good way.

Susan's house has a back entrance in the lane near the end of my street that – until recently – was so overgrown you couldn't really see in. It's the gate that Susan let me out of the first time I met her before term started.

I wasn't really paying attention to the house that night I jumped over the wall. So, if you were to ask me, I'd have guessed it would be big and old with tall, grand windows, and a wide verandah – all that sort of stuff. Spooky, I suppose, and crumbling.

In fact, it's not like that at all. It's big all right, but more modern-looking and square. It looks completely out of place in the middle of the large, overgrown grounds and the only thing that seems right is that it is definitely crumbling. The tiled roof is dotted with patches of green moss and sags in the middle, and one window is boarded up. The walls have graffiti on them. There are weeds everywhere: on the path, in the flowerbeds. In the corner of the lawn, a small bonfire is smouldering in a firepit, a thin wisp of smoke rising from the ashes.

I remember, with a flush of shame, what I said to Susan about her living in a big house. It's big but very run-down and not a bit 'posh'.

I really, *really* don't want to be here. For a start, I'm supposed to go back home straight from school. Mam is working an extra shift packing parcels at the Swift Centre. **We'll talk tonight** her text had said, and that won't be fun. What's more, I should be home when Seb gets back from his goalkeeper training and I'm in enough trouble as it is.

He's got a key, though. A few weeks ago, I'd have been certain he'd snitch on me. Now I'm going to have to trust him . . .

Ahead of me Susan's babbling on as though she's a grown-up showing me around. 'We are making a lot of progress. The place was awful when we moved in, but Mummy reckons it will be shipshape in a few weeks.'

Her mum. I've never met her, but then . . . why would I? 'Is she in? Your mam? Mum, I mean?'

'She has gone to London for some meetings. My daddy may be coming home. Well, I say "home": he has never lived here.' For a second, I think she's going to tell me more about her dad. We're standing at the front door now, which has been freshly painted in smart navy blue. She chews her lip and glances quickly at me. 'He, erm . . .' She stops, then starts again. 'The house was rather run-down. It's the only way we could afford to move here after . . . after what happened.'

Is she trying to tell me something? I look at her, but she has moved ahead of me.

Inside, it's like I'm immediately wrapped in a thick blanket. There is a little lobby filled with houseplants and beyond that is a dark, warm hallway with an old, patchy carpet. The house smells different too. There are cleaning smells, and a warm, comforting spice aroma that reminds me of when Mam cooks curry.

'Shoes!' commands Susan, and I kick mine off. She picks them up and places them neatly on a shoe rack, then hands me a pair of grey felt slippers from a box. She must have noticed my face, although I'm trying hard to look as though this is normal. She does her half-smirk.

'It's Mummy. She's a bit, erm . . . particular about stuff like that.' Susan takes a breath, and I know she's going to tell me more, but at that second Mola's piercing old-lady voice screeches from upstairs in Tibetan. Susan yells a reply, and, when our eyes meet again, we both know the moment has been lost.

There's a small room off the main hallway that is black-dark when Susan opens the door and, when she hits a switch, dim lights illuminate ancient-looking velvet-covered sofas facing a huge screen.

'Wow! A home cinema! Is this where you watch telly?'

I forget – she probably doesn't watch television.

'Not really. It was here when we moved in. But it's great for movies. And Mola uses it to watch her old Indian films.'

She points to a rack of ancient video cassettes in brightly coloured boxes.

I'm confused. 'I thought she was Tibetan?'

'She is. Only there are almost no Tibetan films, and she won't watch Chinese ones, so she likes these ones, in Hindi with English subtitles, if she can get them.'

'Wow,' I say. 'How many languages does she speak?'

'Loads. Tibetan, obviously. Ladakhi, where she grew up. Cantonese if she has to. A bit of Hindi and Nepali. English . . .' She turns back to a cupboard. 'Give me a minute and I'll set it up.'

Susan opens the cupboard to reveal various box-shaped machines with wires coming from them. One I can tell is a DVD player, the other two I don't really know what they are.

I carefully take one or two of the boxed films out of

the rack. Some of the titles are in squiggly writing that I can't understand. Others I can read because the letters are the same as we use, but I still don't know what they mean. One has a picture on the front of a young couple gazing at each other lovingly. Susan takes it from me gently.

'Mola loves her romantic films! Don't you, Mola?'

The old lady is standing in the doorway, watching us and smiling.

'Ah! It's my favourite Dream-boy!' she beams. 'How nice that you come to visit! You watching films?' She points at the one I'm holding. 'That's the one I like best. Such a beautiful story. I watch it every year at least one time. What we watching now?'

Susan takes the videotape out of the bag and holds it up to show her grandmother. 'It's an old VHS that has been lent to us by Mr McKinley. You know – the old man we visited? Malcolm here wants to know what is on it.'

Mola narrows her little eyes. 'It might not be . . . ah . . . suitable for kids, huh? Could be too violent or, or . . . saucy or something, no?'

Susan thinks for a moment, then she says, 'Mola – it's part of . . . it's a school outreach project.' She turns to me. 'Isn't it, Malcolm?'

'Yes!' I say, too enthusiastically, but I think it goes unnoticed. 'Yes, it's a school thing.'

Mola scrunches up her face in confusion.

Susan says, 'Homework, Mola.'

'Ah! Homework! You are a good girl! You must do lots of homework and you will be a diplomat like your *pha*. You must love homework too, boy?'

Ah, she means me. 'Erm . . . I . . . ermm . . .'

'Malky *loves* homework, Mola. Don't you, Malky?'

The old lady nods approvingly and winks at me, as if she'd known all along that I *love* homework. As if.

'I knew it! Susan always chooses very clever friends. Very well. But I will watch with you in case it is too saucy.' She sits down heavily. 'And now you will bring me tea, because you are such a good girl, Susan. And butter cake. And another cushion.'

I sit down on the faded velvet sofa while Mola beams at me, silently delighted that Susan has a friend who loves homework.

CHAPTER 50

Susan reads out from the handwritten label on the cassette. 'It says Scotland Loud And Live – May 1981.' She slots the cassette into the machine and presses 'play'.

The picture is a bit scratchy, the colours are too vivid and blurry, and the sound isn't great, but here it is.

The programme starts with the theme tune, which sounds like it's played on an accordion, and lots of pictures of Scottish landmarks, like hills and castles and that famous bridge, and deer with antlers and stuff like that. The programme title comes up in big tartan letters:

**SCOTLAND
LOUD & LIVE**

**WITH YOUR HOST
ROBBIE FERGUSON**

A grinning man comes down the lit-up steps of the TV studio as the audience applauds and whoops. He has a fat, drooping moustache and long hair over his ears. He's wearing a baggy dark green suit and a tiny, narrow tie and, even if I didn't know this programme was from the 1980s, I could tell it was ancient.

'. . . wonderful programme for you tonight on *Scotland Loud and Live*! I'll be meeting the Dundee woman with Scotland's biggest collection of antique jam jars, our roving, raving reporter, Donny Greig, is finding out how people all over the country are preparing for the Royal Wedding, and tonight he's in Galashiels in the beautiful border country. Are you there, Donny . . . ?'

'Is this the right programme?' I say to Susan.

'What in heaven's name is he wearing?' said Mola. 'He looks like a huge . . .'

'Shh . . . watch.'

The camera cuts back to Robbie Ferguson.

'. . . my first guest tonight. Known to many of you as the Mystic o' the Highlands, Kenneth McKinley toured Scotland's theatres for nearly two decades with a wonderful act that combined mind-reading, levitation – oh yes! – with some feats of mystery that were so baffling that many people began to think he was the real thing! He befriended stars like the Beatles before vanishing from the public eye. Well, he's back. Here's a quick clip of him in action at the Pavilion Theatre, Glasgow, ten years ago . . .'

Here the picture cuts to a stage where a man in a kilt

– easily recognisable as Kenneth – is talking to a lady next to him. The film is in black and white.

'Now, Maureen,' Kenneth is saying in his musical Scots accent, 'I'd like you to take my hand.' The lady does so and the two stand side by side. With his other hand, he reaches down to where a short sword hangs from a belt, and I breathe in sharply.

'Look, Susan! That's the . . . the thing that was hanging over the back of his chair!'

There's no mistaking it. The camera shows a close-up of the carved handle.

'Hold my dirk in your other hand, Maureen, there you go, and, when I say so, raise it up slowly.'

Kenneth allows his chin to drop to his chest as though he is sleeping. Seconds tick by, as the theatre band plays a slow, spooky melody.

'Raise the dagger, Maureen.' She does so, and Kenneth, dramatically lifting his head and widening his eyes, cries, 'Float!'

Maureen gasps. Still holding her hand, Kenneth's feet rise a little way off the stage floor. One centimetre, two, three. The audience starts a ripple of applause that gets louder. Kenneth's feet are now at least ten or fifteen centimetres off the ground. He is floating!

'Oh my!' says Mola, breathlessly.

On-screen, Kenneth lifts his head and says, 'Now, Maureen, please check above me and behind me for

wires or supports of any kind. Careful with my dirk!'
She moves her other hand round him. The crowd
applauds again.

Slowly, he descends until both feet are back on the
stage. He thanks Maureen, shoves the dagger back in its
sheath, acknowledges the applause gracefully and finishes
by saying, 'Ladies and gentlemen. The power of the mind
is a marvellous thing. Thank you for your attention!'

On our screen, the picture cuts back to colour and
Robbie Ferguson in the studio.

'Well, that was then, and he's floated all the way back
to us now! Here to talk about his new venture, the Mystic
o' the Highlands himself, Kenneth McKinley!'

And there he is, in his kilt, sporran and dirk, coming
down the studio steps to the talk-show sofa. He's grinning
at the audience's applause and he's holding an exact replica
of the strange device that is currently hanging above my
and my brother's beds: a Dreaminator.

'Wow! He looks so young!' says Susan. 'What on earth
is he holding?'

I don't reply.

The interview does not go at all well. The show's presenter
seems determined to mock Kenneth and make jokes at
his expense, and Kenneth looks increasingly uncomfortable
when the audience seems to enjoy the taunting.

To begin with, Robbie Ferguson stands facing Kenneth

who is on the sofa. 'Can I start by showing you how I can float?' he says, and the audience titters. Kenneth smiles back, good-natured, but he looks a little wary.

'Stand up,' says the presenter, 'I'd like you to be Maureen. Please take my hand!'

The audience laughs. He turns his back slightly, so he is in a different position from Kenneth who had been facing the audience directly. But then, just like Kenneth had done, Robbie Ferguson starts to float, just a little bit off the ground, but the audience cheers and gasps. It looks amazing.

But then, in a slight jerking motion, he turns his body round until he is facing the audience – and there is a huge laugh from them as they see the trick, and the camera shows a close-up of his feet. He has been balancing on the tiptoes of one foot, which is protruding from the bottom of his shoe.

The audience howls with laughter at the simple trick.

'Come on, Kenneth – admit it! That was how you did it, eh? It's just an old stage trick. I had the studio boys here make up special shoes for me!' The presenter's tone is teasing, but there's a definite edge to it. Kenneth's face freezes in a cold smile.

'Well –' he hesitates – 'that might be *one* way of doing it, but I assure you . . .'

'Don't worry, Kenneth. I know the rules. You can't reveal your secrets.' Robbie pauses for comic timing and shoots a cocky glance at the camera. 'Instead, *I'll* reveal them for you!' Big laugh from the audience, and a close-up of Kenneth looking uncomfortable.

'That's not fair!' says Susan. 'That's not how Kenneth was doing it!'

'Shh, Susan,' says Mola.

Robbie Ferguson goes, 'Och, don't mind me, Kenneth. Just enjoyin' a wee bit o' banter with you, eh? So tell me, O Mystic o' the Highlands – what's that you've brought with you to *Scotland Loud and Live*?'

Clearly relieved that the subject has moved on, Kenneth grins and holds up the device, and the audience goes, '*Ooooh!*'

'This,' he says, 'is my latest venture. I call it . . .'

'I believe you're calling it "*the Dreaminator*". Woooo!' The presenter says this in an exaggerated, dramatic way that makes it clear he thinks it's crazy and the audience titters. 'What does it do, Kenneth?'

'Well, as the name implies, it allows the user, when asleep, to control his or her dreams, so that . . .'

Robbie Ferguson interrupts again. 'You're saying you can dream whatever you like, thanks to these wee crystals.' He reaches over and holds up one of the woven cords with a crystal attached.

'Well, it's not *just* that, Robbie. You see, the philosophy behind this is based on my lengthy studies of a number of ancient cultures. Many of us possess the ability, through practice and meditation, to control our dreams and actually experience them *as though we are awake*. What the Dreaminator does is to combine that natural ability – which is *very* hard to acquire – and put it within the grasp of pretty much anyone. By using the unique qualities of these crystals here to create an undetectable vibration around the sleeper, along with the ancient power of the pyramids . . .'

The presenter's face shows boredom and frustration. He interrupts. 'Oh aye. Can you prove that it works, Kenneth?'

There's a long pause, and the audience sniggers again.

Kenneth says, 'In cases like this, proof is a difficult thing to quantify, Robbie, so I'd say . . .'

'So you *can't* prove it?'

'Well, I know it works for me, and . . .'

'Well, you're bound to say that! You're selling it!'

The audience laughs properly now, and Kenneth glances at them, annoyed.

'I hate that man!' says Susan. 'He's a bully!'

'How much is this selling for, Kenneth?'

'Well, once production commences, I expect it to be retailing for around twenty pounds.'

Now the audience gasps. I do too. 'Is that *all*?' I say to Susan.

'That was 1981,' she says, quickly, not taking her eyes from the screen. 'It would be a lot more now. Shh.'

'. . . you're saying that you haven't started making

them yet? And you're expecting people to pay twenty quid to control their own dreams and you can't even prove it works!'

'We have made some prototypes, but full-scale production . . .'

'Kenneth, with respect. I love you as the Mystic o' the Highlands, but I tell you this much. If you manage to persuade people to shell out twenty of their good Scottish pounds for a load of string and a few pebbles, then that will be your best trick ever!'

He grins at the audience, who are howling with laughter now. Kenneth has no choice but to smile and to pretend that it's all in good humour. But, in the close-up shot, his eyes look moist.

'It's *not* a trick!' he says, struggling to control his voice. 'There are more mysteries in the human mind than we can ever dream of . . .'

'Is . . . is he crying?' I say.

'Looks like it,' says Susan.

Robbie Ferguson is wrapping up the interview. '. . . a great sport and a great entertainer. Ladies and gentlemen – Kenneth McKinley!'

The camera lingers on a close-up of Kenneth and his watery, baffled smile, while the audience applauds, politely.

Susan fast-forwards and the tape spools quickly through the rest of the programme. Kenneth doesn't reappear. The programme credits whiz past and the picture goes black. She has raised the remote control again to press 'stop' when the picture comes on again and I say, 'Don't! Let's see,' and she presses 'play' instead.

CHAPTER 51

There is Kenneth again, on a different stage. This time, though, he's not in his kilt: just jeans and a huge striped jumper. He has grown a little beard, and his hair is longer. Behind him on a backdrop in big letters it says

NEW AGE – NEW BEGINNING
1983

Kenneth is addressing an audience, although it's hard to judge how many people there are. It's an amateur production: the camerawork is wobbly and the sound isn't great.

'My friends,' he says as he raises both arms above his head, 'a new age of understanding and insight is upon us! Together we can dream of a new future. A future free of conflict! A future free of disease! A future of love and brotherhood, in which we use the infinite power of our subconscious to release us from poverty, from sickness, from weakness and from hatred!'

He is mesmerising to watch. His voice swoops, his

arms slash the air in front of him and his hands make chopping motions to emphasise his words. I don't even understand most of what he says, to be honest. It sounds like a sermon by one of those old-time preachers, only there is no mention of God, or heaven, or hell. Instead, it all seems to be about 'releasing our inner powers' and 'coming together to dream a better future'. Kenneth displays pictures behind him of the stars, and ancient temples, the pyramids in Egypt, complicated-looking mathematical formulas, a picture of a human brain, and a Native American chief complete with a huge feathered head-dress . . .

Then he holds up a Dreaminator and the audience applauds. 'This, my friends, will change the world! Control your dreams, and the awesome force of our thoughts, even when we sleep, will create a world of . . .'

Then the picture goes fuzzy and finally black as the tape ends.

Susan turns off the VHS machine and we sit in silence for a moment.

'Wow!' I say.

'Poor Mr McKinley,' she says at last.

'Ridiculous,' says Mola, taking a long and noisy slurp of tea. 'Nothing but cocky-pop. And dangerous cocky-pop as well.'

'Poppycock, Mola,' corrects Susan. 'And why dangerous? It's just harmless, surely? I mean, it can't possibly *work*.'

'This is just a short cut. A very *bad* short cut. Like . . . like eating sweeties instead of proper food.'

I say nothing. If what Mola just said is true, then I have been munching my way through a family pack of Haribos. Every night. While I am asleep.

Mola continues, an air of righteousness settling over her. She closes one eye and turns the other to Susan, raising a single finger, palm out. Although she addresses her granddaughter, I think this is meant for me.

'I have heard of these toys. Pah! They will mess with your head.'

That phrase again! I am surprised. 'You've heard of these Dreamy-thingies?' *Clever, Malky*, I think. *Don't sound too familiar with them.*

'Course I have. Not that one exactly, but others. People always look for a quick solution. They want to control everything. "Control your dreams," he says. Meditation is all about *giving up* control. Just *be*, you know? It takes time and patience to be good at it. But who has time and patience these days, huh? You want everything now-now-now. Click, I want it now! Click, same-day-delivery!'

'Well . . .' says Susan, 'it may not be . . .'

'Don't interrupt, Tenzin. Thing is, when you eat only sweeties, your teeth fall out, you get fat and you die an early death. You understand? Stop trying to control everything. Just let it be. You know – like the Beatles song?'

To my astonishment, she starts singing Mam's bedtime song: '*Let it be, let it be . . .* You understand?'

Susan gasps. 'That's the song Mr McKinley just mentioned!'

Mola's not listening. 'I'm talking to him. Dream-boy over there. He knows, don't you! You with me?'

'Yes, Mola,' I lie. I haven't got a clue what she's on about, and I'm still a bit freaked out at hearing Mam's song warbled by Mola.

Susan is showing me to the door, and she's wincing a little. 'Sorry about Mola. She gets a bit . . . intense sometimes.'

I nod. 'Why does she call you by your last name?'

Susan is puzzled for a moment, then her face clears. 'Oh! Tenzin! That is only my last name in English. It is my first name in Tibetan.'

'That's odd,' I say, and she smiles.

'Not really. My daddy wanted me to have an English name as well, so he chose Susan and then added my first name to make a surname because in Tibet they don't really do names in the same way as you do.' She points to a picture of an elderly man with spectacles and a bald head, in a silver frame on the wall of the little entrance lobby. He has the look of a government minister, or head teacher, except he's wearing dark red robes. 'I am named after this man. Dalai Lama,' she says.

'But that's not your name?'

'Dalai Lama is his title. His name is Tenzin Gyatso.'

'Cool. Is he a relative or something?'

Susan lets out a little gasp of laughter and puts her hand to her mouth. 'No, Malky! Dalai Lama means "great master". He is the world leader of Tibetan Buddhists.'

I nod slowly and – I hope – wisely. 'Like the Pope?'

Susan shrugs and smiles. 'I suppose. A *bit* like the Pope.'

I say to her, 'Are you a Buddhist then?' and she does the exact same shrug-and-smile.

'Sort of. Not really. It's quite hard to be a good one. I practise with Mola.'

It occurs to me that I have never said sorry for siding with Kez that day, and for what I said in the lunch hall earlier. And so I do. She gives her shy smile and nods. 'Thanks,' she says. 'Friends?'

'Aye. Friends.'

I seriously think this whole thing might have ended right there had the next few seconds been different. If I hadn't had that conversation, I'd have been on my way home and Susan would never have found out.

But what happens, happens. And guess whose fault it is?

My phone goes as I'm standing there with my hand on the doorknob, ready to go.

It's Seb. He's FaceTiming me. I think about not taking

the call, but I remember I was supposed to be there when he got back from goalie training . . .

I hold the phone up and Seb's face appears. He's on Mam's laptop in our bedroom, in his green keeper's top.

'Sorry, mate,' I say, trying to head off any whingeing. 'I'm just leaving now. Five minutes.'

'Okay. Are you passing the corner shop?'

'Yeah. Why?'

'Can you buy some triple-A batteries . . . ?'

Batteries? I should have been quicker. I can see where this is going. I try to swipe the phone screen to end the call, but I'm in too much of a hurry, and end up stabbing at it with my finger to no effect. Meanwhile, Seb is still talking.

'The ones in my Dreaminator are losing power. Look – it's not as bright . . .' He tilts the laptop and my phone screen is filled with an image of Seb's Dreaminator.

Susan sees and hears everything and, oh my God, the look on her face.

CHAPTER 52

'You lied to me, Malky Bell. You have been lying to me since the start, haven't you? And do you think I did not hear Mr McKinley say Dreaminator? I am not deaf, you know.'

I've tried to make a swift getaway, but she has followed me down the weedy path and her voice has gone all quiet again. It's like . . . when other people would shout, Susan Tenzin goes the other way.

'All that "shared dreaming" stuff with your little brother?' she hisses. 'It was that . . . that thing, wasn't it? And did you . . . *steal* it? How, Malky? *Why?*'

I sigh. 'It wasn't stealing. It was borrowing, just a dare – banter, you know? I was messing about with Kez Becker . . .'

Susan lets out a small snort of contempt.

'And . . . one thing led to another,' I say.

'Is that the best you can do, Malky? "One thing led to another"?'

I find I don't have a good answer for her. I mumble something and Susan puts her hands on her hips. From somewhere deep inside me, I hear myself murmuring, 'I'm sorry,' for the second time in about a minute.

'Look what has happened, Malky. You stole, you lied, you used this Dream thing with no knowledge of what it might do to your head and it is sending you crazy! It is like my Mola says: you want all of this stuff too quickly, too easily. All that business in school today? That is the dream world escaping from your head. You're lucky it has not happened to Sebastian . . . or has it?'

'No. Don't think so.'

'Good. Maybe he is too young. How would I know? Have you heard about karma?'

I shrug. She says, 'Mola would not like this definition, but . . . bad actions have bad results.'

I shrug again. 'So?'

'So. If you are asking me, then you have to stop using the Dreaminator and return it to Kenneth. It is that simple.'

There is something in her manner that makes me push back and I say, 'But I wasn't asking you, was I?'

She swats away my reply with a flick of her head. 'Oh, stop being so stubborn. You do realise, don't you, what you have done? People suffer because of lies, Malky. People suffer because they stand up for the truth. Why do you think my dad is not here? It is because he stood up for the truth, and the liars in charge do not like that. Truth, and honesty, Malky: in a crazy world, *they are all we have!*'

I want to tell her that I've been *trying* to tell the truth. To Mam, to her, but the mention of her dad distracts me.

'You . . . your dad?' I say.

'Yes. Put in jail in China for telling the truth about Tibet. They . . . they do things differently in China. It . . . it is a long story.'

We stand there for several seconds, glaring at each other, and the pain of Susan's separation from her dad seems to blaze from her dark eyes.

I wonder about sneaking into Kenneth's backyard and replacing the Dreaminators in the shed. My stomach turns over at the thought. I can't do it.

After a moment, I say, 'I can stop using it, sure. But I'm not taking them back.'

'Them? You mean there's more than one?'

I nod and mumble, 'One each.'

Susan tuts then looks at me closely through her big glasses. 'Being honest, Malky, means a bad deed belongs in your past. Being dishonest means it is with you forever. Which do you want?'

In my heart, I know she's right. 'Is that karma?'

'No,' she says. Her voice has softened. 'That's just me.'

Susan takes a step forward until she is standing close enough for me to catch her soap-and-apples smell. 'I will come with you if you want,' she says. 'We go there, you hand them back, you apologise, you say that it was just a prank, or whatever . . .'

'Banter.'

'That's it. It was just banter, you are really, *really* sorry . . . and that is it. What can they do? You said that Andi already knows it was you, anyway. So it will be a piece of cake.'

I raise my eyes to meet her intense gaze. 'Butter cake?'

'Exactly!' she laughs. 'A piece of butter cake.'

'Tomorrow?'

Susan smiles her closed-mouth smile and says, 'Yes. Tomorrow morning. Come round here, we'll go together and we will put everything right. As friends.'

I feel like a heavy box of anxiety has been lifted off my chest.

'Friends,' I repeat.

CHAPTER 53

Mam has texted that she's been held up at work and Fit Billy's cooking our supper again. Second time this week: it's something super-healthy and vegetarian which is okay, but it's got beans in it, and I know Seb will have really bad wind come bedtime. There's good news, though: Mam will have calmed down by the time she gets in *and* she'll be tired; I might even be in bed and avoid the confrontation about my antics in the lunch hall until tomorrow.

'What is this?' says Seb, eyeing the pan suspiciously.

'It's bean stew,' says Billy, proudly.

It's like Seb's been waiting his whole life to deliver this line. He pauses to catch my eye, then says, 'I don't care what it's *been*, Billy. I want to know what it is now!'

I start to tell him off, mainly because I'm angry with him about his FaceTime call. 'Seb! Don't be so . . .'

But I stop when Billy lets out a loud bark of laughter. 'Good one, son! Top banter!' he says and Seb smirks with satisfaction.

I think about taking the Dreaminators down, but then

I realise that I'll have to explain everything to Seb and I'm just not in the mood. Besides, I don't want to scare him, so I'm going to have to lie to him, and Susan's little lecture is still kind of ringing in my ears.

'You're quiet tonight, Malky,' says Billy. 'Is there something wrong?'

'No,' I say and to cover my silence I take another mouthful of Billy's stew.

'Nowt wrong with a bit of quiet, eh?' says Billy, which I'm grateful for.

Later, Seb's already lying in bed when I come in, brushing my teeth. Billy has found him new batteries from somewhere and the Dreaminators are glowing a little brighter, it seems to me. They look more powerful and they scare me.

'Hey – got something for you,' Seb says, and then lets rip with a huge fart that he wafts over to me with the side of his duvet.

I tut and shake my head, which is not the reaction he wants. I try to sound as casual as I can when I say, 'You know what, Lil-Bro – let's not do the dream thing tonight, eh?'

His voice goes up in pitch just like mine does. 'Eh? You're *boring*. Why not?'

'No big deal. I'm just not in the mood, you know.'

'But don't take them down, Malky! They've got new

batteries. We can do the cave-boy one. Ride on the back of a mammuf! We could even make it a . . . a dinosaur. I know there were no dinosaurs when there were people, but . . .'

Only a few weeks ago, I'd have ignored him. Told him to shut up and stop whining. And there would have been *no way* I'd have done what he wanted just, well, just because he wanted me to. I'd have taken the Dreaminators down to show him that I was his big brother and that I was in charge. But things have changed between Seb and me.

Instead, I reach over and turn off his Dreaminator. 'Another time, eh, Seb? Not tonight.'

'Why?' he whines.

'Listen, man, I'm just tired, okay?' I turn mine off as well and climb into bed. I think I'm asleep pretty quickly.

And I'm *definitely* asleep when Seb creeps out of his bed and turns on both of the Dreaminators again, starting the dream that will end so badly.

The dream that begins in our usual cave, and leads to Seb being captured by a tribe of huge Stone Age warriors with spears.

The dream that ends with Seb lying in a hospital bed, unable to wake up.

NOW

CHAPTER 54

And so here we are. Seb is still in a coma, in hospital, and I am back on my unmade bed.

Earlier, I watched silently as Dad took the Dreaminators down from their hooks and now, from my window, I see him toss them carelessly into the back seat of his car. Tony and Lynn from across the road have come over to see what's going on: there was an ambulance outside our house early in the morning, so they must know something's up. Fit Billy's out there as well and they're all talking.

If only I had taken them down last night, none of this would have happened.

Mine and Susan's plan to put everything right by returning the Dreaminators has been well and truly smashed to pieces now. The Dreaminators are lying, tangled and messy, in Dad's car.

I can tell their conversation pretty much from seeing all their reactions. Heads on one side, nodding and concerned. Then Lynn's hand goes to her mouth in surprise, and Tony shakes his head, sorrowfully. Billy leans in, asking for more details, curious about what might have made Seb sleep so deeply, and shakes his head again. They both turn to look at our house and nod. (Dad has obviously told them I'm in, and they're saying they'll keep an eye on me.) Then Lynn puts her hand on Dad's arm and he nods in response before he gets into his car. They watch him go. Billy exchanges a few more words with Lynn and Tony, then turns and comes into our house, using his own key I think, which is new.

Dad said he'd be gone a couple of hours. That doesn't give me a lot of time, but I know what I need to do.

I put my head round the living-room door. Billy's making himself comfortable on the sofa and he has brought his own games console round. He says, 'I'm really sorry about Seb, Malky. I'm sure, you know . . . he'll be okay. Doctors know all about stuff like that.'

He's being kind, so I just nod. He pats the sofa next to him. 'Wanna play a game? I've got *Wolf's Lair*. It was the name of Hitler's headquarters for the German advance on Russia, and you've got to . . .'

'Billy?' I interrupt. 'I'm very tired. I'm going back to bed.' I close the door and head upstairs. As I go, he's putting his headphones on. Even better.

The front door's no good. Tony and Lynn are not exactly guarding me, but their house faces ours, so there's a fair chance they'll see me if I go out, and they'll be worried, and call Dad. He and Mam have got enough to worry about.

So I go out of the kitchen door at the back and, a minute later, I'm through the yard door, down the alleyway and along the back lane before I can even argue with myself.

'Call round tomorrow,' Susan had said. She'll be expecting me. But it's not Susan I need to see.

I'm relieved that it's Mola who opens the door, but there's no more, '*Ah, special Dream-boy!*' stuff. All that is replaced by a dark look of distrust. I get it immediately: Susan has told Mola about me, Seb and the Dreaminators, and Mola is not impressed. I'm sort of glad in a way. It saves me having to explain it all.

'Hello, young man. Is Susan expecting you?' Her voice has lost all of its singsong warmth and almost makes me shiver. She looks up at me standing on the doorstep. She's not in her usual long cotton things, but still manages to look completely round in a baggy T-shirt and long skirt.

'It's you I came to see, Mola,' I begin, but then, from behind her, Susan comes down the hallway. She looks at me in surprise. It's a sunny day, and I'm sweaty from running here.

'Hello. You look terrible, Malky. Come in. What is wrong?'

I look between the two of them and they are both frowning.

'It's Seb,' I blurt out. 'He's not woken up. We were dreaming, and I can't wake him, and he's being held captive by the big guys, but Dad's taken the Dreaminators to hospital, and Mam's there, and Fit Billy's at home, so . . .'

'Whoa, young man! Shh. Steady,' says Mola, holding up her palms. I stop talking, realising that I've been gabbling. She tips her head on one side and looks at me, curiously, like you might gaze on an interesting exhibit in a zoo, then she nods, slowly. The whole thing is oddly calming. 'Come. Follow me.'

We go out into the garden where there's a wooden picnic table and the remains of breakfast. Mola points to the bench.

'Now then. Sit down and have some tea.' Her tone is still brisk: her offer of tea is like a nurse prescribing medicine, but she sounds a tiny bit friendlier.

'I don't *want* any tea . . .' I begin, but then I see her eyes, gentler now, and I stop. 'It's Seb,' I say, again still wondering how much Mola actually knows, worried that she will be angry.

What does it matter, Malky? She already knows, and who cares how angry she gets?

We sit at the table in the shade, and I tell them everything about the Stone Age dream, and Seb being captured.

Neither of them gets angry. Neither says, 'I told you

those things were dangerous, you stupid boy. Look at the mess you've created. Why were you so irresponsible?'

No, they both just listen without commenting, without judging.

Then Susan says, 'What happens now?'

'No idea. The doctors are investigating. They say he's "stable", that it's like a coma. It might even *be* a coma, and that people usually . . . come out of comas, but you can't tell how long . . .'

I trail off. It was saying the word 'usually' that tripped me up.

'Oh, and one more thing . . .' I say and I tell them about Seb's wrists looking red, and the dream I had when I was attacked by Cuthbert, and the pain I felt and the marks that were left when the crocodile bit my arm.

'But . . . but that cannot happen,' says Susan. 'It is actually impossible. Are you . . . ?'

'Yes, I'm sure.' I sink my head on to my hands and slump forward on the table, knocking a plate on to the grass. Mola shuffles along to me, making little clucking noises of concern. From the corner of my eye, I see her arm reaching to me and I think she's going to cuddle me or something, which I'm not really ready for, but instead she taps me twice on the top of my head, quite sharply.

'Hey. Hey! Dream-boy! Don't leave us now. We need you here, we need you present, and fully awake, yes? And so does your brother.'

I lift my head wearily.

Then she says something so quietly that I can hardly hear. 'Why did you do it, Malky? If it was going bad? Why?'

I blink at her, puzzled. Is she trying to tell me off – you know, 'I told you not to mess with this'? I have to think for a long while before I answer.

'I guess I didn't believe it myself. I mean, I knew the shared dreams were really happening, but how wrong could it go? They're *dreams*, Mola! They only exist in my mind. And Seb's.'

Susan stares at her trainers for a while, then she raises her head and looks at Mola, as if she knows a reply is coming.

Mola shakes her head, with a sad smile. 'The internal life, Dream-boy,' she says, 'is as real as anything else. Perhaps even more so.'

CHAPTER 55

I find myself on my feet again, and my voice is louder. Mola does not flinch, but maintains her steady gaze as I say, 'But it's *not*! They are *separate*! You . . . you've got stuff going on in your head, and then there's stuff going on here, in the real word!' I stamp my foot and thump the table to emphasise my point. 'They can't . . . they can't *interfere* with each other, can they? *Can they?*'

Mola gives her serene smile, and this time it drives me mad.

'Stop smiling!' I say. 'It's not funny. You can meditate, you can dream, you can do whatever you like, but it can't have any effect.'

Mola says, 'And your brother's wrists? Your sore arm, Malcom? Your . . . ahh . . . performance at school yesterday? Oh yes, I heard. Were they real, or just in your mind?'

I fall silent and sigh, and sink on to the wooden seat again. I rub my forearm, remembering the teeth-marks of the crocodile. No one says anything for ages. I mutter, eventually, 'I just don't know what to do.'

'Some more tea will help us think. Susan, be a good girl. Malcolm, help clear the table. And for a little while we say nothing at all. Complete quiet.'

Perhaps it's doing something in total silence that clears my mind. A familiar action: clearing cups and plates, carrying them into the house's sparse, neat kitchen, no one saying anything at all. I find a cloth and wipe down the picnic table while Susan boils the kettle. I put fresh cups on a tray, then I load the dishwasher. It makes me feel better.

On the kitchen wall is a photograph of a handsome man with shiny black hair like Susan's. Mola sees me looking.

'My son,' she says.

'Susan's dad?' She nods and I follow her back outside. She makes herself comfortable with a cushion on the wooden planks of the picnic-table bench. I can't sit.

'He is in prison,' says Mola, as matter-of-factly as if she had simply said, 'He's gone to Sainsbury's.'

'Yes. Susan mentioned, erm . . .' I don't know what to say. What *do* you say in situations like that?

At that moment, Susan arrives, carrying a tray of tea things. Mola looks at the tray and makes an approving noise in her throat.

'I don't think you would like *po cha*, Malky,' says Susan, 'so I've brought you regular tea.' She sees me looking a bit embarrassed. '*Po cha* is Tibetan tea.'

'The *best* tea! Everyone loves it,' interjects Mola. 'It is made with tea leaves and . . .'

I can already identify the smell. 'Yak's butter?'

Mola grins. 'Clever boy!'

'But it takes a bit of getting used to,' says Susan.

'Nonsense! I drink it when I was a little girl!'

'Tibetan tea,' Susan says, 'is made by boiling the leaves, then adding butter and salt. It's . . . unusual. I love it!'

Mola beams. 'See? You are good girl, Susan!' She takes a sip of her butter tea. 'Malcolm will not drink that goat's wee.' She grasps the cup that Susan had poured for me and throws the contents on the grass behind her, and says, 'Malcolm? Dream-boy? You all right?' She hands me her cup and says, 'Drink it. It is good.'

Hesitantly, I raise the little cup to my mouth and pause. Something has washed over me, like a cloud obscuring the sun.

I stare at my teacup, inhaling the strange odour, and blinking.

'Am . . . Am . . .' I am finding it hard to talk. I stare at Susan. 'Susan . . . am I dreaming?' Right now?'

CHAPTER 56

'Malky! What do you ask that for? No. No, you are definitely not dreaming!' Susan sounds alarmed.

As quickly as it started, the feeling wears off.

'I'm sorry . . . I just had a sort of . . . flashback.' I shake my head, vigorously. To be certain, I quickly look at the clock on my phone. Everything is fine. 'Float,' I say to myself. I can't float. I sigh with relief.

It was as though something had flicked a switch in my head. A sound? A sight?

No. The smell of the tea!

'I'm all right now,' I say, and it's the truth. I do feel okay, but I don't want to speak for a moment. I look across at Susan and Mola and they are both sitting with their eyes half closed, as though they are enjoying the silence as much as I am. I sip my tea and close my eyes as well.

I can hear seagulls and the soft hum of traffic on the seafront, and the gentle rustling of a tree outside, and a bicycle bell pinging, and away in the distance – so far away that I might be imagining it – a child shouts something.

There's something else as well, and it's a moment before I work out that it's the fluttering of the little flags that form a large cone around the flagpole in the garden, and I'm reminded of the evening – only a few weeks ago, but it feels like a lifetime – when I first heard them, and saw them, and met Mola too.

I feel like, if I could just detach myself further from today, I might hear the sound of the clouds moving, or the high-pitched buzz of a sunbeam, or the soothing hum of the blue sky, and everything will be back to normal.

I can't do it. I open my eyes and find, to my embarrassment, that Susan and Mola are both looking at me. Mola smiles and nods. 'Welcome back.'

'I was . . . daydreaming.'

'Good,' she says. 'More people should try it! Silence is not empty, Malky: it is full of answers.'

'I was thinking,' says Susan, replacing her cup in the saucer precisely. 'Malky. You think that Seb is somehow "trapped" in a dream of your . . . your making?'

I sigh. 'I guess so. I mean . . . that's as good a way of putting it as any. No wonder people don't believe me.'

'Can't he control the dream he is having?'

'I don't really know. A bit, I think. But not enough to wake up, obviously. Something's gone wrong.'

Susan looks over at her grandmother. 'Have you heard about this, Mola? This dream-sharing?'

Mola doesn't look at us, but gazes at a point in the

distance so intensely that I turn my head to see what she's looking at, but there's nothing.

She nods slowly. 'I have heard of it. I had a *lama* – a teacher – who talked about it. He definitely believed it was possible. Maybe belief is all that is required.'

There's a long pause before Susan speaks next, and I hear the seagulls cawing again.

'So . . . Malky . . . could you go back to the same dream?'

I think about this. 'And . . . and do what?'

'Well, you say your powers of control seem to diminish the longer you are in the dream?'

'That's what's been happening, yes.'

'And also the *realness* of the dream increases at the same time? So you get a sore arm from the crocodile, and Seb's wrists get rope burns?'

'I suppose so. Is that what's happening? I don't know for certain.'

'Well, neither do I, of course. But it *sounds* like that is what is happening. Doesn't it?'

I sort of nod, but I don't really know what to say and the garden returns to its previous silence. Mola hasn't said anything. She's just listening, her tiny dark eyes flicking between Susan and me as we talk. Then she gets up, accompanied by a percussion of cracks and pops from her joints, and starts walking up the garden. She pauses to look back.

'You coming.'

It isn't a question.

'These are nice,' I say, referring to the strings of coloured flags that Mola has taken us to. Close up, their fluttering has become a rattle that is noisier than I expected. I add, 'What are they for?'

Mola has turned her face up to the sun.

'They are prayer flags,' says Susan. 'A tradition in Tibet. We say that the wind carries the prayers away.'

I nod. 'Carries the prayers up to God, yeah?'

Susan shakes her head. 'We don't believe in God. Or at least – not like "God" god.' She pauses, lets this sink in and I find myself wishing I had paid more attention during our RE lessons with old Mrs Puncheon at school. 'But we do believe in prayer, and we like to think the winds will carry our prayers of compassion and hope to every corner of the world.'

I stroke a pale pink cotton flag through my hand. 'They're very old,' I say. 'And faded.'

'That is a good thing! It means the prayers are being taken.'

We're both kind of waiting for Mola, who was the one that summoned us to the flagpole, but she is just standing there, silently. Just as it's beginning to get a bit awkward, she looks up at me with such force that I want to turn away, but it seems rude, so I make myself gaze back at her.

'I warned you. You remember? I say, "Inside your head is bigger than outside. It is easy to get lost in there."'

'Mola,' says Susan, protesting. 'Poor Malky's feeling bad enough already.'

Mola flaps her hand as if my feelings were the least important thing in the world right now.

'How old are you?' she says.

'I . . . I'm nearly twelve.'

'Huh. Old enough to know better. My grandfather is a teacher of young children when he is your age. You wanna know what I think?'

She's being so direct and intense that I hesitate and she jumps in again. 'Well, do you, Dream-boy?'

Susan replies crisply, 'Mola. Malky did not come here to be told what to do about Seb by you or by me. It's not his fault. He's just scared.'

'No, Susan,' I sigh. 'She's right. That's kind of exactly why I came.'

'Yeah!' says Mola, pleased. 'He's scared! And should be. Messing with things like that. It's like a video game to you, innit? *Bam-bam-bam*, now I'm dead, press "replay", new life. And now you find out it's real! These things, these dreams, what we call *milam* . . . these are the result of years of study, of thought, of meditation over centuries. Centuries, boy! Then this fella comes along with his . . . his *toy* –' she spits the word out as if it tasted foul – 'and you expect it to be all la-la-la fun-games. Huh?'

What can I say? My mouth has turned down with sorrow and shame, and worse a tear is leaking from one eye. And still this fierce little old lady is going on at me, while Susan stands by, not stopping her. Though how she would, I've no idea.

I say it so quietly that I'm not sure it's even audible above the fluttering of the prayer flags. 'What should I do?'

Mola steps forward and stands in front of me. 'You asking? You asking my opinion?'

I nod.

'Cos, you know, the opinion of one old lady don't mean much. But –' she raises one finger – '*if* you asking me, then I say you go back. You fall asleep under your toy and you do the only thing possible. You go back in your dream. And, while you there, you take the greatest leap into the unknown. And you take your brother with you. You can put right what you have put wrong, Dream-boy.'

I don't understand any of this. It sounds like gibberish. *A leap into the unknown?*

'What do you mean, Mola?' I say, sniffing and wiping my eyes. I'm not going to start crying now, because I am trying to concentrate on what this strange old woman has just said.

'You need to go to the edge of your dream and then go further. Go *beyond*.'

I blink at her, desperate to understand, and she smiles back at me.

'You'll know when you get there. Sometimes the greatest journeys have no map.'

Then she places her palms together and says, 'There. Now it is yoga time. Excuse me. May all things be well – *tashi delek*.' She turns and walks back into the house, leaving me and Susan standing by the flagpole.

Go to the edge of your dream and then go further.

Simple.

Only – with no Dreaminators, how am I supposed to get there?

CHAPTER 57

I take out my phone and look at the time: forty-five minutes have passed since Dad left in the car to go back to the hospital. There are no new messages, but that doesn't surprise me. Mam and Dad are pretty preoccupied.

There's a mossy stone bench in the garden that Susan and I sit on. I think Susan's a bit embarrassed by her grandmother. She says, 'I'm sorry about Mola.'

'It's okay,' I say. 'She might be right. But, even if she is, it makes no difference. I can't get back to the dream. The Dreaminators have gone.'

'What?'

I explain about Dad taking them to the hospital for examination. 'And he definitely won't bring them back home. Especially if I ask him to. He thinks it's dangerous nonsense. He'd get on well with Mola.'

Susan reaches out her hand and squeezes mine. I've never seen another kid do this. It's strange but . . . not embarrassing. I turn to look at her and she seems almost as sad as I am.

She says, 'If only there was another one. A Dreaminator, I mean.'

I stare at the rattling prayer flags. They flap and flutter in the wind.

And something snaps into focus in my mind – an image.

'There *is* another one.'

'What do you mean?'

'A Dreaminator. I know where to get one.' I stand up, quickly. 'Come on. We haven't got long.'

CHAPTER 58

We have about an hour left. That is not long to:

1. Confess to Mr McKinley that I stole the
   Dreaminators from his shed and that I'll
   return them as soon as I get them back from
   the hospital. This part is going to be tough,
   but, as Susan pointed out on the way here,
   it was part of the original plan, anyway.
2. Explain to this very old, sick and confused
   man that – thanks to his invention – Seb is
   now in a coma, trapped in the Stone Age, in
   Cramlington Hospital.
3. Persuade him, in the meantime, to lend me
   the only remaining Dreaminator, currently
   hanging over his bed, so that I can use it to
   go and rescue Seb.

Put as bluntly as that, it sounds ridiculous. But it is
also true, and the only way I can see of getting out of
this mess.

'So – in and out, yeah?' I say. 'We have to keep this quick.'

'You said that the first time we came.'

It was only yesterday that Susan and I had last stood at the top of the yellow-grey sandstone steps that lead up to Kenneth McKinley's front door. Everything *looks* the same: the hardy shrubs in the little rockery, the big bay window with its permanent thin coating of salt from the sea breezes, and the weathered black paint on the front door – but everything *feels* different.

I press the bell. We wait a moment, then I press again. They weren't expecting us, or perhaps Andi's got her headphones in, or he's in the bathroom . . .

Susan and I both turn and look over the fields and gardens, towards Collingwood's Monument and the Tyne path. We know that Andi takes Kenneth there for some fresh air, but he's nowhere to be seen.

I really don't want to give up. I'm pressing the bell for a third time when I hear movement on the other side of the door. Andi opens it, and she looks tired. She's not wearing her carer's smock and her shiny skin seems paler and dull.

'Oh. Hello,' she says, trying to smile but failing.

We all stand there, a bit awkwardly. Why isn't she inviting us in?

She says, 'Did you not get the message?'

'Which message?'

She sighs, deeply. 'I told your Mrs Farroukh. But it was only a few hours ago.'

We both shake our heads.

Andi takes a deep breath. 'I'm sorry to tell you this, kids. Mr McKinley died last night.'

CHAPTER 59

It takes a moment for this to sink in.

Like an idiot, I say, 'Are you sure?'

Andi gives a sad little laugh. 'Yes, Malky, pet, I'm sure. Late last night. Just like that. In his bed. He was very old and . . . I think he was almost expecting it. I'm sorry you found out like this.' She's still hanging on to the front door and we stay on the steps.

I'm wondering what to do. I don't think I'm even sad, not yet. Instead, I'm seeing my only chance of rescuing Seb evaporating.

Susan blurts out, 'Can we come in?'

Andi gives her a funny look and Susan's bottom lip quivers. 'It's just . . . he reminded me of my grandad, and I'd like to take a last look around.'

For someone who never lies, Susan is pretty good at it when she has to be.

'Erm . . .' says Andi. 'Yeah. Why not? Come in.' She clearly thinks this is strange and I don't really blame her. She stands aside and we enter the tall dark hallway. I feel I need to say something now.

'I'd just, you know, like to see his room one more time.'

Oh no. That really does sound suspicious. And morbid. It's not like we knew him well. Andi shrugs and shows us in. I reach for the hand-san and then realise with a pang of genuine sadness that I don't need it any more.

I suppose that is when it hits me. I *liked* Kenneth McKinley. His chair is in the same position. The strange thing is that the cushion where he used to sit is still indented, like Seb's pillow was. I never thought that a bum-print from a dead man could be so sad.

I clear my throat to speak and it sounds loud in the huge room.

'Where is he? I . . . I mean, his body?'

Andi is staring out of the huge bay window and doesn't turn round. 'The funeral directors came first thing. It was all written down. He had moments of pure clarity, when he knew he didn't have long, and he could be very precise. There'll be a funeral, but, like I say, he didn't have any family.'

'There's Uri,' I say.

'What?' says Andi.

'Uri. His son.'

Andi sits down heavily on the green buttoned sofa. 'Malky, Susan. There is no Uri. At least, not now. Kenneth lived in his own little world half the time. Uri died years ago. Decades. Kenneth used to comfort himself by imagining he was still with us.'

273

'But . . . the phone calls?' I say, pointing at the old telephone next to his chair.

'A remote timer. One of Kenneth's . . . fans, I suppose, from the old days, set it up for him years ago, apparently. It would ring every few days at the same time. He knew, of course, but he just liked pretending. He used to say he could reconnect with his son in his . . . his . . .'

She trails off, staring out at the sea.

'In his dreams?' I say, and she turns back sharply.

'Yes. Exactly. It was all part of, I don't know, his "cosmic vision". His hippy stuff. You know he used to be on the stage?'

Susan and I nod. 'We saw a bit on that tape,' she says.

'I thought that was what that was about,' murmurs Andi. 'He did a mystery and mind-reading act, I think. Reckoned he could float!'

I remember the TV show we watched. I say, 'Wasn't it all just a trick?'

'Eeh, I don't know! Probably! But then he got into all of this dream carry-on, with that thing above his bed, and he gave up show business, and he ended up here, forgotten. And now . . . now . . . Oh, sorry, kids.'

Andi digs out a tissue from her sleeve and starts dabbing at her eyes. 'He was a difficult old so-and-so sometimes, but his lonely heart was in the right place and I'm sad he's gone.'

Almost instinctively, I think, Susan goes over to Andi and sits next to her. She doesn't hug her or anything: she just sits. Andi swallows and smiles bravely.

'May I use the bathroom?' I say. I'm now acutely aware that the minutes are ticking by until Dad will be home. It's also not impossible that Fit Billy has been upstairs to check on me and seen that I'm not there.

'Yes, of course. Out in the hall on the left.' Andi doesn't turn round as I leave.

I don't bother with the bathroom, but instead make straight for the room where Kenneth slept. The door is shut and the handle is stiff to turn. There's a loud click when I open the door and I look round, startled, in case Andi comes, but she doesn't. I'm guessing that Susan will have engaged her in a grown-up conversation to distract her; she's good like that, is Susan.

The room is neat. There are still clothes laid out on a chair. But there is only one thing I have come for. I look up at the ceiling above Kenneth's bed.

It isn't there.

How can that be? Why isn't it there? Who's got it?

I step further into the room. Perhaps it has dropped down on the other side of the bed? I find myself tiptoeing, even though I don't need to because of the thick carpet. It's nowhere to be seen, and I'm considering pulling open the drawer of a chest when Andi says, 'This is the second time, Malky!' I swing round with a gasp. 'Just what on earth are you up to?'

'No . . . nothing,' I say, stupidly. The look on Andi's face shows she doesn't believe me.

CHAPTER 60

Andi sighs and unfolds her arms, coming further into the room, followed by Susan who is wearing a pained expression on her face and mouthing 'sorry' for allowing Andi to escape.

'Come on, son. Out with it: what's going on?' she says.

There's nothing I can do except try the truth. 'Have you, erm . . . have you seen a thing that used to hang here? It was like a decoration,' I say, pointing at the empty hook above Kenneth's bed. Andi nods.

'It's gone with him. His instructions were pretty clear.'

'Well, who's been here?' I say, a bit too urgently. I sound rude and Andi looks taken aback.

Patiently, she says, 'I found him . . . deceased . . . late last night. A doctor came first thing to issue the death certificate. The funeral directors arrived a bit later to take away the . . . Kenneth. Did you think you'd just come in and take it? Did he say you could have it?'

My silence is all the answer she needs.

'One second,' says Andi. 'Come with me.' She marches

out of the bedroom that Kenneth died in and where I am beginning to feel very uncomfortable. Susan and I follow her back to the big room.

Andi takes a sheet of paper out of an envelope. She unfolds it and her eyes flick over the lines written on it.

'Buried with him. He knew he didn't have long, poor old soul. He left instructions on here: his "final performance" he called it. He wanted to be buried in his kilt along with his "dreany-mator" or whatever it was.'

Andi's mispronunciation annoys me. 'It's a Dream-inator, and . . .'

'Well, whatever it is, Malky, it's been taken by the funeral directors and placed with him. Dying wishes. I'm sure you'd want to respect them. And whatever the heck you've been up to ever since that first night ends here and now, all right?'

She looks at us as though she's expecting a response. Susan says, solemnly, 'Of course.'

Andi seems reassured. She repeats, 'Of course. Now, if there's nothing else, children, I need to get on. I'm very sorry that this has happened. I was with him for three years. I know for a fact that he enjoyed meeting you.'

'There is one more thing,' says Susan. 'What happened to Dennis?'

Old Dennis! How could I have forgotten about him? Admittedly, he never actually did much except make foul smells and sleep (often together), and I don't think he ever quite forgot that his first encounter with me was that time in the backyard, but still . . .

At the exact moment Susan says his name, there's a scuffling sound from under a couch, and Dennis's old head appears.

'Dennis!' exclaims Susan, and crouches down to scratch him. I honestly don't think I have ever seen a sadder-looking animal. His big amber eyes look up wetly at Susan, and he's not even bothered by my presence. From under the couch, I hear the thump of a single tail-wag: his way of acknowledging Susan's kindness.

'Do you . . . do you think he knows . . . about Kenneth?'

'Oh aye,' says Andi, solemnly. 'He was lying next to him. How he got up on the bed, I'll never understand, but he managed somehow. He understands everything, that dog. And, if a dog's heart can break, then his is in a million pieces right now.'

We're back outside, Susan and I, and neither of us knows what to say to the other, so we walk along in silence until we get to the bench by the sailing club where we had sat before, and it's like we both know that we're going there, and that we'll sit down in the same place. I feel it's something we need to do, having just learned that Mr McKinley is dead.

I wonder if either of us is going to cry, and I keep shooting little sidelong glances at Susan to check, but, every time I do, she is just sitting with her eyes closed, her back straight and her face tipped up slightly into the wind coming off the sea, the wind that carries prayers around the world. So I try it too and we both sit there silently for a while like that. I don't know how long for: probably only a minute or two, but it feels much, much longer.

Susan says, 'They were more alike than either of them would ever think, you know.'

'Who?'

'Mola and Mr McKinley. Do you remember that thing he said the first time we met him? Something like: better to keep your mouth shut and be thought a fool, than to open it and remove all doubt. It's a bit like what Mola says about silence not being empty . . .'

I complete the sentence. 'It's full of answers.'

Susan sighs and nods, slowly. 'What are we going to do, Malcolm?'

We. I like that.

But it doesn't mean I know what to do.

CHAPTER 61

I'm back home and upstairs minutes before Dad gets in. Billy hasn't noticed my absence and shoots off, leaving his Xbox behind. I don't think Dad likes him. Susan said she'll message me later, to check on Seb.

I can't concentrate on anything. I keep replaying in my head the conversation we had with one of the doctors when he said that Seb might be in this state for days, but that they didn't know, and they'd have to wait for the results of tests, and that they were consulting with another doctor in California, but there's an eight-hour time difference . . .

And now everything is lost. My one chance to get the world's last Dreaminator snatched from me.

Dad comes in and flops down on the sofa opposite. I don't even have a chance to say, 'How is he?' He starts talking straight away, in a kind of monotone.

'No developments. At the moment, all they're saying is that he is "stable". They've ordered up some bit of machinery from another hospital that will give them a better look at his brainwave pattern, but it's got to come from Manchester. They're not ruling out infection. In some cases, the body can sort of put itself into a coma in an attempt to fight an illness, but they can't understand why there's no fever . . .'

And so on. I try to take it all in but I can't. Instead, I just stare at the silent figures on *Wolf's Lair*, paused on the screen, mid-battle, waiting for someone to take up the console again.

I have to ask Dad, but I'm a bit nervous.

'The, erm . . . Dreaminators? Did they . . . ?' I want to know if they – that is, the doctors or researchers or whoever – have discovered anything. Perhaps it's a bit early, but still . . .

'No, Malky,' says Dad. 'I handed them over to Dr Nisha. I felt like I was mad for even bothering her with them.'

'So you didn't bring them back?'

Dad's tone is soft, or perhaps just exhausted. 'No, Malky, I didn't. And, until Seb is back with us safe and well, I don't want to hear them mentioned again, all right?'

He sits next to me now and he wants me to meet his gaze, but I cannot pull my eyes away from the screen where the game characters are doing that thing that they do when the game is stopped: you know, they stay still for ages, then they'll move a bit, walk in a circle or something, then return to their resting position, waiting for a player to activate them again.

Dad takes my chin in his hand, gently turning my head to face him. 'Hello? You with me?'

'Yeah.'

'Can I ask you something?'

'Mm-hm.'

He breathes in deeply through his nose. 'Why did you do it, Malky? Last night? You told the doctor that things had been going wrong before, you had had warnings, so why did you carry on?'

'I wasn't going to. Honest. But then . . . Seb started it, and I thought once more wouldn't harm.'

Dad is quiet for a while. Then he says, 'That was my problem, you know? With the drugs. Every time I thought once more won't harm.' He sighs. 'Don't repeat my mistakes, son.'

'But you're okay now?'

'Let's just say I'm okay *for now*, eh?' He hugs me, saying into my ear, 'He'll be all right, son. He'll be all right.'

And I hug him back and I go, 'Uh-huh,' while over his shoulder I'm still looking at the paused game.

Is that what Seb is doing? I wonder. *He's still dreaming but nothing much is happening?*

Is it like he is paused in my dream and waiting for me to reactivate it? There's no hope of that now. Not without a Dreaminator.

I feel my phone buzzing in my pocket, but I don't

think Dad wants our hug to end yet, so I stay wrapped up with him. At last, he gives a big sniff in my ear and then gets up and heads towards the stairs.

'I'm shattered. I can't even think straight,' he calls back to me, but his voice sounds wobbly and cracked. 'Your mam's staying at the hospital. Your Uncle Pete and your Mormor are driving over from Ullapool. We're all taking turns talking to Seb, you know? Trying to keep him with us. You and me'll head back to the hospital in a bit, aye?'

I nod.

'I'm going for a lie-down in your room. Can you wake me in an hour? I'll be out like a light.'

I take my phone from my pocket. There's a message from Susan.

I have thought of something we could do, but I am not sure you will like it.

I wonder if it's the same thing that I've thought of? If it is, I *definitely* don't like it.
Before I can reply, she sends another message:

I am coming to yours.

CHAPTER 62

I meet Susan at the backyard door.

We go into the kitchen and I shut the door so as not to wake Dad. Neither of us says anything: we haven't discussed what 'the plan' might be yet. I'm more nervous than I expected, and we both start speaking in low voices at once.

'If this is . . .' I begin.

'You will not like . . .' says Susan.

We both stop. Neither of us wants to say it, and there's a moment of silence. Susan breaks it.

'Mola sometimes applies her own, ah, *interpretations* to the teachings of the Buddha. And she thinks that Seb is caught in a loop, kind of a mental trap, caused by, erm . . .' Susan bites her lip and dries up.

'Caused by me,' I offer.

'Well, only sort of. Partly. Caused by, I don't know, *messing with things you do not understand* would cover it. And the Dreaminator. I mean . . . crystals? Crystals have always had "mysterious qualities". I looked it up.'

Of course she did.

'Crystals have been used in mystical healing and ancient religions for, well, forever, really. And pyramids too. Did you know, if you place a razor blade under a pyramid, it will not go blunt?'

'Really?' I say.

'Well . . . probably. It is difficult to prove.'

I think I have a better explanation. 'You know when you stop playing a video game, and the characters are still moving but not doing anything?'

Susan gives an embarrassed half-shrug. Of course, she's not much of a gamer.

'Doesn't matter. They become reactivated when you pick up the control again.'

Susan nods. 'So . . . you will have to reactivate your dream.'

I puff out my cheeks in frustration. 'Go back there and what? Get him? How is that going to work?'

Susan says, 'Perhaps it is like Mola said. "Sometimes the greatest journeys . . ."'

We finish the sentence together: "". . . have no map."'

'Except,' I say, 'I don't have a Dreaminator. I had one thought, though: perhaps if we looked on eBay or something, or Gumtree, or, or . . .'

Susan is shaking her head. 'I have already looked. Everywhere. I do not know if he ever even sold any. Maybe after that TV show he just gave up.'

I nod miserably.

'But we *know* where one is, don't we, Malky?' she says.

We stay quiet for a moment, contemplating this.

It's like we're dancing round the subject, and it is Susan who takes the lead next by saying, 'The Dreaminator. It is at Becker's funeral parlour on Front Street.'

I feel cold just thinking about it. 'But where *exactly*? In . . . in his coffin?'

Susan chews her lip as she thinks. 'I don't know, Malky. But I would say . . . maybe? I mean, isn't that what people do? In films and stuff? You are all dead and whatnot, in your best suit – or kilt in Kenneth McKinley's case – and you are lying there with a photo in your hand, or a necklace, or something that has been important to you.'

Is that right? Is that what happens? Susan actually doesn't seem very sure of it. I take a deep breath and say, 'I don't want to do it.'

'Do what, Malky?'

'I don't even want to say it.'

'Say what, Malky?'

I can tell what she's doing. It's crafty. She's making me say it out loud. Once it's out there, it becomes more real. I force the words out.

'I . . . I'm going to have to steal . . . the last Dreaminator in the world from . . . from a dead man?'

Susan smiles – a bit sadly, as though she knows how hard that was for me. 'Yes. But it is not you. It is "we".'

'What's it got to do with you? Why are you helping me?'

She adjusts her specs and looks at me with her deep dark eyes. It's as if I've asked the stupidest question ever. The answer is so obvious to her and, because I know her now, I also know that she is telling the whole truth, and it feels good.

'Because I am your friend,' she says.

Something changes between us in that moment. Whatever happens from now on – whatever happens with Seb – I'm not on my own.

I open up Mam's laptop and, moments later, we're both staring at the outside of a building shown on Street View.

Becker & Sons
Funeral Directors & Monumental Masons

It's a newish-looking building in two parts. There's a reception area with modern glass doors and big windows; next to it, accessible through reception, is a bigger building with a strip of narrow windows at roof level and a set of double doors at one end. I swallow hard. This is a crazy, ludicrous, criminal, dangerous and just plain weird thing to be doing. But it might also be my only chance.

'How do we even begin to do this?' I croak to Susan. I mean, it's all very well to have done dodgy stuff in the past, and got into a bit of trouble, but this is a *whole new level* of bad. Making it even stranger is the fact that next to me is a girl who has probably never done anything bad at all in her life, yet she's the one that came up with the idea.

'I don't know,' she says. 'But we have to do it soon, right? We do not have much time. Tonight, I think.'

At that point, I hear Dad coming downstairs, and I quickly close the window on the laptop. He comes in and looks a bit surprised to see Susan there.

She stands up – *stands up!* – and says, 'Hello. I am Susan Tenzin. A friend of Malky's.'

Wow, grown-ups are suckers for this sort of thing, aren't they? Dad stops, gives her a tired smile and says, 'Hello, Susan.'

'I am very sorry to hear about Sebastian.'

'Thank you, love.'

'I was just leaving, wasn't I, Malky?'

Ten minutes later, Dad and I are in the car heading back to the hospital. As she left, Susan said, 'I'll text you later,' and the thought of that, and what we had half agreed to do, made me go very quiet.

Have I seriously just agreed to do this? I'm not sure,

exactly. I still have half a hope that – somehow – I will get our Dreaminators back at the hospital. The whole thing plunges me into silence in the car.

Dad doesn't really seem to mind. Perhaps he, too, thinks that silence can be full of answers.

CHAPTER 63

Mormor and Uncle Pete are Mam's mam and younger brother and they are already at the hospital by the time we get there, sitting with Mam in the beige waiting room beneath Aslan the lion from Narnia. A box of tissues and empty cardboard coffee cups sit between them. Their eyes are red and puffy. Outside the room, hospital staff walk quickly everywhere, and for a moment I try to imagine I'm just there for something normal, but of course it's never normal being in hospital, is it?

A man in a doctor's coat comes into the room. He explains that Dr Nisha has gone home, and that he is the doctor in charge of Seb's case. I don't remember his name and he doesn't look at me once. He seems nervous and doesn't sit down.

The news is not good. Seb's blood pressure and breathing rate have fallen and, while the doctors are still 'optimistic', it is still too early to say, and they still don't know exactly what's happening to him.

There is talk of the ICU, which I know from TV means 'intensive care unit', reserved for the most serious cases of everything, although Seb is not there. Not yet.

'Can I see him?' I ask the doctor.

I'm on my own with Seb in his room.

I can hear Mam and Uncle Pete murmuring outside, talking with a nurse. Seb looks like he's hardly moved since this morning. He's still for ages, then he twitches a bit – maybe his hand, or his eyes move behind the eyelids, then he'll return to stillness, only his chest moving up and down under the bedclothes. There's a drip attached to his arm, and something else leading from his wrist, and a strip of something stuck to his forehead.

'Hey, Lil-Bro,' I say. I feel self-conscious. No one can hear me, but then Seb probably can't, either, so it's all a bit odd, like I'm talking to myself. There's a chair next to his bed, so I sit down and take Seb's left hand in both of mine. I'd never hold his hand normally, of course, but this is anything but normal. I run my fingers over the raised red marks on his wrist. Have they got worse?

Perhaps, in the dream, he's twisting and turning to get away? Perhaps, like me after the Hitler dream, he's dreaming that he's awake? Or is he just stuck in a static dream-state, unaware of what's going on? I hope it's that. I can't bear to think of him terrified all this time: aware that he is in a dream, but unable to escape it.

The marks are definitely worse. I wonder if anyone has noticed? I'm thinking about telling someone when Seb jerks his arm away and then turns his head on his pillow. For a glorious moment, I expect his eyes to open and his stupid, gappy grin to reappear and I start to smile . . .

He gives a little grunt, then a gasp and a sort of little cough, then his body twitches again. He doesn't wake, but I notice he has started to sweat. There's a few seconds of this; some numbers on a screen above him start changing rapidly, though I've got no idea what any of them are.

Seb's twitches are becoming bigger, and his head moves from side to side. Then there's a beeping sound coming from the machine. It's like he's in a fight with an invisible attacker.

'Seb! Seb, man!' I shout. 'Wake up!'

I look at his writhing head and I gasp: a huge red mark has appeared below his left eye, spreading down his cheek. It's exactly as though he has been punched in the face, and the sweat is now pouring off his forehead. The beeping of the machine continues, and a nurse dashes in, ignoring me, and studies one of the screens. She hits some buttons, the beeping stops, then she goes to the door and calls down the corridor.

'Jez, Aminah! Quickly!' Two other nurses, a man and a woman, come hurrying. Mam and Uncle Pete are nowhere to be seen, and I'm just standing next to the bed, feeling scared and useless.

They all say things like, 'BP elevated one three five over sixty. Heavy perspiration. Heart rate one twenty, ECG spiking, temperature falling thirty-three degrees . . .'

Then the nurse called Jez leans over to look at Seb's face. He touches the raised wound gently with a gloved hand. I can see already it's going to be a big bruise, and I'm hoping that Seb is not in pain.

'What is this? Who was here with him?' says Jez to the others and they all lean in to look at it. Then the three of them turn to look at me.

He says, 'What happened? Did he fall?' Then, more slowly, 'Did you touch him?' It's a moment before I realise what is going on.

They think I hit my brother! I would never do . . .

Okay, there was that time I hit him with the game controller, but that was ages ago . . .

I raise my hands. 'No. No. No, no, no. I didn't touch him. Honestly. It . . . it just came up on his face!' My voice gets higher and louder. 'Really! Why would I?'

If anyone answers that question, I miss it among the people coming and going – quickly but with purpose. Ten minutes later, Seb has been admitted to the intensive care unit.

His condition is being described as 'involuntary coma-like stasis with spontaneous facial and dermal contusion'.

I suppose the doctors know what that all means, but I don't. I hear a lot of, 'Are you sure?' and, 'We need to wait for the results before we know,' and stuff like that.

Back in the waiting room, Mam and Dad sit side by side while I stare out of the window again.

'Malky,' Dad starts, and Mam snaps back, 'Tom. Don't.'

He ignores her. 'Malky. I know you've been violent to Seb in the past . . .'

'Dad! Honestly!' Mam knows that I wouldn't have hit Seb. Well – not hard, anyway, and not in the face like that. They have both seen us fight plenty of times, Mam especially. Apart from the game-controller incident, I gave Seb a black eye once when I pushed him over and his face hit the corner of a low wall; I was grounded for a week after that. Seb once kicked me so hard in the mouth that he split my lip, but he wasn't grounded, because I was pinning him down and Mam said it was my own stupid fault.

Trouble is, Dad's not around these days and maybe he thinks I've turned into a thug. There's a look on Mam's face that tells me she's not *totally* convinced that I didn't hit him. Not *one hundred per cent* like you need your mum to be about something like this. As for Uncle Pete and Mormor, they've come back with coffees and all Mormor wants to do is hug me, which is nice to begin with, but it's getting a bit tiresome.

Whatever Dad is going to say next is interrupted when the young doctor from before returns and holds up a plastic bag.

'We have had *these* back, at least,' he says.

'What?' says Dad.

'Malcolm's dream . . . things?'

'The *Dreaminators*?' I say.

This is amazing – I can't believe it! I'm not going to have to get one off a dead man, after all!

Uncle Pete and Mormor exchange glances: they have no idea about any of this. The doctor sits down next to me. In fact, I soon realise that this is pretty much all for my benefit.

He smiles, trying to make the mood a little lighter, and reaches into the bag. His brings out two broken plastic rings and some tangled and cut wires and it's a few seconds before my mind catches up.

When it does, I feel sick.

The Dreaminators: they've been ripped apart almost beyond recognition.

I stare at them. There's no way I can put them back together.

CHAPTER 64

'They're . . . broken,' I say.

'Yes. Sorry. We have taken them apart, as you can see. We kind of had to, in order to examine them.' He lifts up the tangle of plastic and woven threads and wire to demonstrate that they have been properly dismantled. As he does so, a few of the crystals fall off and roll on to the floor.

I must look pretty upset because the doctor pulls a guilty face. 'Can you, um, get more?' he says.

'No,' I say. 'The man who—' But I realise I can't tell them about Kenneth McKinley. 'The man I got them off at the Lifeboat sale didn't have any others.'

'Ah, sorry about that,' says the doctor. 'Still – we were able to study them, at least.'

'And?' says Dad.

'Well,' says the young doctor, 'there's good news and bad news. Malcolm, you'll be pleased to learn that there is nothing, nothing at all, about these Dream . . . things that could possibly have been harmful to Sebastian. The bad news, of course, is that they have given us no further clues whatever to his condition, but then we didn't really expect them to, did we?' He looks over at Dad for that last bit.

Dad sits back on the sofa, looking satisfied.

I say, 'When you say, "nothing at all", what does that mean?'

'Just that, young man. It's a plastic hoop with a few strings and wires with some small stones . . .'

'They're crystals!'

He doesn't seem impressed. 'If you say so. They're each illuminated by a low-watt filament powered by a battery.' He smiles at me. 'My girlfriend works in the radiology department. They're always quiet today so I had her run all the tests – you know, X-rays and so on? It is exactly what it looks like – a cheap toy. And completely ineffective. Like I say, there's absolutely nothing . . .'

I think it's 'cheap toy' that upsets me the most. I interrupt him. 'It's not! It's not a cheap toy. It's a wonderful invention and the inventor's just died and the only reason that it's ineffective now is because you've pulled it apart!'

The young doctor looks startled at my outburst. 'I . . . I'm sorry, Malcolm. I mean, I could try to fix them if you want, only your dad . . .'

'That won't be necessary, doctor,' says Dad, briskly. 'Thanks for taking so much trouble over a complete waste of time.' He gathers up the bundle of wires and string and plastic pieces and dumps the whole lot in the swing-bin in the corner, then dusts his hands in a 'job-done' sort of way.

He turns to me. There are tears pricking the back of my eyes now and I think he can tell because he softens his tone and sits down with a sigh. Mam's glaring at him.

'Malky, mate. I knew I recognised the name of those things from somewhere. It's been bugging me for ages.' He tuts to himself as if remembering something unpleasant. His eyes flick to the doctor, as though he is wondering whether to continue, then he takes a breath. 'When I was . . . *getting better* . . . there was a patient in our therapy group, Karen. Well into her sixties, maybe more. She said she'd come across a "Dreaminator" years ago and, well . . .' Dad pauses to find the right words. 'She blamed it for her . . . for her troubles. Her addictions. It's all nonsense, Malky. But some nonsense can be dangerous, do you see?'

He waits until I nod.

'Who is this dead inventor anyway? I thought you said you got them at the Lifeboat sale.'

I can feel myself getting red with anger and shame. 'I . . . er . . .'

Dad snaps, 'I hope you haven't been lying, Malky.'

Now Mam gets involved. Since Dad left, she hates

him telling me and Seb off. 'Back off, Tom – he's upset. And keep your voice down. You've no idea what it's like bringing them two up when you don't even contribute enough money . . .'

'Don't go there, Mary, just don't!' hisses Dad. 'At least I wouldn't allow physical violence . . .'

And they're off. I watch this go on, along with an embarrassed doctor and a bewildered Uncle Pete and Mormor. I don't even say anything. I just leave the room, closing the door behind me and managing to hold on to my tears until I'm in the car park, when they come like I've taken my finger off the end of a hose. I can't even see Dad's car, so I just sit on a wall and sob.

I cry for Seb, alone in a horrible dream land, getting worse by the hour. I cry for Kenneth McKinley as well, a sad old man dying alone and forgotten. And I cry for myself, wrongly accused of punching my brother when he's sick. Most of all, though, I cry out of fear: for now I know there is only one thing left I can do.

Of course, the doctor is wrong. I know that much. You can analyse and examine something, and pull it apart as much as you like. But he and his stupid girlfriend didn't ever use it, did they? They never lay underneath it and slept, and shared dreams, and sailed in Spanish galleons, and experienced the whole . . . the whole . . . *magic* of it. Did they?

One thing is for sure, though.

I have to act, and soon. I have to get into Becker's funeral parlour, and steal the last remaining Dreaminator.

CHAPTER 65

Mam and Dad are staying overnight at the hospital in two rooms near the intensive care unit. Mormor and Uncle Pete are driving me home and staying at our house. We're in Pete's car, and neither of them has said a word to me for the past ten minutes. It convinces me that they think:

a) I punched Seb in the face while he was lying in a coma in hospital. *Why would I do that?*
b) If I could do that, then I'm probably responsible – somehow – for Seb's current condition.

Well, they're half right, at least.

As for me, I'm not keen on talking, anyhow. I have enough going on in my head without adding conversation.

I stare out of the car window as we turn left along the seafront towards home. It's an overcast, muggy evening, and the usual breeze from the lilac-grey sea isn't even bothering the leaves on the trees. People with drinks stand outside the Park Hotel, laughing; a small crowd of day-trippers with cool boxes and sandy feet wait at the bus stop; and, a little bit further along the front, a familiar figure walks alongside a slow black-and-ginger dog . . .

'Stop!' I shout. 'Please stop!'

'What's wrong, pal?' asks Uncle Pete, turning back to look at me and making the car swerve a little.

It is definitely her – Kez Becker – and walking alongside her is Dennis.

'Nothing's wrong. I just need to speak to that girl. See? Her with the dog there!'

But we are driving too fast, and we're already way past her.

'Susan? It's me . . . Guess what? I've just seen *Dennis* being walked by Kez Becker by the Park Hotel.'

I'm up in my room, lying on my bed under the hook where the Dreaminator used to be. I told Uncle Pete and Mormor that I wasn't hungry (untrue) and that I was tired (untrue) and that I was going upstairs to read (also untrue).

'What?' says Susan.

'Dennis. Kez has got Dennis – Kenneth McKinley's dog?'

'All right . . .'

'Look. Seb is . . . he's not improving. In fact, he's getting worse. We have to act fast. And Kez Becker is the key.'

'The key to what?'

'Getting the Dreaminator from the funeral parlour!'

'And how will we get Kez to help us?'

'I don't know.' I say. 'I haven't thought of that yet.'

'I see.' She sounds doubtful. 'But . . . it is getting late and Mola is . . .'

'No,' I say. 'We haven't got much time.'

I tell her everything about the hospital, about Seb writhing on the bed and getting the wound on his face, and the ICU . . .

'How soon can you meet me?' says Susan, her tone suddenly changing from doubtful to positive.

'How soon? You mean now?'

'You said it was urgent.'

'I know. But I can't just . . . *leave.* I've got relatives here.'

'You will find a way. Twenty minutes. By the Priory gates. I have an idea.'

I take a deep breath and look in the mirror. Is that me? My blond haystack is the same, my bogie-coloured eyes (Seb's description) and the freckles over my nose . . . they are all familiar. But something has changed. Do I look older? That's silly. A nearly-twelve-year-old can't suddenly look older.

Perhaps I just feel it. I run my hand through my hair, and, as I do, I touch the spot where, weeks ago now, I bruised my scalp when I floated up to the ceiling that very first time. It doesn't hurt now, there's no bump or anything, but it makes me think.

I go back to my bed and lie on it, trying to position my head against the headboard to touch the same spot, and I really can't. Not easily, anyway. I did this the first morning, remember, but I just thought I *must* have bumped my head on the wall. Now I know that I didn't.

The head-bump from my dream became real, just like the teeth-marks, just like the sores on Seb's wrists . . .

It has been going wrong right from the start!

I stand up from my bed, tighten my jaw and say with as much determination as I can: 'You can do this, Malky.'

Downstairs, I hold up a plastic bag with a book in it, trying to behave as if this is the most normal thing in the world. Uncle Pete and Mormor are in the living room, watching television with the sound turned up to loud because Mormor's hearing is really bad.

'I have to take this back!' I shout. 'I won't be long,' and I turn to go, believing for a whole second that I have got away with it.

'Hang on, mate. Where are you going?' says Uncle Pete, muting the sound and making Mormor look up from her phone. 'It's nearly half past eight. It's dark out.'

Okay, okay, total relaxation. They don't know that this isn't normal.

'Oh, it's just a school thing.' *Don't make your voice go*

high, Malky. 'Ahem. Susan left her school iPad here. Earlier. Before. By mistake. And she needs it right now. She's only at the end of the street.' I'm gabbling, definitely, but I'm keeping my voice low.

'School iPads, heh? So modern!' says Mormor, raising her eyebrows.

Oh, please don't ask to see it. There's just a book inside this bag, and our school doesn't use iPads, anyway.

'I won't be long.'

'Who is this that you're meeting?' says Uncle Pete.

Oh, come on! I can see the clock on the mantelpiece eating up the minutes . . .

'Susan. Susan Tenzin. Big house at the end. She's always round here. Mam and Dad know her really well. She's like my best friend.'

Somehow this seems less like a lie than it might have done until recently.

'Well, that's nice,' says Mormor. 'I had a friend called Susan when I was at school, and . . .'

Oh no! She wants to chat!

I add, 'They're Buddhists,' for good measure just because I know Uncle Pete did a mindfulness retreat in Greece last Christmas. 'And they go to bed very early.' He gets the hint.

'Don't be long. Got your phone with you?'

I wave it at him and I'm out of the door before he can change his mind, and I *run* to meet Susan on time.

CHAPTER 66

Susan and I lean against the railings in front of the old priory, facing Becker & Sons, and already I'm creeped out just by looking at it. Susan straightens up and looks at me keenly.

'It is all about psychology,' she says. 'I have been trying to work out how she will think.'

She's good, I'll give her that. She *sounds* as though she knows what she is talking about.

'Option one: we could tell Kezia the truth. Say that you need to get the Dreaminator in order to . . . you know, do what you need to do, and ask her to go into her father's funeral parlour and take it from wherever it is.'

I don't have to think about this for very long. 'Not gonna happen. She won't believe me for a start, and, even if she does, she's not just gonna steal something as . . . what? A favour?'

'Correct. So we have to use psychology.'

She's leading me down a certain path – and, better still, she's making me want to be led.

'Okay, Einstein. How's that gonna happen? Just tell me, Susan.'

She holds her chin and taps it with her forefinger as if deep in thought, although it's an act. She has worked this out already.

'You told me once about Kez Becker's "Halloween Challenge" . . . '

I stare at her, horrified. 'No, Susan. No, no, no . . .'

'It is the only way,' she says. 'How else are we going to get in and have a look around to find the Dreaminator? It will be in a box with a label, or on a shelf, or something. We can not go in and ask for it, can we? The place is not even open, and we can't wait until tomorrow.' She looks at my face, and I quickly hide my expression of terror. She even laughs a little and pats my arm like she does. 'Relax, Malky. You will not be in there long.'

'But . . . but, Susan, man . . .' There is no easy way of saying this. 'There'll be . . . b-bodies. Dead people.'

'No, there will not. I have done some research. They are not just left lying around, you know. They must be securely stored and refrigerated in a dedicated, licensed unit. It is the law, specifically the Public Health Act of 1984. That building over there is just a showroom and a workshop. '

'Are you sure?' I ask, a little too anxiously.

'Almost certain.'

I don't like the 'almost'.

'Half an hour, yeah?' I say.

'That is what you told me Kezia said. She is a strange girl, that is for sure.'

'Ha ha ha! Stranger than you can possibly imagine!' says Kez, coming up behind us and making us jump. She has Dennis on the end of a long rope, and he sniffs around in the bushes near us. For once, he doesn't growl at me. Perhaps he's okay with me when I'm not on his territory.

Kez squeezes in between Susan and me as if the three of us have always been best pals. 'What's up, losers? Very intriguing text message, Susan. How'd you get my number?'

'COMMS contact sheet, obviously. Staying in touch, you know?'

Susan has set this up already? I glance over at her and she catches my eye with a slight smirk.

Kez makes a *pffft* sound. 'Oh, *that*! Ha – you suckers! I managed to get out of that, eh? Told old Farroukh I had "gerontophobia", didn't I?'

She smirks when Susan and I both say, 'What's that?'

'It means a fear of old people. It's a real thing. Said I suffered "psychological trauma" cos of me dad's business. Made it up, of course, but she seemed to believe me. And now you're dragging me away from me regular Saturday night horror film, hur hur! *Night of the Dead* it was, and I tell you . . .'

'Cut out the spooky stuff, Kezia,' Susan says, but not

sharply. 'And let's just get this done, yes? How come you've got good old Dennis, by the way?'

Kez swivels her head between us. 'Good old Dennis? Are you kidding? Stinkin' bag of fur more like! Never stops pooin'. I've said I'll look after it temporarily, like. Wish I hadn't. They found it at old man McKinley's house. Did you hear?'

Susan nods. 'Yes. It was very sad, wasn't it?'

Kez shrugs. 'Aye, very sad. RIP an' all that. Didn't you have to visit him as part of the COMMS thing? Anyway, I've only got it until St Woof's, the rescue centre in Whitley Bay, find a space. They've said just a few days. Which is just as well, because it flippin' reeks and, and . . . oh no. You dirty, horrible brute!'

Dennis has hunkered down for a poo, and I suddenly feel so sorry for the dog. His sad look is still there, and now he's getting shouted at by Kez for something he can't understand.

Kez makes gagging noises and fishes a black plastic poo bag from her pocket. 'I *hate* this bit. Really hate it.'

Susan reaches over and plucks the bag from her hand. 'Don't worry,' she says. 'I will do it.' Quick as anything, she puts her hand in the bag, scoops up Dennis's poo, turns the whole thing inside out and ties the top. She deposits the bag in a bin on a lamppost and comes back, smiling. 'There,' she says. 'Easy-peasy! Good boy, Dennis!' The old dog licks her hand gratefully.

Kez grunts. 'Hmph. Thanks.'

And I think: *Clever Susan! Now Kez owes us.*

'Anyway. What was your text all about?' says Kez. 'What's it got to do with my challenge?'

'Ah yes. Your challenge, Kezia. Let me just reiterate. You say that you will give ten pounds to anyone who will stay alone in your father's funeral parlour at night for half an hour?'

Hearing Susan say it out loud like that makes my bum clench in fear.

There are dead people there!

Yes, yes, I know. Susan reckons there aren't. And you can tell me all you like about the logic of it. Dead people are dead: they can't harm you. There is no such thing as ghosts: I know that too. What possible harm can come to you, just sitting in the dark for half an hour? None at all. You won't even *see* a body: they're all locked away in a huge refrigerator, that is if there even are any.

Still.

Kez says, 'Ah, I dunno, man. Money's a bit tight at the moment, you know? I don't think I have ten quid to me name right now.'

I look at Dennis, and his sad face.

'I'll do it for the dog,' I say. 'You don't even have to give me a tenner.' The words are out of my mouth before I really think about it.

Kez stares at me. 'Hang on. You'll spend half an hour

in there, in the dark, and I don't even need to give you a tenner? All I have to do is hand over this smelly old hound that's going to the rescue home, anyway?'

This is not good. Kez is suspicious. Time for some acting. I stand up from the wall and take a few steps in the direction of home.

'You're right,' I say. 'It's a stupid idea, and far too scary. There's no way I could do that just to own a dog for a few days. Bye.'

'Hang on, hang on,' says Kez, and I know then that she's bought it.

Psychology, Susan called it. Seems like it works.

CHAPTER 67

A lot of the Becker & Sons square building is concealed discreetly behind high hedges, with only the reception bit clearly visible from the street. We've come round to the walled car park at the back, beyond which are thick trees and an embankment leading to the old railway line. It's overlooked by the Beckers' flat, which occupies the whole of the first floor, but there are no lights on anywhere. It's very dark and Front Street suddenly feels miles away.

I look at Kez, and I think, *Imagine living so close to dead bodies!* But of course it's all normal to her. She goes over to one of the long black funeral cars and crouches down, putting her hand inside the rear wheel arch and extracting a set of keys.

'Me dad's forever telling Terry not to leave them there. Good job he ignores him, eh?' she says. 'Right then: you ready for this?'

My heart feels tight in my chest and I can hardly swallow. I clench my teeth and give a short nod as Kez approaches us, jangling the keys. We follow her round to the big double doors.

Susan murmurs so that Kez can't hear. 'Remember. The dead cannot hurt you. Focus on your *real* purpose. Focus on Seb.'

'Hang on. You said . . .'

'I know. I am almost certain. But you know . . .'

Kez has unlocked the double doors and, when she opens them, a soft beeping starts. She turns to us. 'Wait here. I have to disable the alarm.' She slips in, and a few seconds later the beeping stops. Kez reappears and the three of us stand for a moment by the slightly opened double doors.

'All right. Rules,' says Kez. 'Half an hour starting from now. No talking to people on the outside. Don't turn the lights on or you're disqualified. If it gets too much for you, bang on the door and say, "I'm a scaredy-cat, get me out of here!" Ready? Hand me your phone.'

'Not giving it to you after last time. Susan can keep it.'

Kez frowns at us both. 'Fair enough. Doesn't matter to me. Now – have a look.'

I step forward to put my head through the gap in the doors. That's when I feel a hard shove in my back as I'm pushed forward into the dark, followed by a loud clunk as the door slams behind me. It's just like when this whole thing started, when Kez pushed me into Mr McKinley's backyard.

'Malky, are you all ri—' begins Susan.

'Shush. You're breaking the rules.'

After that, silence. Even though I know that Kez and Susan are on the other side of the doors, I'm terrified. It would have been scary enough just sitting there with my back against them for thirty minutes. Instead, I have to prowl around in near total darkness, looking for a dead man's Dreaminator.

The narrow windows just below ceiling height let in a tiny bit of light from outside, but it's a dark night, anyway, and the only streetlight is broken. I blink hard to try to force my eyes to get used to the blackness and after a little while I work out where I am.

The room I'm in is bigger than it seemed from the outside. There are some lockers like at school, a rail with suits hanging from it, a shelf with top hats, and some low chairs. This must be some sort of changing area or staffroom. There are empty teacups on a little table and a sink in the corner. I start looking around for anything that might give me a clue as to where the Dreaminator is, and pretty soon I conclude that it's not likely to be here. Not in this space, anyway. There are some head-height kitchen cupboards which I quickly look in, but it's stuff like mugs and teabags.

A swing door on the other side of the space leads to a wide corridor, also dimly lit by the ceiling-height windows, with three or four doors leading off it, most with little round windows in them. I peer through one:

it's much too dark to see inside. I try the door handle: it's locked.

I freeze on the spot when a beam of white light passes across the ceiling, followed a second or two later by the deep rumble of a big motorbike turning into the car park.

Kez's dad!

I scuttle quickly back through the swing door into the staffroom and go up to the door I came in through. I'm about to thump on it and demand to be let out, but I can hear the motorbike only a few metres away. Then the engine goes quiet and there is an adult voice, muffled through the door, but still audible.

'Hello, love. What you doing here?'

'Hi, Dad. Just walkin' Dennis. He chased a ball and it went round this side.'

Mr Becker chuckles. 'Chased a ball? That's something new. I've not seen him get above walking pace.'

His voice is getting nearer and I hear the jingling of keys followed by Kez's squeaked question.

'You're not going in there, are you?'

'Erm . . . yeah, love. Why sh—'

'Only . . . Mam was asking for you. I think. You should see what she wants. First, like.'

'Aye, well, your mam can wait a minute longer, can't she? I just have to get something from the office. Don't look at me like that. What's wrong with you? Go on, off you go back home. Yes – now, Kezia. Scram. Beat it.'

By the time I hear the key in the lock, I'm in full-on terror. There is nowhere – *nowhere* – in the staffroom that will conceal me if he turns the light on, which he is certain to do.

CHAPTER 68

The swing door is still moving and creaking behind me as Mr Becker comes through the main door, and I'm standing in the corridor, which is now lit up as he turns the building's interior lights on. If he comes down here to get to the office at the other end, he'll find me.

There are four doors leading off the corridor. The first one I already know is locked. I try the second one: that is locked too, and I just know what will happen when I try the others. I can hear Mr Becker's footsteps coming across the staffroom floor.

The third door is locked as I expected. The fourth door has no window and it . . . opens.

I slip through it and almost squeal out loud. In front of me, dimly lit by a single candle burning in a holder, are three coffins. Each one is on a waist-high trolley with wheels. The one furthest from the door has a pleated curtain round the base, concealing the metal and wheels of the trolley.

I hear the swing door creak at the end of the corridor. Mr Becker's footsteps are getting closer and I realise I have left the door open, but it's too late to go back. For a second, I freeze, but, as the footsteps draw alongside the doorway, I dart behind the far coffin and slip under the trolley's curtain.

He stops at the door and goes, 'Oh my goodness me,' in a weary tone. 'What have we here?'

He can't know I'm here, can he? I'm crouched under a coffin behind a curtain: he can't see me. Unless he can hear my heart thumping and that is a distinct possibility.

Then I hear the *beep-beep-beep* of a mobile-phone keypad.

Mr Becker is standing next to me now. If I angle my head down, I can just see the toes of his biker boots where the curtain doesn't reach the ground.

'Terry? Yes, it's me.' His voice is not loud, but I can tell he's not pleased. 'I've just come back to the site to pick up that paperwork and guess what? Not only was the alarm not set, but the door to Store Two was unlocked, and you've left a flippin' candle burning! A naked flame. Well, sorry doesn't quite cut it, Terry. It's a massive fire risk. We're running a funeral home here, Terry, not a bloody crematorium. Yeah, well. Consider that your final warning.'

He tuts as he ends the call, then I hear him blow out the candle and leave the room, locking it behind him, and . . .

. . . locking me in.

As Mr Becker's footsteps die away, I find I cannot move. Ever heard of people being 'paralysed with fear'? Well, that's me. I never thought it could be real, but every time I try to move I freeze up. I'm locked in a dead-dark room with three coffins that have to contain dead people otherwise what are they doing here? It is as though my brain is telling my limbs: *So long as you don't move a muscle, nothing bad will happen.*

I feel like throwing up, and I try to fight the urge to sob, but it doesn't work and I let out a quavering wail of terror. When I realise that my wail of terror actually sounds like the *woo-ooo-ooo* of a Halloween ghost, I let out something that is a bit like a laugh and a scream. I'm crouched under a coffin in total darkness, making these lunatic noises, and I'm a mess.

I guess it helps, though. When I finish, I wipe my face with the curtain, pull it aside and take a deep breath. I crawl out from under the trolley and the room is blacker than black. There are no windows – not even in the door to the corridor – so I really can't even see my hand in front of my face.

The smell of the candle that's just been put out gives me an idea. I grope around until I find it. It's in a metal holder on a little table and on the table is – o*h, the relief!* – a box of matches. Trembling, I take one out, and use it to relight the candle.

I wonder if I preferred it when it was completely dark? Now I can see the three coffins: a white one with flowers painted on it, a black, shiny one with brass handles, and the one that I was hiding under. This is a simpler one in plain wood.

I ease the candle from its holder and bring it over to the coffins. My hand is shaking so much that little bits of melted wax are splattering on the coffin lids, while dark shadows skip and hide in every corner. Each of the coffins, I see, has a pink Post-it note stuck on the lid.

I hold up the light to read the first note on the black coffin. It says, simply, Mr D. Dyson. The next one reads Mrs E. Armstrong. I swallow hard, because I know what the one on the wooden coffin – the one I was hiding under – will say. Sure enough, there it is.

Mr K. H. McKinley.

Before I open the lid, I carefully look round the rest of the room, in case there are boxes of stored items, or shelves or cupboards . . .

Nothing.

I have lost track of time. I don't know when – or for that matter *if* – Kez will be back. But I know that the only chance of getting the Dreaminator is to open the wooden lid and find out if it's there.

With one shaking hand, I hold the candle up; with the other, I nudge the lid, half hoping that it is fastened down so that I won't have to do what comes next. It isn't, though: it moves. I squeeze my fingers under the edge, lifting and pushing until the lid slides away, and I glimpse the white satin lining of the box.

I turn my head. I can't even watch what I am doing with my own hands. My eyes are screwed shut and I push too hard. The coffin lid clatters to the floor causing a tremendous noise in the small room and I drop the candle, but it doesn't go out.

I bend to retrieve it, and rise up slowly, slowly, panting with terror at what I might see. Swallowing hard, I peer in.

There's nobody. More important, there's no body, and I breathe out with relief: a sort of wobbly sigh.

The coffin's not empty, though. Oh no. Right there, resting in the centre of the shiny white satin, is the world's last Dreaminator.

Then I hear footsteps outside again. I grab the Dreaminator and crawl back beneath the curtain.

The doorknob rattles.

CHAPTER 69

'Malky! Malky! You in there?'

I'm not sure I've ever been more relieved to hear someone's voice.

'Susan! Yes! I'm here!' I'm up against the door, but it won't budge. 'Don't you have a key?'

'Only to the outside door. The alarm is going to go off any . . .'

Her last words are drowned out by the piercing *wheep-wheep-wheep* of a delayed intruder alarm. I do a quick calculation. How long will it take Mr Becker to hear that and come downstairs to investigate? Thirty seconds? A minute? Not even that.

There's just no way I'm going to be caught stealing from the coffin of a dead man! I'm still holding the candle and I ram it back into its holder.

'Stand back!' I shout to Susan. 'And get ready to run!'

I shove the Dreaminator down my zip-up jacket. Then I grab one end of the wheeled trolley supporting the biggest, heaviest coffin – the black one – and drag it to the far end of the room. I run, pushing it in front of me. I haven't got long to pick up much speed – maybe five metres – but the weight must help, because the trolley crunches into the door, busting the lock immediately and springing the door open a little. I pull the trolley back and ram it into the door again, forcing it open with a loud bang. The coffin is blocking my exit now, but there is space above so I hop up on to it, and crawl over the top, landing in a pile at Susan's feet. Already I can hear the front door being opened in the reception area.

Susan and I don't talk. Instead, we run – back along the dark corridor, through the staffroom, out of the back door into the rear car park.

The only exit from the car park is the passageway past the reception block. Otherwise there's a wall – a high wall – and on the other side a steep embankment leading down to the old railway line which is now a cycleway. We have no choice. I leap on to the bonnet and then the roof of one of the hearses, which buckles under my weight, but it gets me high enough to grab the top of the wall.

'Come on,' I say to Susan. 'You can do it!'

'I know,' she says and follows me as we both scramble over, landing on the other side in a huge blackberry bush, which snags our clothes and rips our skin as we struggle to get free and down the embankment to the cycleway. I feel something crack beneath my jacket, but I can't stop to check.

Have we been followed? I don't think so. I have heard no shouts, though the intruder alarm is still wailing behind us.

'This way,' I say, pointing in the direction of North Shields, a couple of kilometres away.

And so we run along the track, past back gardens and through a gap in the fence, which tears a long rip in my jacket, and we're in the playground of Seb's primary school, and still we don't stop till we've climbed over the spiked railings and we're at the end of the back lane of Susan's street with her rear gate to our left and my house a bit further on.

It's pretty dark at this end, and there's a patch of grass where I sink to my knees, my chest heaving. With shaking hands, I take out the Dreaminator and examine it. One of the pyramid sides has been bent, and there's a crack in the bamboo hoop, but it's otherwise all right. I hope. Susan is less puffed-out that I am, although she's just as scratched and filthy.

You okay?' I say after a moment, and she nods. 'Thanks for getting me.'

'Kezia just left you!' she says in a tone of disbelief. 'When her dad turned up on his motorbike, she tossed me the keys and told me to make myself scarce and to put them back when I was done. I am sorry. I had to wait until her dad had gone from the front office, and he had reset the alarm. What a . . . what a . . .'

I'm waiting for Susan to choose her insult for Kez Becker. I have never heard her say anything nasty about anyone.

I still haven't. She finishes her sentence with a tut and a shake of her head, and hands me back my phone.

I turn it on and stare at it while it boots up. I'm still panting a little – more, I think, from nerves than exhaustion.

'Oh no,' I say and Susan crouches down next to me. 'What's wrong?'

Eleven missed calls: all from Uncle Pete. Plus two voicemails, and three text messages. Reluctantly, I click on messages. This can't be good news.

Where are you?

Please call – urgent.

Come home now, or I am coming to get you.

That last one was only five minutes ago. I can't call him, I don't dare. Instead, I send a text back.

Sorry. Phone battery died. On my way back.

It's a poor excuse but it'll have to do.

Susan and I face each other on the scrappy patch of grass.

'Do I look as rough as you?' I ask, taking in her mud-streaked, torn clothes, her hair which for once is filthy and messed up, and a deep thorn-scratch on her cheek.

She smiles. 'No. You look great! Tiptop. Never looked better.'

We both chuckle nervously before a slightly awkward pause.

She says, 'Good luck.' Then she leans in and hugs me, pinning my arms to my sides so I can't hug her back, even though I was going to.

'Do you know what you have to do when you use the Dreaminator?' she says.

'Not really.'

Susan chews her cheek in thought. 'Go to the edge of your dream and then go further. That is what Mola said.'

'Do you even know what that means?'

Susan smiles her closed-mouth smile and says, 'Not really. Sorry.' We stand facing each other for a moment, then she says, 'Good luck,' again before turning and walking away and I do the same.

I've gone about ten metres when she calls my name and I look back. 'I might see you there,' she says. I nod and wave, not really understanding or even sure that I heard right.

She might see me there? See me where?

But I soon forget about that. Uncle Pete is standing on the front step when I turn up our little driveway, and he does *not* look happy.

TWO HOURS LATER

CHAPTER 70

I'm lying on my bed.

Sleep? You've got to be kidding. I feel like I have crammed about a week into a whole day, and, if you imagine that that will make me tired, then let me tell you: I am about as far from sleepy as it's possible to be.

Uncle Pete hadn't known what to do, and for that I'm pretty glad.

When I turned up looking like I did, with the Dreaminator concealed under my jacket, Uncle Pete was confused. He's been firm with me before, and once raised his voice at Seb, but I honestly don't think he's ever had to tell me off. The confusion was written all over his face, and I decided I would have to bluff this out.

What choice did I have?

'What the blazes happened to you?' he said. 'And where've you been? Me and your Mormor have been worried sick. I was on my way out to come and get you.'

Mormor was just sitting on the sofa, shaking her head slightly in sorrow or disapproval: it's hard to know which.

To be fair, I felt a bit sorry for them: as well as confused, they did look pretty upset. I could tell Uncle Pete was angry, but he doesn't have kids of his own, so . . .

I bluffed. I lied, in other words. I made up some story about Susan's guinea pig escaping, and having to chase it all round her garden, and I knew he'd never be able to check it out.

I hung my head. 'Sorry, Uncle Pete. I didn't mean to worry you,' I said in a really small voice.

(Ooh, I *hate* having to do that. It's *so* effective on people without kids, yet strangely ineffective on parents and teachers.)

Mormor tutted and muttered something in Swedish, then, 'Malky, *älskling*. Your mama and papa have got enough to worry about. Go and get showered and then into bed. We'll say no more about this. Give me a hug first.'

Oh no. Not a hug. Not when I'm hiding something under my jacket.

'*Kom hit*,' she said in Swedish, opening her arms. 'Come here!'

I hesitated.

'What's wrong with you?'

There was no getting out of it. I leaned into her from a standing position and tried to angle my body away from her, but she kept pulling harder.

She's bound to discover it.

'Hey, what is this?' she said, and I thought I was found out. But she was touching the tear in my sleeve. 'Take your jacket off, Malky, *älskling*. I shall mend this for you before your mama finds out, how about that? Well, for what are you waiting? Get it off!'

At that second, Uncle Pete's phone rang in his pocket and Mormor was distracted for a moment. We both stopped our hug and waited to see what the news was. I could tell from his tone that he was talking to Mam. He hardly said anything, just things like, 'Mm-hm,' and, 'I see.' Then there was a long pause, and he said, 'Oh no.' Mormor's hand went up to her mouth in alarm.

'That was your mam,' said Uncle Pete, putting his phone away and sitting down heavily. 'It's not good news. Seb's condition is getting worse. Tonight is going to be very critical. I'm really sorry, Malky.' His mouth was turned down in a tight, thin line, and his face was becoming pink with the effort of not breaking down in front of me.

Mormor looked up at me, her eyes moist. 'Do you pray, Malky?'

I shrugged. I don't really, except when we have to at school.

'You might want to tonight,' she said, and turned away, quickly. I used the opportunity to dash upstairs. Obviously, they both thought I was going to my room to cry (or pray, perhaps), but I was just eager to get the Dreaminator out from under my jacket.

And so here I am and it's nearly midnight.

The Dreaminator's ring of lights seems to glow with a greater intensity than the ones Seb and I had and seems more green than blue. Does that mean it's more effective?

Uncle Pete's sleeping on the sofa downstairs and Mormor is in Mam's room. The TV went off a while ago. Now everything's quiet. And I'm wide awake.

Then my phone pings with an incoming text message. It's from Susan.

I was not sure whether to send you this, but here goes.

There is a link to tap on, and when I do it opens a picture. It is a scan of an old newspaper article.

Edinburgh Evening News

Mystery death of 'Mystic's' son

2 March 1988. The death of a teenager at the Royal Infirmary of Edinburgh has left doctors 'baffled'.

Uri McKinley, 13, was admitted to the unit on February 23. He had fallen into a 'spontaneous deep coma' and doctors were unable to wake him.

His condition rapidly declined and he died peacefully two days ago. Doctors have been unable to pinpoint a cause of death and the matter has been referred to the Scottish legal authorities.

Uri was the only son of entertainer and self-styled 'Mystic of the Highlands' Kenneth McKinley and his wife Jeanette.

Mr McKinley toured Scotland in the sixties and seventies, but retired from public life a few years ago.

If I had had *any* remaining doubts about the seriousness of Seb's situation, that short article has removed them all.

The more I think about being wide awake, the more it scares me. I *have* to get back into that dream. Seb is in real danger. He could die, like Kenneth McKinley's son.

It's down to me. Everything is down to me.

CHAPTER 71

I look at the clock on my phone. It's now past three a.m. and I still haven't slept.

I lie first on one side, then the other, then on my back, then on my front. Mam says she sometimes reads if she can't sleep, but that would involve turning the light on, which would mean accepting my wakefulness, so I'm *definitely* not doing that.

Twenty minutes later, I've switched the light on. Lying on Seb's bed is *Kobi the Cave Boy*.

Just looking at the pictures gives me butterflies. The empty, sandy landscape on the first page is a bit like looking at an old holiday photograph. And the words too are so familiar.

In the shadows of the cave, the fire flickers red,
And Kobi lies down with a rock beneath his
**   head,**
And pulls the fur blanket until it tickles his
**   nose**

While outside the cave mouth, the cold wind blows.

Kobi feels sleepy and his eyelids close.

Slowly, slowly, like Kobi's fur blanket, the book sinks down and touches my nose and I don't even notice.

And then I'm awake again. Dammit! What was that noise? A *thump!* behind me.

There is it again. *Thump!*

I look at my phone again: 03.42. Just then a message from Susan flashes up on the screen.

Are you awake?

Thump!

The window. It's coming from the window. Somebody is throwing something at the window. I shake off my duvet and open the curtain at the exact second a foam dart hits the glass and makes a much louder thump, making me jump back, startled.

In the little backyard, I can make out a figure with dark hair and a buttoned-up jacket, about to fire another missile. Susan sees me and lowers her arm. She's holding Seb's Nerf gun that he left under the hedge. I open the window.

'I wasn't sure whether to disturb you,' she hisses.

'I was nearly asleep,' I whisper back, trying not to sound angry.

'Good,' she says. 'Catch this. Then go back to sleep. It might help. Good luck.'

She fishes in her jacket pocket and pulls out something. Her aim is good and I catch it first time. I look down at the small packet tied with string, and by the time I look back she's gone, the yard door slamming behind her.

CHAPTER 72

There's a note taped to the package.

Dear Malky,

Sorry I disturbed you. I lay awake wondering whether I should, but then I thought this was too important.

Do you remember the first time you shared your dream with Seb? You said you remembered the smell of yak's butter.

And then yesterday — at school — you said you had smelled it again and you had a sort of 'flashback'.

And again — in our garden, when you suddenly smelled our tea.

And finally — Mr McKinley lighting the cigarette but not smoking it.

Smells and sounds can often trigger the deepest memories. I love meditating under the soft flapping noise of our prayer flags, for example.

And so inside this packet is some yak's butter. Open it, smell it, leave it open near you.

You are a good person, Malky Bell. You deserve to succeed, so I hope this helps.

Your friend,
Susan

And now I really *am* tired. I fumble to open the packet, and, as soon as I do, the sharp smell of the yak's butter begins to fill the room.

I get back into bed and close my eyes. And this time I really do fall asleep, while the Dreaminator hangs above me almost completely still.

CHAPTER 73

It's different. That's all I can say right now, looking round the familiar cave where Seb and I have started so many of our adventures. This is the biggest adventure of them all, and he's not here. I was hoping I'd start this dream where I left Seb – in the clearing with the big guys who captured him. That would have saved time. My subconscious had other ideas.

How is it different? Everything *looks* the same. There's the fire, not even smouldering any more; there's the drawing on the cave wall still: the car that made Seb laugh when he drew it imagining people discovering it in thousands of years' time. Outside, the cold wind blows just like the book says, and little clouds of sand puff up and disappear in the breeze. Even the fish-shaped airship is drifting in its usual place.

I *feel* different: that must be it.

It's not just that I am nervous – although I am. It's that this is no longer fun. Mola's words come back to me: 'It's like a video game to you, innit? *Bam-bam-bam*, now I'm dead, press "replay", new life.'

I find myself saying aloud, 'Well, it's not a game now, Mola.'

'Good, I'm glad you realise it,' she replies. I swing round and there she is behind me and I gasp. 'You took your time, Dream-boy,' she says, but she doesn't sound angry, just impatient.

'I . . . I . . . couldn't sleep. Hang on . . . this is a dream, right?'

The old lady rolls her dark little eyes like a teenager. 'What you think? Course it is.'

'But . . . but how come you . . . I mean . . . ? Are you sharing my dream, or am I just dreaming you?'

'You gonna waste time worrying about this, Dream-boy?'

'No, but . . . why? Why are you here?'

'You might need some help. Actually . . . Susan thought you might need help. Now tell me this: how much you wanna get your brother back?'

What sort of question is that? 'More than anything, Mola! Even more than that!'

She narrows her eyes and nods. 'Hmm. Sounds like a lot. Come on then. We got a run ahead of us.'

She's off. We have to get up the beach, up the hill and across the great plain to the canyon, then on to Gravy Lake, before we get to the clearing where Seb was captured. Beside me, Mola runs without even panting. She has lifted up her ankle-length sarong, and her pale legs, knobbly and veined like a crumbly blue cheese, match mine stride for stride.

Soon we're sprinting across the windy plain, with the Gravy Lake in the distance.

'Mola!' I pant. 'All this super-fast running. It . . . it will use up my dream-control-power thingy.'

'So? You got a better idea?' She's still hardly even out of breath. 'You took long time to get here. We not got time for walking.'

She runs ahead of me and soon we are approaching the canyon with the green river of mint custard. I'm beginning to tire, even though I'm dream-running but still: this is going okay, I tell myself. I stop at the river's edge and sink to my knees, my chest heaving. I count the exposed rocks poking above the surface and forming a route over the water: five steps and I'll be across.

One of the rocks, though, looks longer than I'm used to. Greener, knobbly. And is it . . . is it *moving*?

'Oh no, no, no,' I murmur to myself, and I scramble to my feet again. As I watch, the rock rises up a little more and a yellow eye blinks at me slowly as Cuthbert shoves his snout out of the river and starts gliding towards me.

'Friend of yours?' says Mola, but my throat is too dry to answer. I'm thinking of my options. I could dream up a Nerf gun? They were pretty effective, only . . .

Hang on! What about a *real* gun?

'Good idea,' says Fit Billy who has appeared beside

me, unexpectedly, just like in a normal dream. Instead of dumbbells, in each hand he holds a huge gun. 'Can I recommend this?' He tosses me a gun, which clatters at my feet. 'A classic Thompson sub-machine-gun. Standard US Army issue throughout World War Two. That model's the M1A1, slightly lighter. You wanna be careful with it, son. Canny firearm, that is!'

'Thanks, Billy.' I crouch to pick it up. When I look again, Billy has gone, but Cuthbert is now coming out of the water. The machine-gun is about a thousand times heavier than Seb's plastic Nerf gun and I heave it to my shoulder.

'All right, you! I've got you now.' I squint through the sights, making sure the crocodile is exactly where I want him, and squeeze the cold metal trigger gently, then harder, then harder . . .

The closer Cuthbert gets, the better my chances of hitting him; but, if I miss, his chances of getting me increase hugely. If he does that, I'll wake up, and I can't risk *that* in case I don't get to sleep again.

I let the crocodile get closer and closer. Mola is a few metres away, further up the bank. 'Careful, Dream-boy!' she warns.

Cuthbert's jaws open: a direct hit, right in the gob, is what I need. One last squeeze of the trigger, and

BAM BAM BAM BAM BAM BAM BAM BAM BAM BAM BAM BAM BAM BAM!

The noise is painful in my ears, but I hold my arms and shoulders steady, keeping the gun aimed directly at Cuthbert. I let off another round.

BAM BAM BAM BAM BAM BAM BAM BAM BAM BAM BAM BAM BAM BAM!

I lower the gun, expecting to see the corpse of a huge crocodile lying in the shallows by the river bank.

'I say, old boy. Doesn't seem to be working, does it?' drawls Cuthbert. 'Daresay that's the thing with dreams, hey? Don't always do what you want! Ah well, tally-ho!'

He runs towards me on his stumpy legs, and I drop the gun. I've backed up to the steep bank of the canyon, but I can't get up it because I can't get my hands on the handholds, and . . .

. . . The croc is getting nearer – like *much* nearer. The wall of the canyon stretches upwards and I try again to scramble up it without success. I turn back to Cuthbert, and I can see the glint of his teeth.

'STOP!' I shout. 'Stop! Oh man – please just stop!'

Cuthbert darts his long head forward, his jaws clamping down on my foot with agonising force as he starts to pull me towards the water. 'No! NO!'

From further up the bank, Mola is running to help, shouting, 'Get off him! Get off him!'

I'm wriggling and twisting, but the more I try to pull my foot out of the croc's mouth, the harder he grips me, and I kick my other leg and it can't move properly, because it is tangled up in the duvet . . .

And I'm sweating in bed, my foot is burning with pain, there's a book resting on my face, which is dislodged when I move my head, the Dreaminator glows above me and I realise with a sob of frustration and a surge of despair that I have woken up.

'No!' I thump my head back on my sweat-damp pillow.

CHAPTER 74

Even in my semi-wakeful state, wrapped in my tangled duvet, I know that if I close my eyes I can re-enter the dream I was in. I'll be back asleep. And a crocodile's teeth will be tearing into my foot, and I'll wake up again . . .

The thought of it all makes me wake up more, and a few seconds later there is no going back. I'm wide awake. I can see Seb's empty bed, the moonlight coming through the thin horse-pattern curtains, the blue circle of Kenneth's Dreaminator shimmering above me, the digits on my phone saying . . .

04:28

My mind's still fuzzy. I can't remember exactly when I fell asleep, but it wasn't all that long ago. I was reading *Kobi the Cave Boy* and I drifted off.

I've missed my chance, haven't I?

Even though I am exhausted to the point of feeling sick, I'm not confident I'll get to sleep again. And, if I do, then what? It doesn't seem as though my dream-controlling is working at all any more. I lift my aching foot out from under the duvet. It feels wet from sweat . . . only wetter than that. It is also a bit sticky, but it's too dark to see anything so I turn my bedside light on and let out a gasp of horror.

Blood is oozing from three deep, triangular puncture wounds in my ankle, exactly matching where Cuthbert bit me. The blood is dripping down my leg and on to the sheet, so I get up and limp to the bathroom.

I'm feeling pretty alert now, and I figure the best way to clean up is to use the showerhead that's connected to the bath taps. Then I'll take a towel and wrap my foot tightly.

I see that I'm leaving a trail of crimson drips wherever I move. The shower curtain is pulled closed, concealing the bath. I pull it aside swiftly, and that's when I actually

SCREAM!

Out loud, and long.

Lying in the bath, arms crossed over his chest, wearing a bright blue-and-green kilt, is the body of Kenneth McKinley, who opens his eyes and rises slowly up from the waist, turning his head until he faces me.

'Och, forgive me, laddie. Is this a private dream, or can anyone join in?'

My mouth is flapping but no words are coming out.

'False awakening,' says Kenneth. 'Again. You're having

a dream-in-a-dream. Again. I'm surprised you fell for it a second time. Did you not spot the signs?'

'No . . . no. I . . . I . . . My clock! The time, the numbers . . . they were fine.'

'Oh dear, laddie. That's definitely not good.' He shakes his head. 'Yer mind is losing touch with reality. Ooh, it's a wee bit cramped in here. Like being in a blasted coffin.' He stands up and stretches his back, his ornamental dirk clanking against the taps.

'Aren't you . . .' I stumble because it's difficult to find the right words. It's not a question I have ever had to ask anyone before. 'Aren't you dead?'

He looks at me, a strange half-smile on his face. 'Och, yes, Malcolm. I'm afraid to say I am. Dead as a dodo.'

'So . . . you're a ghost?'

He steps out of the bath and stands next to me. 'Go on . . . touch my hand. See? If I was a ghost, your hand would go straight through mine, wouldn't it? No, you're having a dream, laddie.'

'But . . . you don't *look* dead.'

'Don't I? I'm glad to hear it, lad, glad to hear it.' He leans past me to check his reflection in the bathroom mirror and smooths down his hair. Then he grins at me, looking over the top of his purple glasses.

'Are you all right? That is . . .'

'All right? I'm dead, Malcolm! I'm about as far from all right as it's possible to be.'

'I . . . I don't understand.'

'Of course you don't. It's a dream! Where logic, rationality, sense and good order take second place to strangeness and improbability. But here's the thing, Malcolm – we're in Dreamland. And in Dreamland I'm as alive as can be. Just because you're dreaming it doesn't mean it isn't real, Malky lad.'

'Mola said almost the same thing!' I say.

He doesn't seem impressed. 'Hmm. Did she now? Remember, though, Malcolm: this is your dream, not mine. The only problem is, it seems as though you can't control it any more. That was always the difficulty with the Dreaminator: the control element never lasted long. Try telling your leg to stop bleeding. Go on.'

I look down at my still-dripping leg. 'Stop bleeding!' I say, softly. It doesn't.

'See? You're in your own dream, that's for sure. But you're now at the mercy of your subconscious.'

I tear a strip off a towel and dab it round the bite wound. 'Is that a bad thing?' I say.

Kenneth sighs. 'It's definitely not a *good* thing. I'm sorry to say that, owing to my demise coming a wee bit earlier than I expected, I never got to warn you about it. On a happier note, your subconscious has brought me along for a last visit to the mysterious dimension of Dreamland, so it can't be all bad. I think you may just have to let go and see where the ride takes you. Now come on, we haven't got a lot of time left before you wake naturally, so we can't stop here bletherin'.'

He makes a move towards the bathroom door. 'Wait!' I say, and he turns back. 'We are going to succeed, aren't we? I mean, in rescuing Seb?'

He moves his glasses down his nose to look at me over the top. 'That, Malcolm, is entirely down to you.'

He opens the bathroom door and beckons me through, and I'm back in Kobi's cave. 'Now,' he says, 'follow me and get ready to meet that crocodile again.'

I feel sick. 'Cuthbert? Why?'

'Because I've a feeling that until you kill him, you'll never be rid of him.'

CHAPTER 75

Outside, the mouth of the cave is exactly as before, with the airship drifting in a clear sky and a chilly wind scooping up whitecaps on the waves in the bay. I turn to Kenneth, who seems far younger than when he was . . .

. . . this is going to sound strange, but I'll say it anyway . . .

He seems far younger than *when he was alive.*

He's standing at the cave mouth, hands on hips, his face lifted to the sharp autumn sunshine, the breeze flicking his kilt round his knees.

'What do we do, Kenneth?' I say.

He keeps his face turned to the sky. 'Why do you keep asking me, laddie? It's your dream.'

'I know, it's just . . . you know, I don't know what to do and I thought you might.'

He looks at me and says, 'No. You're in charge, or at least your subconscious mind is, and right now that's all there is of you. That's just how it goes.'

I'm beginning to panic, and I can hear my panic-voice

getting louder and higher. 'But you made the Dreaminator: you must know!'

'Och, I long ago gave up havin' any proper control over my dreams. I used to meet wee Uri and that was about it. I'd just allow my dreaming mind to do whatever it wanted and you know – as you youngsters say – *go with the flow.*'

'And that worked? That was okay?'

'Aye, it was,' he says, smiling slowly. 'And I got to meet my son again.'

'Oh,' I say. 'Of course.'

Kenneth gives me a long stare. 'This is a lot of talking when you've got a job to do, if you don't mind me saying.'

'Can you run?' I ask.

Kenneth answers by bobbing up and down on the spot a couple of times, and then starting to jog up the beach like a much younger man, his knobbly knees working hard and his shiny black lace-ups kicking up sand. I catch him up, limping badly, then for the second time in an hour I find myself running up the rocky incline to where the clock tower will be in 10,000 years' time, through the low, dusty bushes of the Turk's Head pub, crossing the space where the seafront road will be and on to the wide plain that leads to Custard Canyon and eventually the Gravy Lake that one day will be Marden Quarry.

I keep wanting to test my dream-control. 'Fly!' I shout,

and stretch out my arms, but I remain stubbornly earthbound. I try not to think about how I will rescue Seb if I have to do it, you know, *normally*. That is, without the power of dream-control.

We run faster and faster. The agony in my foot hasn't lessened, my chest is hurting, my legs are tired, and we're still only halfway.

As he runs alongside me, Kenneth seems hardly breathless at all, which must, I figure, be a big advantage of being dead. He lifts up his arm to look at his wrist.

'I don't mean to alarm you, wee man, but outside your bedroom it's getting light and you'll be awakening naturally in about half an hour. Maybe less, actually.'

In reply, I grit my teeth, pump my arms harder and lengthen my stride until I can see a small speck in the distance, standing on the lip of the canyon. A moment later, I recognise the tiny, round shape, more or less exactly where I had left her before.

By the time I draw up next to Mola, I have a painful stitch in my side, and I am so light-headed with exhaustion that it stops me noticing how much my foot is hurting. Five seconds later, old Kenneth McKinley, ninety years of age, saunters up in his kilt – breathing no more heavily than if he had just walked up the steps to his front door.

Mola and Kenneth face each other warily for what seems like ages. Mola speaks first.

'So it is you then? You what got them into all this kerfuffling, huh? Your fault, eh?'

'Madam, you could not be more wrong. Malcolm and Sebastian got themselves into all this, ahh . . . *kerfuffling* with no more help from me than the development of the infernal Dreaminator, which Malcolm here stole.' He looks at me with a wry smile. 'Sorry, laddie.'

'How did . . . you know?' I wheeze.

'I didn't, actually. Well, not until you admitted it just now. But Dreamworld or not, the truth will out, as your Wullie Shakespeare said.'

I'm still too breathless to speak properly, but I'd be unable to say anything, anyway, I am so stunned.

Mola does not look as though Kenneth's explanation has satisfied her. She shakes her head, angrily, and says, 'For centuries, people have contemplated the inner workings of the mind, our whole *existence*. Through meditation, through prayer, and then you come along with your toy and look what happens!'

Kenneth seems a bit embarrassed. 'Madam, you may be right. But you are mistaking me for someone who is alive and has the power to change things. That power, alas, is no longer mine owing to my essential, well . . . deadness, I suppose. By the way, I've not been in this dream before, but I don't like the lean an' hungry look of yon fella coming up behind you.'

Mola and I turn and with a lurch in my stomach I see Cuthbert crawling over the lip of the canyon and he's looking straight at me with his huge yellow eyes.

I groan out loud.

CHAPTER 76

Cuthbert heaves himself over the lip of the canyon and takes a couple of scuttling steps towards me before stopping to lick his lips.

'What do I *do*?' I ask.

'Ye'll ken when ye ken is all I ken,' says Kenneth and I have *no idea* what he means, but I don't have time to work it out. All I can think of is running away.

'Follow me!' I say, and I scramble back down the canyon, leaving Cuthbert at the top, struggling to turn round so that he can pursue us. Kenneth comes after me, digging his shoes into the smooth, steep canyon wall, which is about the height of a house and even has windows . . . and a familiar front door with cracked black paint . . .

As he descends, he grunts something at me, and I hear it in snatches.

'If he's been with you a while, then you don't want to run away, Malcolm . . . your greatest fear will always chase you until you confront it.'

Mola slides down, her long sarong riding up past her

knees, and seconds later we're at the bottom together, while Cuthbert looks down at us angrily from the canyon's edge, snapping his jaws. We haven't got long, I know it: he'll be after us soon enough.

When she gets alongside me, Mola grips my arm and points to where, midstream, three more crocodiles are gliding towards us through the pale green custard.

'It's getting worse. Can't you stop them?' she says.

I shake my head. 'It doesn't work like that, Mola. Not any more. Look.' I point at the crocs and say, 'Stop. Turn around!'

Nothing happens and they get closer to us, about thirty metres upstream.

I glance up to check on Cuthbert's progress at the exact moment the beast launches himself down the steep, muddy slope towards us, rolling and sliding and flapping his tail. I stare helplessly, my head swivelling between Mola, Kenneth, Cuthbert and the three crocs.

We are trapped. I look across the custard river to the bank opposite: it's our only escape, if we can outrun, or outswim, the crocs.

'What should we *do*?' I wail, while Mola and Kenneth shake their heads, sympathetically.

'It's your dream, Dream-boy. No one else is in charge. Just like life. But seeing as you ask . . .' She's looking at the river. 'Your brother is on the other side, right?'

I'm ahead of her. 'Come on! Into the erm . . . custard!'

I'm knee-deep already, and Mola is too, but Kenneth is lagging behind. 'Come on, Kenneth – we have to be faster than those crocs!'

Mola and I are midstream. The three crocodiles are getting closer. Kenneth calls out to us: 'You don't have to be faster than *them*. You just have to be faster than me! I'll take care of these wee scunners, but you, Malcolm – good Scottish name that, by the way, did I ever tell you? – you have to deal with yon big lad.' He points to Cuthbert. 'Here – you might need this! Catch.'

He unhooks his dirk from the sheath at the side of his kilt and tosses it to me. I watch it twirl and spin in the air, glinting in the sun as it arcs towards me, and I know – don't ask me how, I just *know* – that if I raise my arm I will catch it perfectly, and I do. It lands with a *thwack* in my palm, much bigger and heavier than I had expected.

At the same time, the liquid around me stops being thick green custard and becomes a regular river, flowing with cold water.

Everything is becoming more real.

And it's at that moment – the exact moment that I curl my fingers round the carved handle of the dirk – that I begin to surrender. I give myself up to whatever will happen and start to trust in my lack of control.

Let it be, let it be, let it be, let it be . . .

CHAPTER 77

Kenneth is wading through the water towards the three smaller crocodiles. His musical, gentle Scots accent has been replaced with a guttural city growl. 'Right, come oan, ye hockit wee jobbies. Ah'll gie ye whit fer! Leave me pal alone!'

Behind me, Cuthbert has entered the water with a splash and is gliding quickly towards us. I turn to Mola, who is out of the deepest part now, and nearing the other side. I push through the waist-deep water, my feet slipping on the rocks on the bottom.

'Mola! Help! Kenneth!' I cry – pointlessly. There is nothing anyone can do. I look upstream to where Kenneth entered with the crocs.

Nothing.

Kenneth has gone. Cuthbert has gone too. I swivel round in terror, alone in the middle of the river.

'Kenneth!' I shout. 'Kenneth!' A scrap of blue-green tartan floats past me on the fast-moving water.

Mola shouts back. 'Forget him, Malky. He was dead already.'

That's when I see it: the huge creamy-white belly of Cuthbert just below the surface of the water, barrelling towards me as he turns and grabs my leg in his jaws, pulling me under the surface as I suck in a mouthful of river.

This can't be happening! Wake up! Wake up!

I can't shout because I'm underwater, but, if my thoughts could yell, they'd be deafening. I have forgotten Seb, I have forgotten everything in my desperate bid to fight off this beast that is churning up the water and twisting my leg, as if trying to wrench it off.

Around me I can see the water turning a misty red from my blood, and at some point I struggle to the surface, taking a gurgling, desperate breath as my head breaks free of the water. Cuthbert has let go and I manage to half swim, half stagger a couple more strides to the far bank, where I can see Mola screaming, 'Malky! Malky! Behind you!'

I turn to see Cuthbert less than a metre away, swivelling once more to expose his belly as he opens his jaws for a final attack, the attack that will surely finish the fight. My right hand is still gripping Kenneth's dirk and in a last, desperate effort I add my left hand to steady the blade and plunge it downwards – carelessly, furiously, knowing it is my only chance.

Half of the crocodile's belly is above the surface, and the razor-sharp steel shaft slips silently into the skin, all the way to the knife's hilt, opening up a massive gash but without stopping the beast. His tail thrashes round me, and I lose my grip, sliding below the water again, which is now a swirling mass of blood – Cuthbert's and mine. Through the mist, I see his mouth open, ready for a last attack, his glassy yellow eyes fix on me and I screw my eyes shut, ready for the end, for there isn't anything more that I can do, and then . . .

Nothing.

I'm standing now, near the shore, and I can hear Mola shouting, 'Malky, Malky!'

Swallowing hard, gasping for breath, I look to my side where the body of Cuthbert lies upside down, nudging the dry bank, his purple guts spilling into the water, the cross-shaped handle of the dirk jutting out of the flesh. I stagger away until I'm lying, choking, at Mola's feet.

Then I see something move inside the gaping corpse. In the space where the crocodile's guts once were is a shape that rises up out of the split belly.

The slimy mound straightens out and I see that it is the back of a person who has been crouched down inside the beast. The human creature – stinking crocodile innards clinging to his clothes – stands up, removes his spectacles, and wipes a sloppy clot of blood from his eyes and beard before stepping out of the crocodile's body with a squelch.

'Dad?' I croak, and he nods, puffing out his cheeks.

'Aye.'

'What are you doing here?'

He looks around, bewildered. 'I wish I knew, Malky.'

I look behind me to where Mola was standing a moment ago. She has gone, and I turn back to Dad.

'Is that it?' I say. 'Aren't you supposed to say something, you know, inspirational at this point? Something properly . . . Daddish?'

Dad spits a bit of crocodile innards on to the ground and says, 'Well. According to your mam, Malky, I gave up the right to say how I'd bring you up three years ago, and so . . .'

'That doesn't mean you can't tell me stuff! Like now, for example. Can't you just tell me what to do? Isn't that what dads are for?'

He shakes his head, sorrowfully. 'I'm sorry, son. I guess I'm not that sort of dad and never have been.'

'But why, Dad? *Why?*'

He takes a step towards me, but I shrink back: he stinks of crocodile guts. He sinks to his knees and looks at me, his face streaked with blood, and shakes his head.

'You want the whole lot *now*, Malky? The drugs, the depression, the divorce? It's going to take more time than you have, son.'

He's right, of course, and I feel my shoulders drooping in despair.

Then he takes a deep breath and says, 'How about I

tell you that I love you instead? And your brother. That I always have and always will.'

I turn to face him. 'That would be good. I guess.'

He gives a sad little nod. 'Aye. Well, it's true. I love you, then and now and always.'

I smile. I didn't know how much I needed to hear this.

'Listen, Malky,' he says, 'I'll be better in future, I promise. But you've got a job to do, and I'm not the one to help you.'

From behind me comes an urgent voice. 'How much longer you gon' be, Dream-boy?'

CHAPTER 78

I turn, and there is only Mola. My dad has gone.

Mola holds out her hand to help me up and we stand, soaking wet, looking back where we came. My foot and leg are in a terrible state, but the agony I should be feeling is less than I expected. Perhaps it will come later. There are no crocodiles to be seen.

'I . . . I think we just did something pretty amazing,' I say to Mola, panting. She sniffs and shrugs.

'Not over yet. And we are running out of time.'

She's right, of course. I have known it since the start of this dream. No way am I going to get through this on my own. I have been trying to dream up help – Kenneth, even my dad – but I am not in control.

What did Kenneth say? The sun is coming up in the real, awake world? That would make it way past six a.m., and I'm normally awake by six thirty, even without an alarm. If you account for the time that has passed since Kenneth said that . . .

'I should say we have about fifteen minutes,' says Susan.

What? Where did she come from?

'You look surprised to see me. Do not be. Instead, let's get going. Hi, Mola. Sorry I am late. I was so nervous I could not sleep. But it worked. You were right.'

My head swivels between them. 'It *worked*? What worked? What are you doing here?'

'I came to help. I hope that is okay.'

'Well, yes, but . . . am I dreaming you?'

'Actually, I think we are all in this together. But, right now, there may be more important considerations, Malky.'

I turn my head away from the wind in order to listen better. From afar, I hear Seb.

'Malky! Help!'

Without saying anything, the three of us start to run towards his voice.

CHAPTER 79

When we reach the big rock, I hold up my hand to Mola and Susan. We stop and crouch down behind it.

I hear Seb again: 'Malky! Help me!'

Inching my head past the rock, I see the group of Stone Age people, led by the biggest one with the square moustache. Two dogs sniff the ground. Craning a little further, I can see Seb, lashed to a large stake driven into the earth, with his hands tied behind his back. Next to him, similarly tethered, are three more people: our friends Kobi, Erin and Farook. Only, like the custard river becoming water, they have totally lost their cartoonish quality. They are no longer drawings come to life, but real people.

I was last here, what? Two nights ago? It feels a lot, lot longer.

Poor Seb is terrified and wriggling, trying to loosen the rough ropes that are binding his wrists, and drawing blood with the effort. He's in the middle of a flat, dusty area, about the size of a tennis court, that has been cleared of bushes, with larger rocks and big logs positioned round it.

More seconds are ticking by and I weigh up the options.

We could run at them, armed with nothing? In a fight between two eleven-year-olds and a short, round old lady, and a group of Stone Age adults armed with long wooden spears, I know who is going to win. My dream-controlling abilities are close to zero now. If I am captured, the same might happen to me as to Seb and I will be trapped forever in a dream of my own making. And what if I am killed? Will I die in real life, or will I just wake up?

Either way, I will not have Seb.

I feel a dig in my side from Susan. She points at some trees on the other side of the flat ground where something big is moving among the trees. I strain to see, but just get flashes of white and brown, and . . . hair?

Susan whispers to me: '*Mammoth.*'

As she says this, a sounds erupts from the trees: a loud, trumpeting growl as though Dennis, Kenneth's old dog, has been crossed with an elephant.

'That's our distraction,' she whispers. 'Well – that and, erm . . . *that.*' She jerks her thumb behind her, and I think I manage to stifle my shriek of horror.

Shielded from the view of the gang tormenting Seb, Susan's grandmother has stripped *completely* naked and is smearing her body with handfuls of mud and dust. She's rubbing it all over her prominent belly and her . . . and her . . . well, everywhere, really. Including her hair.

In fact, especially her hair, which is now standing on end, aided by large amounts of dirt.

I concentrate on looking at Mola's head because I don't really want to look anywhere else.

I manage to speak, but it comes out as a croak. 'Is . . . is this *my* dream? Am I imagining this, because that's your grandmother and I don't want you to think . . .'

Susan puts her finger to her lips to shut me up. 'You have done a lot, Malky. You have killed Cuthbert. Let me and Mola do this next bit.'

She beckons me to follow her towards the clump of trees. She turns back and gives a thumbs up to Mola who returns the gesture. She doesn't seem to care at all that she is a mad, nude old lady covered in mud.

Half a minute later, and Susan and I are alongside the clump of trees, and we still can't be seen by the group, who are about thirty metres in front of us, circling Seb and the book characters with spears and growling dogs.

Are they going to *kill* him? He's only seven! He shouts out for me again, and I want to run forward and grab him, but I know that I can't.

I hear another roar from the woods and feel another surge of fear. Then the mammoth emerges from the trees, filling my vision, and I freeze, staring.

It is twice my height and shaped like an elephant. It has a trunk with long grey bristles, two enormous, curved white tusks and a patchy, coarse coat of reddish-brown hair. It is furious, and I have no idea why it's staying where it is.

No idea, that is, until it sees us, bellows again and starts to charge.

Susan and I shrink back, instinctively, but we need not have bothered: the beast is tethered to a tree by means of a thick, rough rope of dried plant fibres tied round its front right leg. It takes a step and is stopped instantly. Like Seb's wrists, the mammoth's ankle has been rubbed raw and bloody.

Susan moves towards it. What's she *doing*?

But then she beckons for me to follow her, and I think of Seb, as I inch nervously forward, towards the enormous animal.

'Quick,' says Susan, crouching down near the tree. 'We haven't got long.' She has a large, flat stone in her hand that she is using to hack at the rope where it meets the tree trunk. With every blow, one or two tiny fibres fray and snap, but it's not breaking fast enough, while over by Seb the group is getting closer to him. They have started a haunting, rhythmic chant.

I can't bear to watch as they lower their spears. I'm on my feet, ready to run at them, but Susan holds up her hand to stop me. 'Not yet, Malky. Please. Wait for Mola.' Her efforts at cutting the rope are getting slower as she tires.

'Let me,' I say. Susan sits back, exhausted, and I take the flat stone from her hand, bashing the remaining strands furiously.

So furiously, in fact, that I don't hear the arrival of a figure next to me. Instead, I see to my right the glint of metal. A dark-haired boy of about my age is holding out a knife to me.

'You left my dad's dirk in a crocodile's belly. It might be useful!'

It's Susan who recognises him. '*Uri?*' she says.

Uri? Kenneth McKinley's son?

What's *he* doing here?

CHAPTER 80

Susan is rolling with this dream world more easily than I am, and she smiles at Uri while I just stand there, mouth open.

'You know my name?' says Uri.

'Yes!' says Susan. 'We knew your dad. I recognised you from the photograph on his table!'

The boy nods and smiles, shyly. Bewildered, I look between the two of them. '*How?*'

'Does it matter?' says Uri. 'Some things just *are!*'

'You're not wrong there, son!' says Kenneth, stepping out from behind a thick tree, his kilt ripped to shreds, exposing his legs, which are no longer skinny and old but young and muscled.

'Kenneth!' I gasp. 'What . . . how . . . I mean, you were killed by the crocs . . . weren't you?'

'You're forgetting, laddie: I was already dead. But the rather splendid thing about your Dreamland is that death doesn't seem to matter. Wouldn't you say, son?'

I splutter for a reply, until I realise he's talking to Uri, not me.

The two of them look at each other with a love that seems to radiate heat and slow down time.

Uri steps forward, and Kenneth pulls him into a hug. They stay there for what feels like a long time, and I glance at Susan, who is wiping something from her eye.

'We're together forever now, son,' says Kenneth. His hair is no longer white, but has the golden sheen of his photograph on the Dreaminator box. His deeply lined face seems to get smoother the closer he holds Uri.

'Yes, Dad,' says Uri, smiling.

Then Kenneth turns to me. 'Use the dirk, laddie. It's a lot easier. This is *your* Dreamland, remember?'

I nod, dumbfounded.

He faces his son again. "Come on, Uri, let's go: we're only in the way here. Wee Malky here's got a job to do.'

'Wait!' I say. 'Will . . . will I see you again?'

Kenneth looks at me over the top of his glasses. 'Who knows, laddie? Some pals of mine once said, "*Let it be*," and it just *could* be, you know?'

He holds out his hand to Uri, and the two step back behind the tree. Uri raises his hand in a shy goodbye, and then they're gone.

CHAPTER 81

At this point, two things happen at the same time.

One is that I slice easily through the remaining strands of rope with the dirk.

The other is that, from a little distance away, comes a scream unlike any I have heard before.

I twist round to look. From behind the large rock where we hid, Mola has emerged, naked, in full view of the gathering. Her arms are in the air, her feet wide apart, and she is yelling something at the top of her voice. She looks absolutely inhuman and totally terrifying and whatever she is shouting sounds like a blood-freezing war cry.

The group circling Seb stop immediately and stare in astonishment at the wild, muddy woman now running towards them down the rocky slope.

At the same moment, the mammoth, finally free of its tether, crashes out from the trees. Susan and I dive out of the way and it charges towards the kidnappers, honking and hooting and tossing its head furiously.

The hunters shriek in terror as the angry mammoth thunders across the dusty ground towards its captors.

The dogs have fled into the woods. With a flick of the mammoth's vast head, a tusk sideswipes the lead man and sends him flying through the air to land in a heap a few metres away. The others turn and aim their stone-tipped spears at the bellowing animal, screaming in fright as it charges again.

Between Mola and the mammoth, no one is paying any attention to Seb. Susan and I run round the side of the clearing towards the stake where he is secured. I hear a shout and turn my head. One of the tribesmen has spotted us and starts to run towards us, but is knocked over by a mighty swing of the mammoth's trunk and sprawls in the dust.

The others have surrounded the animal, and one of them throws a spear, which lodges in its neck, causing it to howl, but it doesn't stop its rampage.

Susan and I are behind Seb now. I don't even have time to say hello or ask him how he is. Instead, I start cutting through his wrist-ties, nicking his flesh at the same time in my frenzy and – good old Seb – he doesn't even complain, though I feel him wince. Seconds later, I've cut through.

For a moment, Seb just looks at me, and time seems to stand still. We don't speak, but we're sort of talking with our eyes. It's hard to explain.

And what our eyes say is: *You're annoying, but you're* my *brother.*

Then I grab Seb by one bloody hand, Susan takes the other and we start to run to the other side of the clearing.

'Wait!' says Seb, pulling us sharply to a halt. He wriggles free and runs back to where Kobi is still tied to a stake.

'We haven't got time! He's not even real!' I scream, but it's no good. Seb is behind Kobi, frantically cutting through the knotted vine with Kenneth's dirk.

To my side, I see that Mola has picked up a discarded spear. She holds it in both hands and bares her teeth at the large, hairy man coming towards her, slowly, with a chilling confidence.

'Mola! Come now!' Susan cries.

'No! Run, children, run!' she shouts.

The big man takes another step and swats aside the spear with a massive hand as easily as if it were a pencil. Mola is defenceless, but stands her ground as the man reaches for her throat with one hand and a stone club with the other, his teeth bared in fury.

Kobi wriggles his hands free from his loosened bonds, smiling his thanks to Seb with a stuck-out tongue before taking the dirk and turning immediately to the one called Erin, beginning to free her in turn. Seb and I start to run, and I am trying so hard to ignore the increasing pain in my croc-bitten leg.

Then Mola is being lifted from the ground by her throat and Susan shouts, 'Mola!'

At the same time, Mola shouts, 'Wake up! Wake up!' and the large man is left clutching at . . .

Nothing.

Before our astonished eyes, Mola has just vanished from Dreamland. There isn't time to wonder at this, because the small crowd of Stone Age warriors have decided not to try to fight the mammoth any more, but to run.

And they're running in our direction.

CHAPTER 82

I'm still reeling from the disappearance of Mola before my eyes. It was like some awesome magic trick: one second she was there, the next . . . gone. But I can't think about it, as Susan, Seb and I run through the trees and out on to a large open plain leading to the river and, beyond, the open sea. We have come in a wide U-shape, and our pursuers are by now a fair way behind us. Far enough, in fact, that we slow down and get our breath back.

'Look!' says Seb, pointing at a clifftop ahead of us. 'It's the priory, I mean . . . it's the cliff where the priory will be.'

He's right. We're standing exactly where Tynemouth will be, with its ruined castle and priory on the clifftop. A building that will not be built for something like nine thousand years and will be a crumbling ruin by the time I am alive. But the cliff is more or less the same. To our right is the Tyne river, to our left King Edward's Bay and, beyond it, the Long Sands and Culvercot – all of them unnamed, at least unnamed in English. Beyond the cliff a massive grey storm is building up.

'Let's go to the cliff edge,' I say. 'We can climb down to the bay.'

'And then what?' says Susan.

'We'll get away,' I say, but I already know what she'll say next.

'*And then what?* You have to make a decision, Malky. This is your dream, remember.'

In the distance, our attackers are coming nearer.

'I don't understand!' I wail. 'I don't know what to do!'

'I'm going to wake up any minute, Malky. I can feel it. And you too: you are going to wake up naturally, and if that happens you won't have Seb with you.'

'How do you *know* this?'

She looks at me, pleadingly. 'I *don't*, Malky. I don't *know* anything! But what I do know is that you have to let go of yourself. Let go of your *self.* Allow the . . . the universe to do its thing and just *let it be.*'

'*What does that even mean?*' I shout.

We're on the very edge of the cliff now, and I peer over. Yet, instead of rocks, and waves crashing on to them, it is as though the storm clouds on the horizon have swirled below me. I look up and can see no sea, no horizon – just a grey fog of emptiness and my stomach tightens.

'I'm scared, Malky,' says Seb. 'They're getting closer.'

Then a man's voice, with an accent like Mola's, says, quietly but firmly, 'Go to the edge of your dream, Malky. And then go further.'

I turn away from the cliff edge and where Susan stood is now a middle-aged man in a simple suit of faded blue cotton, a number printed on his chest. His hair is straight and black and streaked with grey, and a patchy beard clings to his hollow cheeks.

I don't even need to ask who he is, and I have given up questioning the logic of what is happening.

Susan's dad.

When he smiles, serenely, and nods in a way I have seen Susan do countless times, it is as though he can read my thoughts and approves.

Susan runs to him, and holds his hand, beaming up at him.

'What if I jump?' I say, gazing at the grey void. 'What will happen?'

'Go to the edge, Malky,' says Susan. 'And then go further.'

Then she and her dad disappear, just like that; like a light going out.

The hunters are getting nearer; I can make out their faces now, and I know there is no way back. Seb and I are trapped on the cliff edge.

'This is your dream, Malky. You have to control it,' says Seb.

'I can't, Seb. I can't control anything any more.'

'Don't let them catch us,' he pleads. I'm back to being big brother, feeling responsible for him and terrified that it's down to me.

But that's how it is.

They're much closer now – only metres away – and the one with the club has raised it in readiness for . . . for what?

When I look at Seb, he just nods.

'Let's do it,' he says. 'Let yourself go, Malky!'

I close my eyes in fear of the blow and, when I open them, I see the Dreaminator above me. A thin morning light is coming through my curtains. It's morning.

No, no, no, no! I can't wake up yet! I close my eyes again, and I'm back in my dream. The stone-club man has taken a step nearer.

'You have to let go of your *self*,' Susan had said.

'Go to the edge of your dream, Malky. And then go further,' her dad had added.

I grab Seb by the wrist, feeling the slick of blood beneath my palm, and as the stone club swings at me I push off with my good leg on the edge of the cliff, pulling Seb with me backwards, into the swirling fog, with the rising sun blinding me . . .

Nothingness rushes up to meet us.

CHAPTER 83

My eyes are still screwed up against the sharp sunlight.

I open them.

I wake up.

The morning sunshine is slicing through a gap in the curtains, hitting my eyes, and I can make out the shape of the Dreaminator above me. If I screw my eyes shut, I'm not back on a cliff-top with a stone club swinging at me.

I am – I *definitely* am – awake. I lie there, panting, and bring my hand up to my face. It's sticky with blood. Everything comes back to me – everything. I don't know how long I'm lying there. A minute maybe? I turn to Seb's bed – and he isn't there. But then I realise, *Of course he isn't there. He's in hospital.*

Is he awake, though?

I hope he's awake.

I get up. I can't shake off the idea that I'm still dreaming. Is this another dream-in-a-dream? I check the bathroom: no Kenneth McKinley in the bath. I go to wash the blood off my hands, then check the bathroom door in case a crocodile comes through.

I grab a toothpaste tube and read the words: *Extra Freshness!* I dash back to my room to check the clock: 06:30.

The words, the numbers, are all clear. I am not dreaming. 'Float!' I say. I don't float.

I am *not* dreaming. My leg is aching, my arm is crusted with dried blood, but I'm definitely not dreaming.

Something smells odd, though. I look up at the old, original Dreaminator. It is still there, but blackened, smouldering, thin wisps of smoke curling up from the singed feathers, the fine gold threads burned to nothing – a ruin.

I'm relieved in a way. But then I think . . . what if I have to go back? What if I've killed Seb? All the negatives start circling in my head. *Without the Dreaminator, what happens if . . . ?*

My swirling thoughts are cut off by my phone ringing on the bedside table. The caller ID says it's Mam.

I hardly dare pick up the phone. I'm in a daze, and later I will find it hard to recall this moment, but for now I put the phone to my ear.

'Hello?' I say.

'He's back,' says Mam, and then she starts laughing and crying at the same time. I know how she feels.

CHAPTER 84

'He's back! Mormor! Uncle Pete! He's back – Seb's awake!'

The next ten minutes are the happiest chaos I have ever known, with Mormor crying tears of relief and Uncle Pete running up and down the stairs, and Fit Billy ringing on the doorbell because he's heard the commotion through the walls, then dashing over the road to tell Lynn and Tony, who come over in their dressing gowns and slippers . . .

And then I'm sitting in the back of Uncle Pete's car, heading to the hospital. It's early and Tynemouth is quiet; the Beckers' funeral parlour looks as though nothing at all happened there last night. As we drive past, I keep my head down when I see Kez's dad coming out of the side lane with Dennis on a lead.

'*Inte så fort, Peter!*' says Mormor who reverts to her native Swedish when she's anxious. 'Not so fast!'

'*Ja, ja, Mama!*' he laughs in response, and speeds up slightly, making her tut.

My phone is in my hand as we zoom up the near-empty A19 to Cramlington Hospital. I'm just about to call Susan when it buzzes in my hand, making me jump.

'He's back,' I say straight away. There's a long pause on the other end, and I wonder if she's heard me. 'Susan . . . ?'

'Yes, Malky, yes! He is! Oh, I'm so relieved. We've been waiting for you to call.' Then I hear her shouting, 'Mola! It worked! It worked!' I can hear shrieking and whooping and I say, 'Thank you, Susan! Thanks a *lot*!' Then the line goes dead as my phone loses reception.

Wait. So they actually *were* in my dream? And Kenneth too?

I don't know why any of that should surprise me, actually.

Anyway, I can't think about it because Uncle Pete has overheard. 'What worked? Who were you thanking?' he says.

Should I tell him? Should I explain the whole thing again? There's no more reason to believe me now than there was before, and any evidence is charred and melted and still hanging above my bed.

So I half lie.

'Susan and her gran meditated in a very special way,' I say. 'They prayed underneath their prayer flags, and the prayers were carried on the wind.'

'That's nice,' says Uncle Pete, and Mormor nods in approval.

'Prayers can be like dreams, Malky,' she says. 'Sometimes prayers are answered, just like dreams can come true.'

'You're right, Mormor,' I say through a grin. 'You're dead right.'

I'm in the back seat so they can't see as I roll up my trouser leg to check my wounded leg, which is almost completely healed.

CHAPTER 85

Dr Nisha is back on duty. She comes in while we're all gathered round Seb's bed, and we stand aside while she does things like shine a light in his eyes and tap things on an iPad. When she's done, she tells us that Seb will be kept in hospital a little longer 'for observation'.

'All of Sebastian's functions appear to be normal, ' she says with a puzzled smile. 'The injuries on his wrists and face have almost completely disappeared, which everybody here is saying is remarkable, and I have to agree. I have never seen anything like it. Are you feeling all right, Sebastian?'

He grins his gappy grin in reply and holds both of his thumbs up. 'Pretty awethome!'

Dr Nisha sighs. 'I warn you now: it may be that we never know exactly what happened. I can tell you, though, this was a close-run thing.' She picks up a clipboard and flips a couple of pages. 'His heart rate, for example, went crazy very early this morning. The duty nurse reported "very disturbed sleep, twitching, thrashing, excessive REM" – that is—'

'Rapid eye movement,' I chip in, just because I'm feeling smart.

'Yes. It seems like he was having an extremely vivid dream.'

I say nothing, of course. But all of the adults – Mam, Dad, Uncle Pete, Mormor – exchange looks and I just *know* they are thinking about the incident yesterday with the deconstructed Dreaminators. Mam's gaze eventually settles on me and, when our eyes meet, I know this won't be the last I hear of it.

Dr Nisha looks at her notes again. 'At six twenty-six, we thought we had lost him. Sebastian's heart and brain activity stopped for twenty-two seconds.'

I do a quick metal calculation. That would have been the time Seb and I took our big leap off the cliff, and for a moment – just a second, really – my stomach turns over with the memory.

The fear, the sun in my eyes, the people chasing us, the fog below . . .

'You okay, Malky?' says Dr Nisha. 'I know this is upsetting. It's odd – at the precise moment his heart rate was most extreme, he said something, didn't you, Seb?' She smiles at him. 'He opened his eyes, and said, "Let's go, Malky!"'

I say, 'It was, "Let yourself go, Malky!"'

Dr Nisha gives me a funny look. 'Actually, you're right! How did you know that?'

Eventually, the rest of them all head off for breakfast, but Seb's already had his, and I'm just not hungry. So the two of us stay in his little room next to the intensive care unit. He's not hooked up to anything. He's sitting in his bed, propped up on fat pillows. There's only one thing I want to know.

'What happened to you?' I say. 'When you were asleep, and you were dreaming, and tied to that stake, and being beaten . . .'

Seb's eyes look up as if he's retrieving a memory.

'Oh yeah,' he says. 'That wasn't nice. But . . .'

'Wasn't nice?' I am amazed. 'You mean . . . you don't remember it all?'

He thinks again. 'Not really. Not all of it.'

'Do you remember the mammoth?' I start laughing. 'Naked Mola?'

'Naked *what?*'

I realise that he has never even met Susan's grandmother.

'Thing is, Malky – this was your dream . . . wasn't it? I was just . . . in it, somehow. Now it feels just like it was a nightmare, you know? Not nice, but . . .'

I look again at his wrists. His bad dream is retreating from his memory like his wounds, and I could not be more relieved. I'm standing over his bed and I don't know why I do this thing, maybe for the first time ever, but I kind of fall forward and gather my little brother in my arms and squeeze, and he squeezes back.

'I love you, Seb,' I say, and he laughs and says, 'Yeah, whatever.'

Then he quickly adds, 'Hey, did you see the wound on my thigh?'

'No. What is it?'

He pulls back the bedsheet. 'The doctors are a bit worried. Here.' He lowers the waistband of his pyjamas to expose his thigh and the top of his buttock. 'Can you see? There. Look closer. *Closer!*' I bend over until my nose is almost touching his white bum. I still can't see anything.

That's when he lets off a *huge* fart, right in my face, and turns nearly breathless and purple with laughter.

I think it's Seb's way of saying, 'I love you too.'

CHAPTER 86

Later that day, Seb's discharged from hospital and Dad's heading back to Middlesbrough. He and Mam are over by his car while Seb and I wait on the same wall where I had been just a couple of days ago. Seb's in his goalie top, of course.

Seb nudges me. 'Look at Mam and Dad!' he says, and when I do I see they are laughing!

Okay, not exactly laughing, but Dad has said something with a smile, and Mam has smiled back at him. Then she nods warmly and puts her hand on his forearm and keeps it there for a little while, then she moves away, beckoning us to follow her to Uncle Pete's car.

'Lads!' calls Dad as we get up and go over to him. The three of us stand a bit awkwardly for a moment. Eventually, Dad says, 'Erm, how about you's two come and see me soon, eh? Middlesbrough versus Luton? I can get tickets?'

I have never been to a proper football match before and nor has Seb, whose face splits into a big grin. His favourite goalkeeper plays for Middlesbrough.

'Awethome!' He puts his arms round Dad and then recoils. 'Dad! You . . . erm . . . you don't smell too good.'

Dad's brow furrows and he sniffs his hand. 'Sorry, pal, I know. I've had this strange smell clinging to me all morning. Since I woke up, in fact. I've had a shower, honest!'

I step forward and sniff. 'Crocodile guts,' I say and his head jerks round as he stares at me, open-mouthed.

'What? I . . . I had a . . . I can't remember, but . . .'

'You had a dream about being inside a crocodile?'

'Erm . . . yeah. How did you know *that*?'

I shrug. 'Just a guess, Dad. I daresay the smell will wear off, though.'

He looks at me closely. I don't want to tell him more, not yet, anyway. Mam calls us to hurry up, and Dad laughs and gets into his car.

'I hope you're right! Boro v. Luton. See you then!'

CHAPTER 87

I'd only been back at school a couple of days and already I was standing in Mrs Farroukh's office. This time, though, I was not in trouble. Susan was there as well.

'You don't have to go if you don't want to,' said Mrs Farroukh. 'But I am going and you will be welcome to join me.'

That's how, three days later, Susan, Mola, Mrs Farroukh and I are among a dozen or so people at Holy Saviour's Church for Kenneth McKinley's funeral. Kez Becker is there too, with Dennis slumped under the front pew.

'Bless him,' says Andi, looking round the empty pews. 'Poor old Kenneth really didn't have anybody, did he?'

In addition to us, there's a couple who lived in the flat above Kenneth who Andi knows slightly, and another carer called Rosemary who did Andi's days off.

In the centre of the church is Kenneth's coffin with a tartan scarf draped over it. I have seen the coffin before, of course, but here it is much less spooky. I have never been to a funeral before, but this is fine. The vicar, a lady with a deep voice and a nice smile, says some prayers, and then looks to the back of the church. We follow her gaze, and from the furthest pew comes an old man with a big white moustache, walking slowly with a straight back down the aisle.

He turns to face the small gathering and clears his throat. I look at Susan. His face is familiar somehow, but I don't know where from.

'Good morning, everyone,' he says in a soft, clear Scottish accent. 'My name is Robbie Ferguson, and I did Kenneth McKinley a great injustice.'

I glance again at Susan who draws a small rectangle in the air with her fingers, and I nod.

This is the man who interviewed Kenneth on the TV show we watched!

'Kenneth had a successful career north of the border, working in theatres with a mystery and mind-reading act, which always concluded with his famous floating illusion. By the 1980s, he had embraced a more, ah . . . *philosophical* approach to his mysteries, and, on the television show that I presented at the time, I ridiculed him.'

The man pauses and lowers his head for a moment.

'I'm not proud. I played it for laughs. I demonstrated an old party trick and told everyone that that must have been how Kenneth did his wonderful levitation. The truth is, that floating illusion is a secret he has taken with him. I mocked the business venture into which he had sunk a modest fortune: a harmless toy that claimed to shape your dreams. Hardly anyone bought one. His career declined and never really recovered. And then there was his son, Uri – named, of course, after Kenneth's friend, the world-famous psychic entertainer, Uri Geller . . .'

Susan has reached over and is gripping my hand hard. We both know something is happening before our eyes, but we don't know what.

'As some of you may know, little Uri died in 1988. One night, he fell asleep and remained asleep for days. It was as though he were in a coma. Doctors could not revive him and, after several days, poor wee Uri passed away. No one ever knew why, although it was said that Kenneth's wife, Jeannette, held him somehow responsible. They parted shortly afterwards.'

Susan's grip on my hand tightens.

The old man straightens his back and turns to address the coffin directly, as if Kenneth can hear him. I don't think I breathe. 'I'm sorry, Kenneth. If your life was made harder by what I did, I hope I have tried to make amends.'

Robbie Ferguson nods, clears his throat again, then walks back down the aisle, out of the church, and out of our lives.

The vicar is on her feet again, smiling weakly. I don't think she was expecting that. She seems relieved to have something to do when she says, 'Malcolm?' Susan gives my hand a final squeeze and then lets it go.

I reach under the pew and bring out a flat box, wrapped up like a birthday present. 'Go on,' murmurs Mrs Farroukh. I stand up and walk slowly to the front, where I place Kenneth's gift-wrapped, burnt-out Dreaminator on top of his wooden coffin. Kez's dad, standing at the side of the church in his undertaker's dark suit and tie, has no idea what is inside, or how I got it, and never will.

'Thanks for your help with Cuthbert, Kenneth,' I say, too quietly for anyone else to hear.

Outside the church, there's a freezing-cold wind and we're all sort of hunched up, not quite sure what to do. Andi says to us, 'Well, that explains *that*,' and gives a little nod of satisfaction.

'What explains what?' I say.

'The people at Helping Hands, the care agency I work for, never really knew who paid Kenneth's bills. A "mystery benefactor" would deposit money every month to pay for his care. I guess that was that Robbie fella's way of making it up to him.'

A few metres away, something is going on between Mrs Farroukh and Kez's dad. They are deep in conversation and Kez's dad is nodding a lot, then he has to go and supervise the loading of Kenneth's coffin into the long black car.

(I've already looked, and there doesn't *appear* to be

any damage on the car bonnet from where me and Susan jumped on it.) Mrs Farroukh is beaming.

'Well, that's all sorted then,' she says. 'I've just cleared it with your father, Kezia. You, erm . . . opted out of community visiting, although your dad says he has no knowledge of your, er . . . phobia.'

I glance over at Kez, whose expression is stony.

Mrs Farroukh continues: 'So I'm assigning you new duties with COMMS. From next week, you will be leading a new initiative: the Great Beach Clean! From Tynemouth to Culvercot, keeping our wonderful beaches clean of marine waste, broken glass and dog mess! Thank you so much for agreeing.' She claps her hands. 'Isn't that *marvellous?*'

Kezia's face is a picture, and it's all I can do not to laugh at the thought of Kez collecting dog poo. She replies with as little enthusiasm as she can get away with, 'Yes, miss. Marvellous.'

Susan and I are standing with Mola and are just about to get into Mrs Farroukh's car to go back to school when Andi comes over. 'I almost forgot,' she says, breathlessly. She hands me a carrier bag that she's had with her all morning.

'Kenneth often told me about his dreams. None of them made sense. But after you'd left the last time – you know, when we met on the river path? – he told me, "Give the lad this. I think he might need it."'

I put my hand into the bag and my fingers curl round a familiar object and I pull out Kenneth's dirk, complete with the leather sheath and belt. I can't say anything at all: my head is swimming.

Andi says, 'He added "good luck with Cuthbert". Well, like I say, he often didn't make much sense, poor old soul. But you know – it's a nice thing to have, eh?'

She smiles at me and I manage to whisper, 'Thank you.' I catch Mola's eye. She is smiling and she gives me a knowing little wink as if that explains it all.

I wish.

ONE WEEK LATER

CHAPTER 88

'Come on, man – we'll be late!'

'Do I look all right?'

'Seb, man, you can wear what you like so long as it's clean, Susan said. It won't make any difference to your ugly mug, anyway.'

At one point, not very long ago, Seb would have complained at that. He'd have whinged. He'd have threatened to tell Mam that I was being mean. I'd have sneered back at him, and then we'd be fighting and Mam would have to separate us, and . . .

Oh, you get what I mean. Instead, he says, 'No – *your* ugly mug.'

I know: hardly top-class banter, but he's only seven. Anyway, we're on our way out of the front door when Fit Billy and Mam emerge from the kitchen where they've been chatting all morning. Honestly, the amount of tea he drinks at our place, I sometimes wonder if he simply doesn't have a kettle of his own. They're supposed to paint the new fence today, like it's a two-person job. They're grinning like mad.

'Boys!' says Mam, with a funny catch in her voice. 'Where are you going?'

I stop in the doorway. 'Sorry, Mam. Susan's invited us over for Tibetan butter tea and cake. She says she's got a special surprise and not to be late.'

Mam's eyebrows go up. 'Really? For both of you? Only me and Billy have got a surprise as well, haven't we, Bill? Something to tell you.'

Billy nods and puts his big arm round Mam, which is a bit unusual, but maybe she's cold because the front door's still open.

'Don't worry,' says Billy. 'It'll wait, won't it, Mary?' He winks at her as we run down the path.

In Susan's garden, the strong breeze is making the prayer flags flap so noisily that the people there are raising their voices a bit to be heard.

Susan meets me and Seb at the back gate and leads us down the path. She says, 'Look at you two – smart and shiny!'

There are people there I have never seen before, plus Mola in a grand-looking crimson sarong. Everyone is dressed up, and I'm glad I put my best shirt on. There is a table laid out, and I spot butter cake and one or two other things I don't recognise among normal stuff like sandwiches and crisps.

'You must be Malcolm,' says a slim lady with hair

exactly like Susan's and the widest, warmest smile. 'And Sebastian. Tenzin – I mean, Susan – has told me all about your . . . ah, adventures. I am Susan's mum. Or "mam" I believe you say here.'

'Very pleathed to meet you,' says Seb through a mouthful of butter cake. Susan's mum pretends not to notice that he has sprayed her with crumbs, and grins back. 'You too, Sebastian. We are very lucky you are here. Now excuse me.' She glances at the sky. 'The rain may not hold off much longer. We need to get on.'

She moves away and claps her hands together. People put their teacups down and stop talking while Susan's mum takes a deep breath and begins a little speech.

Of course, it's in Tibetan. Seb looks at me, puzzled, but I just shrug. People seem to murmur approval, and there's the occasional ripple of applause. At one point, Susan's mum breaks off to dab her eyes, and people go, 'Awww!' and smile.

I look around for Susan. Where is she? She can help me understand just what's going on. I notice a little table supporting the framed photograph of the Dalai Lama decorated with flowers and some tealights flickering inside long glass tubes.

I edge over to Mola, who is smiling with such force that I can't help grinning as well.

'Mola,' I hiss through my smile. 'What's happening?'

'Shh. Special guest coming out now!'

As she says this, everyone turns and from inside the house shuffles Dennis, with a man holding his lead. Everybody chuckles and cheers and claps, and so do I because I've guessed what is happening, and I'm pleased for Susan that she gets to keep Dennis.

She'll certainly be a very responsible owner of an older dog and I'm very happy for her. Mind you . . . it's a lot of fuss to go to for adopting a dog!

People, including Susan, are crowding round the new arrival, and chattering with delight. There's a clap of thunder, and people go, 'Oooh!', while the wind picks up and further rattles the prayer flags. One or two people are carrying plates indoors as the first spots of rain come and amid the hubbub I lean over to Mola and say, 'Susan must be very happy.'

'Oh yes. Now she has her dad, she is very happy girl.'

I nod and smile.

Hang on. Wait.

What? I didn't hear properly. She didn't say *dog*, did she?

'I'm sorry, Mola. What did you say?'

'I say, now she has her dad, she is very happy girl!'

Her . . . her . . . Oh my God!

Seconds later, I've pushed through the people surrounding them, and I'm *whooping* with delight for her, and I've grabbed her in a big hug and spun her round and then I've hugged her very startled-looking dad, who I'm not at all surprised to see looks just like he did in the dream, and he smiles and hugs me back; I've even hugged Dennis.

And there, with the rain spotting my shirt and the wind flapping the flags to a frenzy, and Susan smiling and Sebastian scratching Dennis's head, I understand just how lucky I have been.

CHAPTER 89

The rain has stopped now, and Seb and I are splashing our way back home through the puddles.

'What do you reckon it was that Mam and Billy wanted to tell us?' says Seb.

'Haven't a clue,' I say, happily. It's probably something to do with the fence, but I don't really care.

'Hey, Malky. All that Dreaminator stuff? We've been talking about it a lot, yeah?'

'Mm-hmm.' We certainly have. In fact, Susan, Seb and I have talked about little else for days. I have had no more waking dreams, and nor has Seb. Just normal, crazy ones that we both forget shortly after waking.

'Thing is, Malky, I've stopped talking about it to other people. Not Erin, not Hassan . . . I reckon they will think we're nuts.'

'I think you may be right, Lil-Bro.'

'So, we don't tell anyone, eh?'

I put my arm round his little shoulders and smile.

'Seb, my friend, I wouldn't dream of it.'

THE END

Acknowledgements

Any book is a collaborative work, and I owe thanks to countless people - many of whom I don't even know - who have played a part in making this story reach you.

Chief among these is my editor at HarperCollins, Nick Lake, whose thoughtful advice is always sound and helpful; also Samantha Stewart and Jane Tait, whose contributions are often disguised as small changes but which have a big impact. Thanks, too, to my brother Roy Welford for reading an early version and making valuable suggestions.

Last, but certainly not least, thank you to the booksellers, librarians, bloggers, teachers and others, for whose consistent support and recommendations I am hugely grateful.